LOVE CHARMS FOR THE CLUELESS

SULA ALBA

To everyone who keeps trying to run away from love.

CONTENT NOTES

This paranormal romance book features on-page steamy scenes. It does also touch on several sensitive topics and themes. If you'd like to know more you can find a full list on my website: https://www.sulaalba.com/content-warnings

Take care and happy reading!

CHAPTER ONE

"Violet, they're calling you in," said Beatrice, looking apologetic.

A sense of dread blossomed in Violet's chest. When she turned to Ellie Rodriguez next to her, she received only a shrug in response. If an issue arose that concerned the whole firm, the senior associates would have summoned them both.

This was Violet's mistake.

Violet trailed behind Beatrice to Carl Calloway's office. She expected to see him upset or at least angry, but Carl, the managing partner, smiled when she walked in. However, standing next to Carl, Scott glowed red. Anger seeped through his usual indifferent facade. His jaw appeared sharper as he swallowed back an insult. He pushed his dark hair back from his face with an irritated swipe of his hand. Noting the differences in their reactions, Violet knew she would be fine, and her concern evaporated.

"You asked to see me?" she asked.

"Yes. Scott says he assigned Ellie to proofread the cover letters for the exhibits for the Michaelson case, but she gave them to you to do," said Carl, placing the stacks of paper on the desk. His round face had never lost its childish appearance, and he had the energy of a sitcom dad. He'd often meander in their conversations together, leaving nuggets of wisdom for her to keep. Violet didn't mind him so much if one could get over his incessant chatter.

"She had a family emergency at home. I didn't mind doing it for her." If she could call boning your recent comatose boyfriend an emergency. But who was Violet to get in the way of true love?

"I gave them to Ellie for a reason." Scott rifled through the cover letters, showing Violet the red pen markings on every single page. "Ellie is more detailed orientated than you." He huffed, his furrowed brow making his angular face appear harsher.

Violet thumbed through the pages, confused by what she saw. She had combed through every page for hours. There was no way she had missed this many mistakes.

"I'm sorry. I thought I had gone through them thoroughly. I don't know what happened."

Scott looked close to a seizure, but Carl just laughed. "Listen, you don't go to law school to write perfect cover letters. That's what paralegals are for, and interns. Just be more careful next time."

Scott turned to Carl, waiting for him to say something else. His dark eyes almost bulged out of their sockets when he realized Carl was moving on. Violet tried to hide her smile. There wasn't much that Scott could do to make her look bad in the eyes of the partners. She had made sure of that during her first week at her internship.

She knew Scott would be a problem the moment she met him. Scott had told Carl and the other partners he had caught Violet scrolling through her phone when she was supposed to be working. Violet could have explained that nobody had given her any work to do yet, so she hadn't been neglecting some enormous responsibility. Or she could have told them she had the e-book version of her textbook on her phone and read ahead for one of her classes. Instead, Violet got even. If Scott Pruitt was going to be a problem for her, she would be a problem for him.

One sunny morning as Scott poured himself coffee in the break room, she spiked his coffee with slippery elm. With a quick flick of her wrist, as Scott turned his back and the powdered herb dissolved into his hot coffee. She whispered her spell as she walked away, imagining his tongue swelling the next time he tried to speak ill of her to their bosses.

"I'm sorry, Carl. I promise I'll be more careful next time. If Scott wants, I'll go over it again with Ellie. He's right; she is more detailed oriented."

Scott opened his mouth, but nothing came out. His face reddened, and he looked close to choking on his own spit. He fought her spell, and Violet internally panicked but kept her cool.

"Well, there you go. We can all move on. Right?"

Violet nodded, but Scott sat fuming in his seat, unable to say anything more about her. The effects of the slippery elm should have lasted a few months, but she thought it might be time for another dose.

Violet held nothing but disdain for Scott Pruitt. He was cold, demanding, and full of himself. He was a junior associate, yet acted as if he owned the place. She didn't know why he had chosen her over the others to torture. Ellie wasn't as convinced that he hated Violet in particular, pointing to all the instances that he had assigned last-minute work to her and the other interns. Yet Violet couldn't shake the feeling that he hated her.

She remembered the anger that flowed through her pores as he sat opposite her in front of the partners, berating her for her lack of professionalism. Violet wanted to strike him. How dare he? She had only been there for a week anyway. His impression of her was wrong, but he would never change his mind. So she didn't bother trying to change it. With the slippery elm in his system, she knew he wouldn't be able to gossip about her, no matter how hard he tried. And if the look on his face was any sign, he wanted nothing more than to spew out every negative and awful opinion he had of her every chance he got.

"How did it go?" asked Ellie, as Violet sat back at her desk with a hard plop.

"It wasn't too bad," said Violet, stretching her arms over her head.

"Seriously?"

"Apparently, I'm not detail-oriented. Whatever, I'm sure it was Scott trying to get me fired, but I have him under my control."

Ellie stopped typing and narrowed her eyes at Violet. "Under your control, how?"

"It's just a little herbal mix to keep him tame," said Violet with a mischievous smile curling her lips.

"Does Molly know what you're doing?" Ellie's eyebrows shot up towards her hairline.

"Molly doesn't need to know. Plus, I'm careful."

"There are a lot of things about you, Violet, but careful isn't one of them," laughed Ellie, turning away to finish looking up case law in the database.

Ellie referred to the events of a few weeks ago. Violet and Margaret broke the coven's rules and killed Ellie's boyfriend Derek after he had attacked Margaret. After Ellie almost died by binding her soul to her resurrected boyfriend, it took the coven binding her soul to River to send Derek back to the spirit realm.

Violet had paid for that death spell after Derek came back to life, and weird undead vultures attacked the coven. But Molly didn't seem to care that she had killed Derek because he had almost killed Margaret. Molly seemed more concerned about Violet skirting the coven rules and almost getting them exposed. Derek was an asshole, a murderous one at that. Hadn't Violet done a good thing protecting her friend and killing him?

Witches didn't operate in the black and white notion of good and evil. The primary rule was to not disturb the balance of nature. Ellie had done far more damage by bringing Derek back from the dead than Violet had by killing him. Yet Molly brought Ellie into the coven with open arms, and while Violet was happy about it, she couldn't help but think Molly forgave Ellie a little too quickly. She liked Ellie and her attached to the soul boyfriend, River. However, Molly had iced Violet out since. She would never put Violet in danger by kicking her out of the coven, but she didn't trust her anymore. It bothered Violet, though she hated to admit it.

"Will you help me with these cover letters?" she asked Ellie. Ellie swung her chair over to her, and they worked in silence. She scanned the documents, circling things that Violet hadn't even noticed. She didn't want to give Scott the satisfaction of knowing that he was right about one thing. Ellie was better suited to this than she was.

As if sensing Violet thinking about him, Scott's loud steps approached their desks. Violet didn't bother looking up, preferring to ignore him.

"Violet, I need you to come with me to the law library on campus. There is case law that I can't seem to find on the database, but I can find it in the library."

"Why do I have to come?" Violet's head shot up.

"Because Ellie is doing the work that I gave her three days ago to complete and everyone else is busy doing the work I assigned them."

"What's this for exactly?" sighed Violet.

"For the witch client."

Violet didn't look away from Scott, but she saw in her pe-riphery Ellie spilling her coffee over her textbooks. Violet didn't understand how Ellie had hidden her witchcraft from her for as long as she had. Ellie's feelings were always so painfully obvious.

"Fine," Violet said.

"We'll go in my car."

"No thanks. I'll take my car."

Violet didn't think there was anything worse than being stuck in a car with Scott. As she gathered her things to head out, she amused herself by thinking about his horrible taste in music. Corporate rock with a hint of ska. She giggled to herself. He was too boring even for that. He probably just listened to NPR all day.

As she climbed into her car and followed him to the library, she wondered why they were going analog for their information. The law firm was defending a client accused of murder, but the prosecution focused mainly on her means of killing him. Witchcraft.

When Eve Miller came into the office to speak to her lawyers, Ellie and Violet tried to figure out if she was an actual witch. Mortals had long come up with stupid ways to uncloak witches. Burning, drowning, marks on their skin, and a whole other mess of ways that just ended with mortals dead.

In the witch world, there were three ways to figure out if a person was a witch. The first being a magical signature, an aura of sorts that flowed around them or their magical workings. Signatures were easy enough to hide, not from spell works since that required too much magic, but they could suppress one's own aura with practice. Most of the coven suppressed their signatures. Molly didn't trust all witches not to rat them out. Violet normally didn't suppress her signature, but when she entered the coven, Molly insisted.

The second was blood. A few drops in a mixture of water and mugwort did the trick. If the water stayed red, the person was mortal. If it changed color to any color but red, they were a witch. The major drawback to this method was getting ahold of the blood. Blood, like hair, nails, skin, or organs, could be dangerous if the wrong person got a hold of it.

Finally, and this was what Ellie did when she met the client; she held her hand. Ellie tried to feel the vibration. The magic coursing through her veins. A sensation so minuscule only other witches could pick up on it. When Ellie went to the bathroom to report what she'd learned, it didn't surprise Violet to learn that the woman was, in fact, mortal. The trials had only caught a few genuine witches. The rest were mortals with an enemy somewhere who wanted to watch them suffer.

Mortal or not, nothing about Eve's trial so far was fair. The prosecutors held a news conference, tainting the jury pool. The judge had revoked her bail for a second time, and he ruled the "magic" at the crime scene could be used as evidence. Violet didn't understand why, since the man had died from a gunshot wound, not a spell. Rumors circulated that the prosecution intended to roll out their key dark magic expert, Craig Nelson. A "reformed witch" who now traveled the country, testifying at trials on his exaggerated expertise. A snake oil salesman, thought Violet, if there ever was one.

They reached the library, and Violet got out of the car and approached Scott. His dark hair had a reddish-brown color in the sun, and he squinted in the light. Despite the snow not being forecast, the weather was turning for the worst, and the cold wind cut through Violet's sweater as they hurried inside.

"What are we looking for?" Violet asked in a low voice. She regretted not bringing her coat. The library was at least warmer. She peered around, seeing the library packed with students. Finals were a few weeks away, and she felt like a slacker seeing everyone else studying.

Scott smoothed his dark hair back, and Violet tried not to pay attention to how his hair fell in waves around his face. He pulled out two small folded pieces of paper from his jacket pocket, holding them between two long fingers. He handed her one, and she read the two book titles written in his scrawl. Both had to do with 17th-century witch trials.

"You find those and I'll look for my books." He showed her his list and saw at least ten books on it. Violet guessed that he didn't trust her and her poor attention skills to find all the books he needed.

"Fine," said Violet and turned towards the stacks. He'd already written the dewy decimal numbers on her paper. So she wandered through the stacks, trying to find her way.

Her hands brushed the spines of the books. She liked the silence. Scott had put her in a foul mood. Coming here was a nuisance, but the silence was almost worth it. Her fingers landed on the book she needed. She pulled it off the shelf and flipped the book open to a random page, skimming through the words. She caught the words 'purity test' and shut it with a loud thud. Hopefully, this would help. Eve didn't deserve what was happening to her. None of the convicted over the past couple of years deserved it either.

A loud bang shocked Violet into dropping her book. She stood still, not registering what she heard. It seemed like someone had set off a firework in the library. Violet's heart raced, and her blood rushed to her ears. No one in the library moved. Violet strained to hear something else, the peaceful silence now turning ominous. Half-aware that everyone in the library was doing the same as her, waiting for the inevitable second boom.

They came quickly. They weren't fireworks, but gunshots. People were running, hiding, but she stood in the middle of the aisle. Too terrified to move. The pops continued; the screams only got louder. Violet did the only thing she could do.

"I am invisible.
My body shall disappear
Your eyes will glide over me
No shadow shall appear
You cannot see me."

She repeated it over and over under her breath. Her heart racing all the while. She heard something distinct from the running, slow, heavy footsteps. The gunshots stopped. How many people were dead? The mere thought of victims made her sick.

She repeated the spell, over and over, until she saw the heavy footsteps step towards her aisle.

The gunman wore body armor, a huge assault rifle at the ready in his gloved hands, and his face obscured by a helmet and mask. Time slowed, and he stayed in the aisle for a small eternity. Had her spell worked? She wished to see his eyes, but she didn't dare move to get a quick glimpse.

He turned and continued walking down the aisle. Violet's breath came out choked, her hands shaking as she covered her mouth to stifle a sob.

The library was silent again. The heavy footsteps sounded further and further away. She stayed put until another shot made her jump, and a cry that sounded all too familiar to her reached her.

Scott.

Chapter Two

Violet couldn't stay stuck anymore. Stealing a deep breath, she ran towards Scott's cry. The only sounds in the library were her hurried footsteps as she jumped over abandoned backpacks and textbooks. She could no longer hear the slow footsteps of the gunman. Unable to confirm her invisibility without a mirror, she had no time to waste worrying over it.

She raced south, peering into each aisle before continuing on to the next one. Worry bubbled in her stomach as every aisle turned up empty, save for the abandoned books and bags.

Where was Scott? She wished he would make more noise, even a gurgle, letting her know he was still alive. But she didn't find him until she reached the last aisle.

Scott lay splayed on his back. Blood pooled beneath his left side. He was awake, but his eyes glazed over her face as she kneeled closer. She couldn't make out how bad his wound was under his sweater. Sweat clung to his brow, and his breathing sounded shallow to her.

She cursed under her breath. Her mind raced, trying to figure out what to do. If the gunman returned, they would be exposed and defenseless. The floor they were on had a couple of study rooms. She had no choice but to take him there and hope the gunman wouldn't find them.

Violet was unsure of how she would carry him. She lifted his arm, looping it around her neck, and braced herself as she pulled him up. He gasped awake, startling her enough to almost drop him. His eyes blinked fast, adjusting to the light. Violet struggled under his weight, and they fell together on the floor.

"Violet?" he asked.

She panicked, realizing she wasn't invisible anymore. "Can you sit up?" she whispered. "Please, Scott, I need your help."

He lifted himself gingerly, sucking in air, as the skin around his bullet wound pulled. She draped his arm again around her neck and shoulders. He struggled to pull himself to his feet, and most of his weight crashed onto her shoulders.

She didn't have time to think about how heavy he was or about his blood smearing on her favorite pink sweater. She dragged him towards the study rooms. The doors hung ajar, their doorknobs shot through, but it was the only chance they had.

She helped him to the floor before returning to the door. She pushed one of the heavy chairs against it, hoping it would at least hold it closed. Not satisfied with her makeshift barrier, she ran to the desk and pushed as hard as her strength allowed, but it wouldn't budge. There was little else in the room to barricade it except for a whiteboard Violet couldn't pull from the wall.

She turned her attention to Scott. His eyes were closed again, and his breath labored in his chest. Violet was no doctor, but he didn't look good. She pulled off her sweater and placed it against his bullet wound, stifling the blood. At least she thought she needed to. She wasn't sure what to do. Years of watching medical shows hadn't prepared her enough for this moment. The cold made her shiver, and she cursed herself for wearing such a thin shirt under her sweater. But after a moment, she couldn't be sure if it was the cold that made her tremble or her growing fear as Scott's face continued to pale. She pushed down the panic building in her chest. Scott depended on her not having a breakdown.

"Scott," she whispered. His eyes opened at that. Violet jumped back, but relief rushed through her. She reached into her back pocket and found her phone. Someone must have called for help by now. Could she risk calling 911 while the gunman might be close enough to hear?

"Violet," called Scott loudly, and Violet shushed him.

"Hey, don't worry. You're okay, but you have to be quiet," she whispered.

"Violet," he repeated. She shushed him again. She would have covered his mouth if she wasn't afraid that it would block his breathing.

"Please Scott. Everything is going to be okay," she lied.

His blood continued to gush out, and her arms shook from the pressure she placed on his wound. She wasn't sure how much more blood he could lose before it became critical.

Suddenly, she heard it again. The same dragging footsteps from before. She held her breath, afraid of the gunman hearing her gasps. She repeated the spell again, changing the words to include Scott. Her hands grew warm on his body. She'd never used the spell on two before and prayed it would work. Her whispered spell grew fainter and fainter as the footsteps grew louder. She stopped as the door jostled. The gunman pushed hard against it, and the chair rattled on the other side.

She trembled, but she dared not move. She couldn't, even if she wanted to. Scott needed her to keep the pressure on his wound. The gunman pushed against the door harder, forcing the chair to the ground and tearing the door from its hinges. Violet was sure she squeaked, but she managed to hold back her scream.

He was in. Violet stopped breathing. She placed a trembling hand on Scott's lips.

The gunman stopped at the door, and she wished to see his eyes again. Like this, he appeared robotic and thoughtless, but bloodthirsty. At least if she saw his eyes, she would know another human did this. She wasn't sure what was worse. A human or a monster.

His head moved, scanning the entire room, left to right. Violet thought he looked like he was looking for something. He didn't move from the doorway, but the attached light on his gun passed by her and Scott three times.

The gunman turned away, and Violet didn't have to wonder why, as sirens grew louder and louder outside the building. The gunman ran out, and Violet breathed again.

She turned to Scott. He was still breathing, but his chest barely moved. She pushed his hair away from his face, smearing some of his blood on his forehead.

This asshole really has me saving his life right now!

She hated him, sure, but not enough to let him bleed out. She had no issue with killing assholes, but she wouldn't compare Scott to a murderer. He was just an annoying coworker!

It didn't take long for Violet to hear the sounds of the police. Their shouts echoed through the still library. People still hiding in the library called out for help. She wanted to answer too, but her voice seemed to stay stuck in her throat. When she croaked out a "HERE", it sounded foreign to her. Like her voice wasn't her own.

The police located them, one of them saying something that Violet was only half listening to. One officer tried to pull her away from Scott, but she fought them. Thrashing away from the man, she placed her hands on her blood-soaked sweater again. She was being silly. Why was she fighting with them? They were going to help him. But in that moment, she felt that if she let go of him, she would never see him again, and the thought frightened her.

A voice broke through her hazed head, a steady and warm voice, and she turned to see a man in a full SWAT uniform standing over her. "It's okay. We'll take care of him." She didn't understand why, but that was enough to pull her from the fog.

She was aware of being taken outside. The cold, waking her skin with goosebumps. Someone placed a jacket on her. Night surrounded her, and she realized she had lost track of time.

How long had she been in the library?

Chapter Three

Violet woke up startled, and she lay in the early morning autumn darkness, staring at her ceiling. Surprised that she was in her own bed and not in the library anymore. Her sleep hadn't been restful. Every dream dissolved into a nightmare of her searching for Scott. As hard as she tried, she couldn't dream of anything else. Every thought, waking or asleep, was about him. About the library and the gunman.

She found her phone dead, realizing she had forgotten to charge it before passing out the night before. Guilt churned in her chest when she saw the thirty missed calls and hundreds of texts from the coven once she turned on her phone. She texted them all back, explaining she was okay. But she didn't want to tell them about the numbness or what had happened. Not yet. She could barely think straight. She didn't mean to worry them, but writing a thorough explanation of the entire ordeal was too much for her to handle.

It was hard not to succumb to the numbness creeping around the edges of her thoughts. But no matter how much time seemed to stand still in the library, life outside it continued, and there were a few things she needed to take care of. Violet called Ellie first.

"Violet! Are you okay?"

"I'm fine," her voice cracked. "I just called to ask you to tell the firm I'm not coming into work today."

"I won't have to. They're closed today. Didn't you read the email? They think this was a targeted attack."

"What?" asked Violet.

"They shot Scott."

"I know he was shot. I was there."

"He was the only person shot."

"But I heard lots of gunshots? How was he the only one shot?"

"I'm not sure, but the firm is very serious. They're upping security today."

"Okay," Violet felt her heart racing. A targeted attack? But why Scott?

"Violet, do you want me to come over?"

"No, I'm fine. Do you know if Scott is okay?"

"I haven't heard anything," but her voice faltered on the other end, as if withholding bad news.

Violet said her goodbyes and reassured Ellie that if she needed anything, she would call her. She hung up the phone, rubbing her eyes hard. Something about the way Ellie hesitated worried her. Or was she just too on edge, reading into something that wasn't there?

Violet couldn't be sure either way. She got up and started getting ready. She was halfway dressed, with her hairbrush stuck in a knot, when her phone rang. Margaret's name shone on her phone's screen. Violet's heart sank. She should have called her first.

"Violet!" Margaret's voice rang out, and Violet held the phone away from her ear. "Why didn't you call me last night? I was so worried! We were all worried! The only reason I didn't show up at your door was because Rosie located you and found you in your house!"

"Believe me, it wasn't on purpose. I'm sorry, Maggie. Yesterday was a lot, and I just wanted to sleep."

"I'm sorry, Vi. I was just worried, but I'm glad that you're okay. Do you want me to come over?"

Violet couldn't help herself as the emotions she'd been pushing down for hours bubbled up. She wiped her tears away, but once it started, Violet couldn't stop it.

"Oh no!" said Margaret. "Please don't cry, Vi! I'll be there right away."

Violet wiped her tears, smudging her freshly applied mascara. There was one reason she didn't hesitate in killing Derek, and that was Maggie.

They'd met in middle school. Classmates bullied Violet for her modest clothing that was always about two hundred years out of fashion. It also didn't help that she had proselytized to them as children, either. The only reason her parents even let her enroll in public school was because of all the impressionable souls needing saving. But no kid wanted to hang out with a classmate who told them they were going to hell in every conversation.

The bullies often teased Margaret about her freckles covering every inch of her body. They also thought her to be weird. No one spoke of it aloud, but Violet had often heard the whispers about her family. Her grandmother sold love spells. A boy in their class blamed her grandmother for why his parents divorced. Another swore she saw Margaret's mom and dad buying pig parts for their spells. A tongue to silence the gossip, and a heart to bind their love forever. Margaret never defended herself, which made the rumors ten times worse.

Ostracized by all their classmates, they came together. By the time they'd met, Violet had stopped trying to push her parents' religion on her classmates. They never forgot what she did, but Margaret forgave her. Violet had never believed the rumors until she caught Margaret talking to an older woman, who disappeared when Violet wandered into her room. Margaret then let her into the family secret, telling her all about the magic she grew up in.

"A witch?" asked Violet.

"Yes," Margaret chewed on her bottom lip, but even through her nervousness, she didn't look like she regretted telling her.

"Do you guys have magic powers?"

"Nothing that special. My mom gets visions of the future, and my grandma can control the weather."

"The weather?"

"Not a lot, just what's above our house, usually."

"What about you?"

"I don't have any powers. Not all witches do."

Violet's mind raced. She peered around them, but everything in Margaret's room appeared normal, even down to the Hello Kitty plushes on her bed. Margaret wasn't as scary as her parents had made her believe a witch would be. If anything, it seemed much more normal than her home.

"Who was the ghost?" asked Violet.

"My great-grandmother, she helps me."

Violet bit her lip, her heart racing, the question poised to spill from her mouth before she could phrase it well. "Can you teach me?"

Violet wasn't born a witch, and her parents would be the first to turn her in to the authorities if they knew what she was now. She'd grown up in an old-fashioned brimstone and hellfire family. Love, they explained, from God was unconditional, yet there were so many rules. So many conditions she had to obey if she wanted to be saved. Belief and faith alone were not enough for salvation, and they reminded Violet daily that she was never enough, either.

At first, Margaret's revelation scared Violet. She couldn't tell her parents. If they discovered the witchcraft, they would do more than just pray for Margaret and her family. They would subject Violet to all sorts of exorcisms by her church. Would they even have believed her if she'd told them she hadn't taken part in any spells? Probably not. This was a secret she had to keep. But it wasn't the first secret she had kept from her parents. Like the stolen lip gloss kept in the bottom of her underwear drawer, or the R-rated movies she had sneaked into with some of the other kids in her church, this too she would keep hidden away.

Margaret and her family had taught her everything she knew. They let her copy the family spells in their book of shadows. Most spell work was universal, but every family had its own recipe. When Violet would flip through Margaret's family spell book, she often wondered how many generations had kept the book. How many generations of loving families touched the book? Were they loved unconditionally, too? The way Margaret was by her parents?

This was all before the trials, and Margaret trusted Violet not to spill her family's secrets. Violet never trusted her parents. Thou shalt not suffer a witch to live. Violet didn't doubt her parents might kill her now if they found out about her. However, they knew nothing about her, and Violet made sure of that.

Violet had stopped talking to her parents when she told them she'd been accepted into college. It appalled them that she had even applied to secular schools. They accused her of many things that night. Someone had brainwashed her. The Devil controlled her and led her astray from God. She'd been too scared to say anything back, but decided never to speak to them again.

She'd gotten the occasional message from them over the years, a perfunctory praying for you. But they didn't seem all that interested in speaking with her further. She figured they were too ashamed of her. Not after the incident.

It must have been hard for them to show their faces to their friends after she left. Violet hoped it was hard and that the congregation still talked about her in hushed whispers. Her parents would never know peace then, and that pleased her.

"Come over later tonight," Violet told Margaret. "I have some things that I have to do first."

They set a time, and Violet continued getting ready. She felt a little better crying over the phone to Margaret. A night in with her best friend was exactly what she needed. But she still had one thing she needed to do before then.

Chapter Four

Scott heard noises around him. A symphony of beeps that told him he was at least alive. Somewhere in the world, he breathed, and his heart pumped blood throughout his body. He wasn't fully conscious until 6 a.m., after a scream startled him awake, but staring around him in the hospital, he found himself alone. It might have been the noises, the insistent and steady chimes, or the nurses gossiping in the hallway. There was no commotion or other person in the room. No one could have let out such a blood-curdling scream.

He took stock of himself. As far as he could tell, his limbs were all accounted for. His head was on his neck. There was soreness but no pain; no doubt the painkillers worked overtime. When he felt assured that nothing physically seemed to be missing, he tried to remember.

The name flashed through his mind like lightning. *Violet.* He looked around at his surroundings, trying to find his phone. Was she safe? Was she shot? The events of the day before were painfully out of reach. Hard as he tried, the memories came back fragmented, shards of images that his mind wanted to forget.

Scott had heard the first shot. He had been confused, thinking they were fireworks. He cursed at himself for not recognizing the sound of gunfire. His mind always worked like that. Rationalizing and assuming the least worst plausible scenario first. The shots continued, people screamed and ran; that's when the panic set in. He needed to find her. He needed to keep her safe.

Scott remembered running. He bumped into others doing the same. The book list he gave her raced through his head. He needed to get there before the gunman.

He tried in vain to remember the gunman. Had he even seen him before the shot? Scott remembered the pain. A singed, burning smell and a blinding pain.

What then? Nothing came back, and it frustrated Scott. He hated feeling out of control. He didn't even drink very often because he hated the sensation of losing any control of his faculties. This felt worse. Like a dream skirted around his mind.

There was blood? Her sweater? Something with her sweater? It came to him like an old blurred photograph. Its edges burned and frayed. Violet kneeled over him, shushing him.

"You're awake?" A nurse with graying brown hair stood at the doorway to his room. "How are you feeling?"

"Okay, considering."

"How's your pain on a scale of one to ten?"

"Four, I guess." She reached for the IV bag, but he stopped her. "I need to know. Were there other survivors?"

"You're the only casualty that came in."

"The rest were dead?" His heart hammered in his chest, and the surrounding monitors beeped embarrassingly loud.

"You're the only person hurt. Nobody else," she assured him. She reached into the bag and handed him his phone. She finished up while Scott looked on, dumbfounded.

How was he the only casualty? Was it a hit? Who had he pissed off lately? No one immediately came to mind. Unless some disgruntled client got even, but it didn't seem right.

When the nurse left, he started scrolling through his phone. He needed to let someone know that he was all right. But as he swiped through the numbers, an unwelcome knot formed in his stomach.

He didn't want to call anyone. What was the point? He was alive, right? He wondered whether his father would be awake at this hour. If he would even answer. His brother would be mad if he woke him up during the early morning hours.

His first instinct was to call work. Beatrice would be there by now. She could email him his work, tell Carl what happened, and forward any calls to him. He put his phone away. His concern for work over family spoke volumes. But he had avoided his family until now. Why change things for a shooting he survived?

A knock on the door diverted his attention from his pitiful contact list. Violet stood in the doorway, and Scott stared, surprised, unsure of what to say. She wore a dark blue sweater, and she had pulled back her dark hair into a ponytail. It was surprising to see how well she held herself together, given what they had endured. She had the same haughty look about her as she surveyed him. His heart monitor beeped louder with his increasing heart rate, and he resisted the urge to unplug it from the wall.

"Hi," she said, approaching him slowly, almost wary that he might strike like a coiled snake. His eyes darted from her face to the small prickly cactus she placed on his bedside table.

"What? No flowers?" asked Scott.

"Flowers die," she said. "And anyway, I thought this fit you better."

Is she saying I'm like a cactus?

"How are you feeling?"

"Like death," he said.

"Be serious," she frowned.

"I got shot; this is as serious as I get." He waited for her to say something, but when she didn't, he continued. "Did you know I was the only one who got shot?"

"I did. Also, the firm is closed today, something about upping security."

"So they think the shooting is related to the law firm." It made sense to Scott. But why target only him? The shooter could have gone directly to the firm for real damage.

"Do you think it's because of some people that we defended?"

"Well, I don't have a lot of enemies, Violet, so probably." She was quiet again, and he hated it. Why was she here? To make him feel awkward? "Thank you, by the way."

"For the cactus?"

"For saving my life." His eyes remained fixed on her as she looked away, finding her reaction curious.

"Yeah, well, I'm hoping you're gonna go easy on me from now on. Seeing as I saved your life and all."

He laughed, her response surprising him, but winced as the laughter pulled at the stitches on his side. She reached out to stop him from moving.

"It's okay. I'm fine, really." There was a silence again, but unlike before, Scott didn't feel the need to fill it.

"Scott—" started Violet.

"Scott?" a jarring voice cracked through their silence. He turned and saw a woman by the door — short, with a black bob and teary brown eyes.

Shit, he thought, *Piper*. He couldn't believe he had forgotten to call Piper.

"Scott? Are you okay?" She lunged forward, grabbing him in a painful hug. Scott glimpsed Violet. Her cheeks burned bright red, and her face was stuck in an uncomfortable frown. No intern should be privy to this aspect of his life, and it embarrassed him.

"Why didn't you call me? I waited last night for you to call! And then I saw the news! And I called your brother and your father, and they didn't know what was going on! They told me you would have called if it were serious, and look at you!"

"It wasn't serious Piper, I'm fine. And I was just about to call you. I only just woke up."

Piper, as if sensing the lie, sharply turned towards Violet. "Can you believe it? He forgot to call his girlfriend."

"You know what, this seems like a private thing, so I'm gonna head out," said Violet. "I'm glad you're feeling better," she added as she hurried out the door.

Scott turned to watch her leave, sensing Piper's eyes burrowing into his face. He didn't want Violet to leave; he could use a buffer right now. Piper's presence near him was making him increasingly irritated. As he turned to Piper, he waited for the inevitable fight.

Chapter Five

Margaret slipped her straw through her face mask's opening. She pursed her lips and sipped her margarita while Violet explained what had happened at the hospital.

"So he didn't tell her?" Margaret asked with a gasp.

"I guess not. She was pissed. Frankly, I'm surprised he would even have a girlfriend." Violet peeled off her mask and massaged the leftover essence into her skin.

"Why is that surprising? Is he ugly?"

Violet got a flash of him in her mind. The dark hair, sharp jawline, and dimples that she had no clue existed until today, when he laughed at her joke. Did he really never smile in front of her until now? "He's not like hideous, but he has an ugly personality. And anyway, I'm not surprised he's a bad boyfriend, too."

"I'm sure it really was an accident." Margaret peeled her mask off too, flinging it towards the trash can. Violet knew she would say something like that. Leave it to Margaret to always see the good in everyone.

"Maybe, but he didn't look happy to see her there."

"Was he happy seeing you?" asked Margaret.

Violet hesitated. "Next question," said Violet, grabbing her empty glass.

"Hey, come on now! Was he?"

"It was probably a fluke. I think he's just grateful I saved his life. And anyway, now I can hold it over his head, so he stays nice the rest of my internship. Who knows, maybe I'll be able to finesse a letter of recommendation from him. That'll for sure piss him off." Margaret rolled her eyes, and Violet took her glass into the kitchen. She refilled her margarita to avoid further interrogation.

Piper's interruption had rattled her. She didn't understand why. What did it matter that he had a girlfriend? She didn't like Scott in that way. She hated Scott. Saving his life was the right thing to do, not because she cared about him but because even though he was a total asshole, that wasn't reason enough to not save him.

She was nothing to Scott. She was a nuisance, a disgruntled coworker, a thorn in his side, but nothing else. Scott was nothing to her but an asshole in an industry of assholes that viewed her work as less than because she was a woman. It was a good thing he had found someone who would date him because he would probably grow old and die alone otherwise.

Margaret walked into the kitchen, handing her glass to Violet. "Refill, please," she singsonged. Violet grabbed the blender and poured the rest of it into Margaret's cup.

Violet hadn't realized how badly she needed her friends today. Ellie had stopped by earlier, dropping off a lasagna that Violet and Margaret had already devoured half. Lenore had come an hour after Ellie, setting up protections around her apartment, and she left Violet a small golden locket.

"Don't open it," explained Lenore. "It'll protect you."

Violet only nodded. The coven knew that when Lenore gave them something, no matter how small or big it was, it would come in handy later. Lenore didn't understand how her gift worked. Her serendipitous offerings had saved Lola from a bad date, found a well on Molly's property, and helped Margaret find a great house selling under market value.

Violet's fingers rubbed the daffodil on the front of the locket. Her fingers found the inscription on the back: A. T.A. This was a family heirloom, and she couldn't believe Lenore would part with it. Or that anyone would care so much about her to give her something so special. Throughout the day, she got messages and love from all her sisters. Little gentle reminders they cared, except for one.

Violet sat back down on the couch, and Margaret flipped through the movies, trying to decide which one to watch.

"Has she said anything?" asked Violet.

"Who?" asked Margaret.

"You know who?"

"Molly? She's cold with me too."

"But is she icing you out as badly as me?"

"Has she not talked to you since everything with Ellie and River?"

"She sent me a message this morning saying she was glad that I was alright."

"That's not too bad."

"It's in the tone."

"She was the one who got Rosie to track you last night."

"Yeah, but Rosie would have tracked me regardless."

"She's pretty pissed, but she'll come around."

"Maybe, but she doesn't even care if Derek was going to hurt you! If it's not done her way, then she doesn't care." Margaret didn't respond. Violet turned to her, finding Margaret's gaze faraway. "Shit, sorry Maggie. I didn't mean to bring it up again."

"It's okay."

"No, it's not. I won't mention that night or Derek ever again. I promise."

"Thanks."

Margaret said nothing for a while, her eyes barely focused on the TV. Violet bit her bottom lip until she tasted blood, feeling horrible for bringing Derek back up again and unsure how to make it right.

"I've noticed something about you lately," said Margaret, breaking the silence.

"I'm only crankier because second year law school is a lot worse than I thought it would be."

"No, not that. You have a habit of saving people's lives. You noticed that?" Margaret sniffled, and Violet knew she was trying hard not to cry.

"Well, I would have done a lot more than just kill Derek if he had killed you, trust me."

Violet meant every word. She loved Margaret. If Molly was upset that Violet had put the entire coven in danger to protect Margaret, so be it. She didn't regret it. The only regret was not making the bastard suffer more at her hands. He had suffered a lot, but that was mostly Ellie's doing.

Without Margaret, Violet wasn't sure if she quite belonged in the coven or if she wanted to continue practicing magic. Margaret knew she would be a powerful witch. Violet had an innate gift for magic. Lots of mortals did. As a child, she would self-induce fevers when she wanted to come home from school early. She made Lucy Mannings' hair fall out after she teased her about her own greasy braids. If she practiced and learned, she could channel her magic. Violet and Rosie were the only two in the coven who weren't born witches, but developed their skills later on in life.

Violet often thought she wasn't as powerful as the rest. They had real power. Molly especially. There was a reason she was the leader. They didn't need to vote or discuss it. Molly's power emanated from her, like silky tendrils touching everything around her. She was still the only witch Violet knew who could cast without saying a word.

"It's about intention," Molly once explained to her. "Feel it. Feel it as if it has already occurred."

Molly's hands wrapped around her middle and warmed Violet's skin through her thin shirt. Violet's eyes were closed as she tried to will anything to happen. But as much as she pushed, nothing did.

Violet grew angry thinking about Molly. If Molly was going to stay upset, so could she. They could ignore each other forever. Molly was not stupid enough to kick her out of the coven. If she kicked out Violet, Margaret would leave with her. Ellie would leave, and the others could too, if they were upset enough by it. To be alone was to be unprotected, and Molly would never risk their lives.

Violet paid little attention to the movie. It was more to Margaret's taste. A romantic drama full of period costumes and accents. When the movie ended, Margaret asked if she was tired enough to sleep. Violet only nodded, her eyes already closing. The alcohol had long covered her senses with a welcomed dullness.

They climbed into Violet's bed, and Violet kissed Margaret on the forehead. Margaret only smiled as she settled onto her side.

"Thank you for taking care of me," she said.

"You're welcome," Margaret said. Her eyes fluttered closed.

Violet closed her eyes, waiting for sleep to take her away. Away from the confusing day with Scott, away from her ongoing fight with Molly, away from the shooting.

She lay there for hours, and sleep never came.

Chapter Six

Scott had spent the better part of his week off working. He told Beatrice to email him any motions and paperwork, and talked to clients over the phone. He hated to stand around doing nothing, and using work as an excuse, he could avoid the calls from his family.

Piper had done more damage than he realized. Her frantic calls to his dad and his brother opened up an excuse for communication, and he hated it. Scott had no clue how she had gotten their numbers, but one thing was for certain—Piper was incredibly resourceful and had a talent for uncovering information online. He had used some of her skills before to help in a case. He never imagined she would use those skills on him one day.

She didn't know his family. Why would she? He'd never told her, and he never wanted to tell her. So, when he learned of the calls, it seemed like a betrayal. Since then, he dodged his father's calls. His brother stopped calling after the third day of no answers, but his dad was as stubborn as Scott. Piper unknowingly had encouraged his dad to reach out to him again, and it infuriated him.

To avoid his family and the piercing guilt building up, he buried himself in work. Family calls were easy to ignore if he had an excuse. Carl had called Scott earlier in the week, telling him to take it easy. There was no need for him to work right now. The firm would take care of everything. Scott didn't listen, and he found himself with a lot of time after asking Piper to return to Philadelphia.

"Are you sure?" she asked. Her brown eyes betrayed her shock at his request.

"I don't want to keep you here. You have school, right?"

"I do, but Scott, I want to stay with you."

"I'm fine. My side doesn't even hurt anymore."

"That's not the point."

He hurt her. It was plain enough for Scott to pick up, but he needed to try something, anything, to make her leave.

"It won't look good if you stay here and neglect school. I know how tough your program is."

"I don't care about school. I care about you."

"Maybe you should care less about me. Please, Piper, I just need you to go."

Her shoulders slumped in defeat, and she turned quickly away to hide her tears. She wanted nothing more than to stay with him and take care of him, and he was being an absolute dick to her. He noticed the weird joy it brought her to change his dressings and wash his back in the shower. But Scott hated having to depend on her. He needed her gone.

Even though he still could have used some of her help, when he kissed her goodbye, a restlessness left his body. He was more at ease knowing two states separated them, although he got the sense this relationship was about to end.

Now that his week of rest was over, he felt a sense of unease as he drove to the office. There was a sense of security in his home. His high-rise apartment had cameras and security in the lobby. Stepping out now, he couldn't help but look at every passerby for a little too long. Scott didn't know exactly what he was looking for. He had no memory of the shooter. He had tried to remember, but the harder he pushed, the further away the image of the shooter became. Every person now was a suspect to him.

Two security guards immediately greeted him when he entered the office. They instructed him to put his bag on the conveyor belt for the metal detector. It took him by surprise, but he didn't fight it and did as he was told. This was what the email had meant by higher security, and here he had expected them to invest in better cameras. He didn't realize he was going to be greeted by fake TSA officers.

After the security officer gave him a quick pat-down, he walked into the lobby. A flock of secretaries and associates gathered around him, asking if he was alright. They meant well; he knew that, but the sudden attention made him uncomfortable.

No matter how many 'I'm fines' he threw at them, they didn't seem to believe him.

He wanted to run to his office but thought better than to be rude to the secretaries, especially Beatrice. She'd done him a few solids over the past couple of years. Luckily, Carl interrupted the ambush of associates after a few minutes.

"Scott!" His booming voice quieted the surrounding chatter. "Glad you're back. Come into my office, please."

Scott said his apologies to the secretaries and followed Carl.

"How are you feeling?" he asked as Scott sat on a chair opposite Carl's desk. Carl didn't sit on the chair, preferring to sit on the desk to be closer to him.

"I've been better," said Scott, finding Carl's proximity unnerving.

"Terrible what happened, but listen, I know you and I have been wracking our brains to figure out who wanted to hurt the firm. I've spoken to the partners, and they believe it may be retaliation."

"Retaliation for what?"

"For defending the witch."

"We've defended witches before."

"The political climate has shifted. Even defending a witch can be seen as an endorsement at this point."

"You're joking, right?"

"There have been attacks at other law firms all over the country for exactly the same reason."

"Can I remind you we're defending her from a murder charge?"

"Yes, but murder by the means of witchcraft. We can't win this one, and anyway, she's not worth losing you or anyone else at this firm."

The red on Carl's neck spread to his face. He didn't like to be questioned like this, especially not by a junior associate, but Scott had been at the firm for almost four years now. His opinion mattered, even if Carl didn't want to hear it.

"So you're just going to drop her?"

"We're referring her out."

Carl studied Scott, waiting for him to say something, but Scott said nothing more. The wound on his side pulsed. Perhaps coming in today was a bad idea after all. He stood up and left before he said something he would regret later.

Scott's anger threatened to spew out the longer he stayed at the firm, but he couldn't storm out and return home. Not without the other ruthless social-climbing associates trying to take his spot.

He sat down quickly when he entered his office. He tried to catch his breath, finding it odd that the trek from Carl's office to his had winded him. The wound on his side throbbed, and the bandage felt itchy on his skin. Normally he could ignore those kinds of things, but today he felt especially strung out.

Scott didn't care about this witchcraft business. He opposed the laws against witchcraft because he saw them as unnecessary government interference, not because he supported the targeted group's faith. He didn't believe there were actual witches. People who played with medicinal herbs and fires, sure, but witches who cast spells and danced with the devil? There was no way. He didn't want to defend this client because he thought it was some moral obligation to defend her people from tyranny, but because that was his job. Witch or no witch, the law guaranteed everyone a lawyer. Who was he to decide whether what she did was right or wrong?

He couldn't pretend it was all about his selfless indignation. This client was his first real case, where he was the lead lawyer since becoming a junior associate. They gave it to him and the other junior associates because nobody else would take it, but that was fine. This was the first proper case where he was going to prove his worth to the firm. Now he had nothing, and that poor woman was going to start over with another firm.

Scott made his way to the lounge to pour himself some coffee. He mostly grunted and used one-word answers to his colleagues' questions. They left him alone eventually, although some lingered around as if the gunshot had altered his personality. But they soon realized the same prickly, short-tempered man hadn't disappeared. Scott figured they probably felt some obligation to check up on him and make sure he was okay. But his sour mood affected everyone around him, and they all cleared out of the lounge.

Scott looked in the fridge for the creamer when someone cleared their throat behind him. He sighed, no doubt another person wanting to listen to the firsthand account of his survival.

He turned around, hoping his scowl would scare them off, but was surprised to find Violet standing behind him.

"You're back," she said, reaching into the fridge to pull out the coffee creamer she liked. Cookies and cream, he noted, a gross choice. He preferred his coffee with a splash of a sensible creamer, like vanilla. He wasn't a monster.

"I couldn't stay home anymore. I had too much work here."

"I've heard you've been working this whole time. You seriously don't even know when to stop, do you?"

"Is that a compliment? Because I think you just called me hardworking?" he smirked.

"It's an insult," she said curtly, but she smiled. She sipped some of her coffee, leaning against the counter. He'd never noticed the mole on her right cheek before, just below her eye. It suited her. "How—" she started.

"Please don't ask me how I am. I'm tired of that question. If I hear it one more time, I'll smash this mug on the floor."

"Okay... bit dramatic."

"It's been a bad day."

"Already?"

"Yes." They sipped their coffee in silence, but it didn't bother Scott. He didn't think it bothered Violet either. "Is this your first day back?" he asked.

"No, I've been here all week."

"Seriously?" he asked.

"Well, I wasn't actually hurt. So, none of my professors gave me a break."

"That's fucked up."

Violet shrugged. "It was a nice distraction, I guess. Carl was nice enough to tell me to take a few days off, but I need my internship hours. So, no break."

"I would tell you to take a break before you burn out, but I don't think you would take my advice."

"You're right, I won't take it, but you should think of taking yours."

"I'm fine, just perfect."

"Is this a new tactic to not alert the other associates that your spot might come up for grabs?"

Scott chuckled. "These idiots will never take my spot."

"Maybe not, but I could."

Scott raised an eyebrow, but Violet looked serious. "You'd be the only true worthy opponent."

"Now who's doling out compliments?" She stared into her cup, but when she looked up at him, it startled him. Those large gray eyes had no bottom, and he grew uncomfortable under her gaze. He could drown in those eyes.

"Anyway," Scott said, turning away, "I should get back." Violet nodded, not saying anything else as he left.

He walked past her, getting a whiff of her sweet vanilla perfume. Violet was beautiful, sure. Scott noticed it before. It was hard not to. She was tall, with long dark hair that cascaded in waves down her back. She had a small upturned nose and long lashes that fanned out against her cheeks when she peered down. He wanted nothing more than to pinch the fat on her hips.

He'd always kept her at arm's length, however, because it was important for his job. The last thing he wanted was an office romance with an intern, of all people. It would look horrible on him, and if they broke up, which they inevitably would, he couldn't stand being in the same building as his exes. The awkwardness of it all made him cringe.

Violet was beautiful, smart, and, he hated to admit it, at times, funny. There was nothing there for him. He questioned the degree to which his feelings had shifted since she had saved him. He was grateful for sure, but was that clouding his judgment now?

Scott sat back in his office, and he pushed away his thoughts about Violet. There were more pressing matters to attend to. Like what to do with Eve Miller? He yawned and rubbed his tired eyes. He might have snapped a little too hard at Carl.

But he hadn't slept well since the shooting. Every night was the same. He tossed and turned in bed, waiting for sleep to come. When he eventually drifted off, he only dreamed of the library. Some nights, he would run away from the gunman. In others, he ran to find Violet, searching down each aisle as his chest constricted with each step. He almost never found her, and when he did, she was always dead.

He would then wake up in a cold sweat, his heart beating against his ribs. No matter how hard he tried, he couldn't fall asleep again. Although some nights he was fine with it because his nightmares were so unbearable, he preferred to stay awake.

He hadn't slept over three hours a night since he left the hospital, so he set up a doctor's appointment to fix it.

Sleep or no sleep, he had a job to do, and it gave him an idea.

He learned Carl would be back in the office in an hour, but he couldn't wait, and Scott called him.

Carl answered with a disgruntled hello, still upset at Scott from their fight earlier.

"Let me keep the client," started Scott.

"Scott—"

"Listen, nobody else works on the case. Just me. You can make that clear to the press however you like. But if someone is out to intimidate me from working with this client, I won't back down." Scott waited as an exasperated sigh was all Carl could muster on the other end. "I get not asking to sacrifice anyone in the firm, but what about me? I don't mind putting it at risk."

"Careful, Scott, you make it sound like a death wish."

"Not a death wish, sir, just stubborn."

"Fine," Carl said on the line. "But nobody else helps. Understand?"

"Yes," said Scott, and for the first time all day, he felt like himself again.

Chapter Seven

Violet couldn't believe the text message when she read it.

Maggie: Meeting at BB. Molly says come!!

The coven meeting didn't surprise her. They used to have them at least once a week. But that was before Violet killed Derek. Before Ellie resurrected him and he threatened to expose the entire coven. Molly had become suspicious of the possibility of someone seeing something the night the coven killed Derek together. As a precautionary measure, she thought it best for everyone to keep their distance, at least temporarily. The girls in one form or another always hung out, but they were extra careful because of Molly.

No, the meeting hadn't surprised her, but what had been surprising was that Molly had asked her to come. Had the ice queen finally melted? Violet didn't expect to be brought back into the fold, but as she parked outside of Books & Beans, a small part of her wondered if maybe Molly had forgiven her.

She hadn't stepped foot inside the place since everything had happened, which was hard since it had been one of her favorite places to study. Other coffee shops didn't quite meet her strict requirements for a perfect study space. They needed to be small and intimate, but not a hole in the wall. There needed to be chatter, but not so loud that it distracted her from her work. Plus, other coffee shops didn't let her order coffee and pastries for free like Molly did.

Violet didn't get out of the car. She needed her buffer. She needed Margaret. The minutes ticked by, and she observed the animated conversations and laughter of the coven inside, but she continued to wait. It looked as if Rosie was telling a story. Her hands waved in front of her face as Ellie and Lola laughed. After some time, she spotted the familiar bright blue of Margaret's car approaching. As they entered the cafe together, Violet clung to her, using her as a shield.

While the others greeted Violet, she received a tight smile from Molly. Violet hadn't seen her in weeks, but she appeared the same. Her high cheekbones made her appear haughtier, and she peered at Violet from behind her long lashes. Checking her up and down as if she was looking for something to reprimand.

"Hi Molly," said Violet.

"Hello, Violet," Molly replied.

They stared each other down, the silence tense between them. The others watched them, unsure of how to interject.

Rosie whistled, "Okay, who's hungry? Lenore is bringing the pizza." As if on cue, Lenore came in, her arms overloaded with pizza boxes.

"Oh thank Goddess," said Rosie, helping Lenore put down the boxes.

"What did I miss?" asked Lenore.

"Nothing," said Lola. "You came right on time, as usual."

They ate the pizza before discussing anything. Nothing could get done if they were all hungry. The coven learned that valuable lesson when Rosie threw mugwort instead of motherwort into a cauldron and almost blew up Molly's house once. They also fought more when they were hungry. Violet hoped that there would be less tension now, but she stayed quiet as she chewed a slice that tasted like cardboard in her mouth.

When everyone finished eating, and they settled onto the couches, happy and satiated, Lola asked what was on everyone's mind. "Are you bringing back the weekly meetings?"

"I'm not sure yet. Things were calming down, but that was before the shooting," Molly looked at Violet. Violet heated under her sweater, feeling like Molly accused her of something. As if it were her fault, she was caught up in a shooting.

"That has nothing to do with the coven," said Violet.

"You were there," said Molly.

"Yeah, but it wasn't about me. He didn't shoot me."

"What happened?" asked Lenore. "We've all avoided asking to give you time to deal. But are you okay telling us now?"

"I haven't really wanted to think about it."

"You don't have to tell us if you're not comfortable," said Ellie.

"No... I think I can talk about it." She told them everything. Exactly as she remembered it. The shots, how she couldn't move, the spell to make her invisible, the gunman missing her, and her finding Scott. She explained having to move him into an abandoned study room to treat his bullet wound.

"There was a moment I thought was a little weird. When I was in the room with Scott, the gunman came back. I used the same spell to make us both invisible, so he didn't see us, but he stayed there a lot longer than I thought he would. He looked like he was looking for something."

"What do you think it could have been?" Molly sounded serious. Violet thought she looked curious, her eyebrows furrowed with a hint of worry.

"I'm not sure. Maybe he was looking for Scott again? Like to make sure he finished the job or something?"

"He could have shot Scott in the head if he really wanted to kill him," said Lola.

"I guess. So was it all just to send a message?" asked Violet.

"There's a lot we don't know. For one, we can't rule out that this has nothing to do with the coven. We haven't been careful lately." That stung, and Violet knew she was speaking about her. "We all got lucky with River labeling all of Derek's victims as an animal attack. We got lucky that nobody walked in on what we were doing to Derek. But we can't be sure that we covered every single one of our bases. So for now, wards and protection spells. Got it? And we have to be extra careful."

"There's another thing," said Ellie. "The law firm is convinced this was a targeted attack because of a client who's charged with murdering her husband by witchcraft."

"Is she really a witch?" asked Rosie.

"No, I checked. She's mortal," said Ellie, "and they've taken everyone off the case but Scott."

"What?" asked Violet, whipping around to look at Ellie.

"Didn't you hear? Beth told me this morning. She heard Scott and Carl shouting when he came back. Carl wanted to get rid of the client. He said he didn't want to put the whole firm at risk. Scott was really upset by it, but told Carl that he would work on the case alone. Carl isn't letting anyone help him."

Violet stayed silent. Scott would really risk his life like that for a woman accused of being a witch?

"Regardless, that doesn't change things, does it? Either way, the shooting may have happened because someone hates witches. So it still stands. Protection spells everyone. Carry it with you," said Molly.

Official coven business ended there, but nobody was in a rush to leave. They laughed and bantered, the atmosphere reminiscent of old times before Violet screwed everything up. Molly went behind the counter, and she and Lola spoke in hushed tones, away from everyone else. As much as Violet wanted to keep the freeze-out going until Molly apologized to her, she needed something. With no other option, she took a deep breath and reluctantly approached the counter.

"Molly? Can we talk?" Molly glanced at Lola and, saying nothing, Lola left. But Violet swore she could sense the entire coven's eyes on her back.

"I was wondering if you had anything to help with sleep?" asked Violet.

Molly looked surprised. "To fall asleep?" she asked.

"Yeah, and to stay asleep, too. I haven't been sleeping well since the shooting, and I've tried lavender and chamomile, but that is as far as my herbalism skills have been able to take me."

"And they haven't worked?"

"No, they haven't. And I know there is stronger stuff, but I am a little apprehensive about the dosage."

Molly sighed and smiled, and for a moment the glacier between them thawed a little. "I'll bring something by tomorrow."

"Thanks." Violet didn't want to push her luck. She turned and joined Margaret and Ellie, feeling a little lighter than she had in weeks.

The next day, Violet walked into Scott's office. She had knocked four times, but since he didn't answer, she barged in. He shot up, startled, making her heart race. He would be jumpy after the shooting, and she wasn't sure why she thought she would be any different. He straightened his tie, and Violet realized she had never seen him so disheveled. His eyes were bloodshot, and his hair stood askew. He struggled with the tie around his neck, which had tightened in his sleep.

"Oh, shit. I'm so sorry," she said.

"What is wrong with you?" he asked, his hand was on his chest as if to steady his heart from the outside. His entire office was a mess, with boxes upon boxes with overflowing paperwork. Violet stepped over the piles and tripped over a tipped box.

"I'm sorry! I didn't mean to scare you, but I knocked!"

"I had headphones in!" He was so mad his nostrils flared with each heavy breath. He looked funny, and Violet smiled at the sight, even though she hadn't come to antagonize him.

"What were you listening to, ska? You're working!" Violet's anger flared up, matching Scott's fury.

"You think I listen to ska?"

"You look like the kind of guy who listens to ska."

"What does that even mean?"

He stood up, and Violet noticed a vein on his forehead twitching. Normally, she took a lot of satisfaction in angering Scott, but she had to remind herself of the reason she had gone into his office in the first place. Some old habits were hard to break.

"Listen, I'm not here to fight."

"Really? You just wanted to barge in and insult my music taste?"

"So," said Violet, unable to help herself, "you do listen to ska."

"I don't okay." She could swear Scott fought off a smile, or maybe it was a grimace. It was hard to tell with him.

"I'm actually here to offer my help. I heard you took the witch case on your own, and I want to help."

"No one else can work on this, Violet. Carl was very explicit about that."

"I know that, but I want to do it anyway. I won't tell Carl, or anyone else. I promise. I'll work on it on my own time, away from the office if that helps. But I want to help. I know I'm not as detail orientated as Ellie, and you'll probably have to look through my spelling, but—"

"Okay," interrupted Scott.

"Okay?"

"Yes, okay. You can help, but no one else hears about this, understood? We don't need this killer coming after you, too." Scott grabbed a notepad from his desk and wrote something down. "My phone number," he said, handing it to her. "I'll tell you more later, but I'm thankful for your help. As you can see, I'm kind of drowning in paperwork."

"Your work is pretty hard without interns and paralegals, huh?" asked Violet.

"Yeah, I feel like an intern again." He rubbed his face with his palms, messing his hair again as he moved them into his scalp. "Get out of here before Carl gets suspicious."

Violet got up and struggled to leave through the mess when Scott's voice stopped her. "And by the way. I wasn't listening to ska."

Violet smiled and closed the door behind her. She skipped to her desk; her smile still on her face.

"You look happy," singsonged Ellie.

"What?" asked Violet.

"Why are you smiling so much?"

"No reason," she said, her voice tinged with secrecy. She turned her attention back to her work, determined to ignore Ellie.

Why was she so happy? She remembered Scott and his messy, dark hair. The smile plastered on his face as she left his office. No, not a smile; it was a smirk. Scott was incapable of smiling. He was incapable of feeling joy. Still, the question lingered. Did she like him?

Violet cringed. Absolutely not.

CHAPTER EIGHT

Scott was careful in assigning Violet work. He slipped papers on her desk as he walked by and left cryptic messages on her phone with the vaguest of instructions, but she tried her best to get it done. She knew if Carl found out about her involvement, Scott would probably get fired. While Violet may have loved the idea a month ago, she now kind of looked forward to seeing him at the office.

It was hard to keep up with everything. She had her school readings, assignments, publication applications, and now had extra secret work she needed to do on top of her usual work at her internship. She was almost glad she only got four hours of sleep a night, because without that extra time, she had no clue how she would get any of her work done. But the insomnia was causing other issues.

She had fallen asleep several times during class, but Ellie constantly elbowing her awake saved her from getting caught. She almost crashed her car into a tree on the way to work. And every time she tried to read anything, she had to reread the same sentence at least ten times to understand it. It made all her work ten times harder.

Still, while difficult, she found a sense of satisfaction in helping Eve Miller. It would've been unfair to drop her case. Whoever had killed her husband tried to frame her as well for being a witch, but that made disproving it difficult. There were no other suspects since the police stopped looking early in the investigation, assured they'd caught the right person. The evidence found at the scene appeared ritualistic. Although Violet thought there was nothing ritualistic about a couple of scented candles and a kitchen knife.

"The evidence is all circumstantial," Scott explained one afternoon in the lounge. Everyone had cleared out as soon as Scott entered. He wasn't the friendliest person before the shooting, but since then, his natural social repellent seemed stronger. It took only one scowl to make the most extroverted person scamper away from him.

"They have nothing to pin this on her, but that won't be our job. Our job is going to be to prove to the jury that she's not a witch. Also, their biases will mean we're going to have to protect her harder from the witchcraft charge."

"It's so stupid. She's being accused of murder, not of being a witch. Shouldn't they focus on the actual murder part of it all?" asked Violet.

"You would think. But juries can be swayed, and if the prosecution is harping on her murdering him for a satanic ritual, then that's what they're going to mostly focus on." He gulped down his coffee. Violet sensed his eyes on her, but she continued to stare into her cup as she mixed her creamer like it was the most fascinating thing in the world.

"So what next?" asked Violet.

"Next, we need to cast a wide net for witnesses. I have the numbers of her therapist and the people closest to her. I need to at least interview them to know if they'll be helpful in our case. Also, I need to set up a time to help Ms. Miller learn how to respond to questions the defense asks. That'll take a while. I need to respond to the motions sent over by the prosecution."

Scott stopped, rubbing his head like it was about to explode. He poured himself more coffee, but Violet noticed his hand shaking as he did so.

"I can set up the meetings," she offered. "If you send me a copy of the motions, I can research what we'll need to answer them."

"Thanks, that'll take a lot off my mind. The case law you emailed me last night helped a lot."

Violet beamed, a small part of her liking the compliment. "You read that last night? I sent it at like four in the morning?"

"I had time." He moved swiftly past her comment to discuss more matters of their case, and Violet took out her phone to take notes. After a moment, Scott stopped, and Violet glanced up to find his gaze curious.

"What?" she asked.

"Who knew all I would need for you to not hate me was to get shot?"

Violet smiled, but she narrowed her eyes. "If it keeps happening, there's only so far my niceness will go."

"I underestimated you, Violet."

"That's almost an apology, but since we're stuck together until this is done, I'll give you more time to plan a better one."

Scott raised an eyebrow. A small smile was on his lips as he sipped more of his coffee. There was no malice in the look. If anything, he seemed glad to be near her. Something had shifted since Violet had told Scott she would help with the case. After a couple of weeks of wading through the mountains of paperwork and writing motion after motion, she didn't *hate* him anymore. But she still harbored a mild dislike.

Violet thought of him as less of an idiot. Sometimes she even agreed with him on some of his takes at meetings. That was bizarre. It's not that he previously had bad ideas before, but they were bad ideas because Scott had proposed them. She used to think that everything Scott said was dumb and uninspired. She used to get annoyed at how he would run into people completely unaware of others around him. He was ugly — well, not *ugly* — but his personality made him ugly. Other girls sure would fall for his shiny black hair, and his muscles, and his abs, and the dimples that showed up when you least expected it, but not her! She wanted substance in a man, and Scott was as interesting as toast.

Violet would help him, she would work for him, but she didn't want to start *liking* him. So, she had come up with a plan during her nights of sleeplessness. Their interactions had to be limited. She wouldn't stay with him for longer than ten minutes alone in a room. She also told herself she would stop noticing the good qualities in him. Focus on the scowl, focus on the eye rolls, focus on the fact that he most definitely listened to ska but wouldn't admit it. Her plan seemed perfect, but Scott seemed hell-bent on making it difficult for her.

While they kept their work a secret and they interacted little in the office, there were moments like this, alone in the lounge, that made her sweat. Moments when she noticed the small things again. Like his dimples when he smirked, or the way he looked so intrigued at what she had to say. The nice things about him that, for whatever reason, came out more in her presence.

Scott, she figured, of course, was unaware of all this. While sure he acted a little nicer towards her, Violet didn't think that he treated her any differently than he had before. He was still rude when she made mistakes, and he still glared at her whenever she made a quip. Nothing for him had changed, but here she *liked* him. She wanted to gag.

"Violet?"

"What?"

"Did you hear what I just said?"

"You were talking?" He glowered again, and Violet smiled.

"I asked if you looked through discovery yet?" He huffed, his self-control working on overdrive, but he hadn't yet snapped at her. The others in the office hadn't been as lucky. Violet caught one intern sobbing in the bathroom after a run-in with him. She could see his patience wearing thin, but she resisted the urge to push him again.

"Not yet. I'll get it done tomorrow."

"Great." He set down his cup to refill it.

"Isn't that like your eighth cup of coffee today?" she asked.

"You're counting?" his eyebrow lifted.

"No, it's just that's a lot of coffee. I mean, it's three in the afternoon."

"You're drinking coffee, aren't you?"

"Decaf; that much caffeine will mess with your sleep schedule," Violet knew because she had been trying everything to fall asleep. She stopped drinking caffeine after lunch, meditated before bed, exercised well before she slept so it didn't energize her, and took baths to relax. Not that any of it helped.

"I'll be fine," he snapped at her, spilling the coffee on the counter.

"Sorry for caring," Violet said, rolling her eyes. She put her mug in the sink and left.

Focus on that, she thought to herself. *His irritating, grating, and whiny voice. What an asshole.*

CHAPTER NINE

The next morning, Violet forced a brush through her matted hair, trying to get ready for her internship when she got a call from Ellie.

"Don't tell me I'm late, Ellie. I already know that! I overslept, and I can't find my evidence textbook!" she yelled into the phone as she winced from the pain of forcing a hairbrush through her hair.

"You left it in class the other day, along with your sweater. I have them, don't worry. Anyway, that's not why I'm calling. Have you seen the news?"

"What news?" Violet's thoughts started racing. Was it Scott? Did the shooter find him and finish the job?

"I'll send you the link. But the firm is closed today because someone broke into it."

"What? By who?"

"I don't know. But I called you because I know you don't check your email in the morning, and you would have been the only person to show up at the office!"

"Thanks, Ellie," she said.

She checked the link. The firm had been more than broken into. Violet couldn't make out the words written in red paint on the entrance. She scrolled down further, hoping the article would have reported on the message but found nothing. The article only reported that someone had broken into the law firm and that the firm was trying to take stock of everything to make sure nothing had been taken. This didn't seem like a robbery to any of the police because nothing of value, like the computers, had been stolen.

It was an odd thing to happen, and Violet's thoughts went to the shooter. What were the chances that someone would break into the law firm after targeting one of their lawyers?

Violet lay on her couch, grateful she didn't have to go to her internship but worried about the unknown. A part of her wanted to drive to the firm, but what could she do? She hated to admit it, but maybe Molly had been right. The shooting, the break-in — it was a mortal issue, not a witchy one. But the memory of Scott's glazed eyes in the library filled her with worry again. She pushed it aside. She needed to use her day and catch up on the reading for school and finish some of her assignments.

The previous night had been another failed attempt at sleep. Molly's tea didn't help, and Violet didn't want to mess with the dosage to take more. Molly had warned her that the blend included poisons and that if she took more than she recommended, it would be lethal. Frankly, Violet felt so exhausted that at least she would rest if she were dead.

Feeling happy that at least she would get some work done, Violet undressed and put on her pajamas again. Sure, she was tired, irritated with herself, and the killer who wanted Scott dead probably vandalized the law firm, but at least she could stay in her pajamas all day. Her happiness dissipated faster than she thought possible as a knock on her door made her jump.

She looked through the peephole to see who the annoying person knocking on her door at seven in the morning could be and almost fell over. Scott stood outside her door. She pulled her face away from the door, confused and freaked out. How did he know where she lived? Also, what was he even doing here at her apartment?

Her eyes dashed over everything in her living room. What was suspicious? Violet ran to her windowsill and moved the ward and hid it behind some plants. She dashed to her bedroom—not that he had a reason to be there—but what if? She pulled out the charm bags from under her pillow, on her windowsill, and by her vanity, and threw them in her laundry basket. She frantically hid the spell books under the bed when she heard the knocking grow louder. Her phone rang in her pocket, but Violet quickly ignored Margaret's call. She had more pressing matters.

"Violet?" he called, knocking on the door harder. She had no choice now. She ran back to the door and winced as she opened it.

Scott wore a long coat over a black sweater and jeans. He carried a box of paperwork and what looked like donuts and coffee stacked on top.

"Can I come in?"

She wanted to say no and slam the door in his face, but something in her told her it was too late. She stepped aside. He strode in, setting everything down on her coffee table. He took in his surroundings, and Violet tried to ignore the judgment in his eyes.

"How did you know where I lived?" she asked first as he took off his shoulder bag.

"I looked you up in the employee directory. I found your address there," he said it as if it were obvious.

"Okay, but what are you doing *here*?"

"The office is closed." He took off his coat and set it on the couch.

Since when did he have burly arms? She looked away. It felt wrong to see him dressed this casually. Like off-duty Scott, was more personal than the Scott she saw every day in suits.

"Yes, but—"

"And our work doesn't end because the office is closed." He opened the box, showing her the paperwork inside. "I emailed you this morning that I was coming over. Didn't you check it?"

"I don't read my emails in the morning. Also, why didn't you call or text?"

"I was in a hurry this morning, and I was already emailing people in the firm."

"Scott, you can't just come into my house! And anyway, I heard we can't get anything from the office because they wanted to make sure that someone didn't take something."

"Well, I didn't take this from the office. I took it home last night." He sat down on her couch and started rifling through the box's contents.

Violet watched as Scott got comfortable, leaning back and reading from the stack of papers in front of him. Her anger didn't bother him, and he seemed to take some kind of sick pleasure from it. He stretched his arms behind his head, and his sweater rode up his stomach, revealing a dark patch of hair, and Violet busied herself with something else, pretending that she saw nothing. It's not that he didn't look muscular before. She could tell even in his button-downs that he obviously had a gym membership, but this? Just when Violet thought she was going to have a good day.

"Is that coffee for me?" she asked.

"The one on the left." He didn't peer up from his paper.

"Why not the one on the right?" If he was going to irritate her and ruin her day, the least she could do was annoy him back a little. Maybe then he would leave faster.

"Because the one on the left has that disgusting cookies and cream creamer you like."

"Oh," she said, picking it up. She sipped it, unsure of what to think about the fact that he noticed something so small about her. Defeated, she sat down and slumped next to Scott. He didn't even glance at her as he passed something for her to review.

They read in silence, but Violet couldn't concentrate on hers. Her head spun, ruminating over the coffee creamer. *It means nothing. He's an observant guy. He would be for a lawyer.* No matter how she tried to turn it in her head, it still felt personal.

"Why did you take a box of discovery to your house?" She didn't want to work. She figured if she annoyed him enough, he might leave and never come back. What she needed was for him to stay far away from her.

"To work on." His annoyance crept into his voice.

"So you spend all day at work, working, and then you go home to work some more? Your girlfriend must really love that."

"We were long distance, so she never lived with me," he said.

"*Were?*" She didn't mean to say that out loud, but the word stuck out like a thorn.

"We broke up," he said.

Well, if it was serious, he would be more choked up about it, thought Violet. Yet he said it like it was an errand he ran. Pick up dry cleaning, drop off mail, break up with long-distance girlfriend.

"So you brought work to your house because you can't stop working?" she asked. She needed to change the subject. Talking about ex-girlfriends gave her traitorous heart some hope.

"I couldn't sleep, so I thought I would work on something."

"How did you know you would have trouble sleeping?"

"Because I haven't been sleeping since the shooting."

"What like at all?"

"A few hours at most." He looked up from his paper, and Violet realized the look on her face probably concerned him because he then asked, "Why are you asking?"

"Because I haven't slept since the shooting either. At most, like four hours, but sometimes it's more like two."

"That's funny, because I thought the reason you took so long to open the door this morning was because you were asleep."

"Why would you think that?" she asked.

"Well," his eyes scanned her from neck to feet. A sudden wave of self-consciousness washed over her, causing her to shiver.

"Oh, the pajamas? I put them back on once Ellie told me the firm was closed." She stretched her arms, her pink cat pajamas in full display for him. Couldn't she have been wearing something cute? Except, she reminded herself, she didn't want to seduce him. Her kitty pajamas were all he would ever see of her loungewear.

"So, you haven't slept either since the shooting?" he asked.

Violet took a good look at him. Her anger before had stopped her from really noticing the small details. He had deep and pronounced dark circles under his eyes. His stubble looked patchy, as if he'd accidentally missed a few spots while shaving. Now that she looked closer, he looked more haggard than she'd ever seen him. The man was falling apart.

"No. Try as hard as I might, it just takes forever to happen, and then it's always like a restless sleep."

"Nightmares?" he asked.

She hesitated. Something about telling Scott her dreams felt a little too intimate. "No, at least if I am dreaming, I don't remember these dreams."

"What are you taking to help?"

"A shit ton of melatonin and an herbal tea. You?"

"Sleeping pills."

"Do they work?"

"No. It's strange, isn't it? That neither of us can sleep?"

"I mean, I get why you wouldn't be able to sleep, but I wasn't even shot."

"It was still a traumatic situation all around." Scott had finally put the papers down on the coffee table, and Violet sweat under her cat pajamas, afraid of what he would say. "Where were you, by the way?"

"What?" she asked.

"I was looking for you. When I heard the shots, I ran through the library looking for you and then, well..." he didn't continue, but she didn't need him to.

"You didn't have to come get me."

"Yes, I did. I brought you there. You were my responsibility outside of the firm."

"I hid under a desk," she lied. "I hid until the shots stopped, and I went looking for you."

"I can't imagine what that was like for you, because for me everything kind of ended after they shot me. I have no memory of it." He hesitated, turning to his papers, before abandoning them again. "Can you tell me what happened?" His brown eyes were penetrating, making her nervous, like he was trying to read her mind.

"If you want to know, I'll tell you." She needed to edit some parts, namely the invisibility spell, but she kept the story roughly the same. Scott listened, but stared at the wall as Violet told him how she had found him. How she had carried him to the abandoned study room, trying to stop the bleeding. She didn't tell him about the gunman coming back. How could she explain how they escaped that?

Rather unlike him, he didn't interrupt or ask for clarification. Maybe he understood that telling the story was hard for her, too. She'd lied to him earlier. She had nightmares almost every night, and in all those dreams, they ended with him dead. Talking about it made her heart race, as if she were still in the middle of the stacks.

When she finished, they sat in silence for a moment, but it felt comfortable for Violet. If she had filled in the holes for him, she understood he would need time to process it all.

"Did I say something to you?" he asked. "When I was unconscious or barely conscious or whatever. What was I saying?"

"You were only saying my name. Loudly, I might add. I kept shushing you because I was scared the gunman would hear you and find us."

"Maybe I didn't register that it was you who was taking care of me. I was still trying to find you."

"Perhaps. But he didn't find us. He never came back."

"Why not just finish the job?"

"Maybe he thought he did enough for it to be fatal."

Scott shook his head, not satisfied with it. "It makes no sense."

"Well, he was a bad shot. And I'm glad for it," said Violet, grabbing another stack and putting it on her lap.

"You are?"

"Just because you're an asshole doesn't mean you should die."

"That's the nicest thing anyone has ever told me."

"Don't get used to it." Violet turned back to him when the silence irritated her nerves. She found Scott with the same satisfied smirk.

"You're not like I thought you were," he said.

"Well, it's not like you gave me a chance. My first mistake and you were trying to get me fired."

"Not fired, I promise you that. Just reprimanded."

"Why?"

"I didn't think you were serious."

"Why? Cause I'm a girl?"

"No—"

"Please," she interrupted.

"Will you let me finish?"

Violet rolled her eyes, motioning with her hand for him to continue.

"I didn't think you were serious because you rolled your eyes when I told you to get off your phone."

"What? That's even worse!"

"Lawyers have attitudes; that's fine. But try that in front of a judge in the future and you'll jeopardize not only your career but your client's future as well. This isn't a game, Violet."

"I never thought it was *Scott*, but you're not a judge. And you have to trust me. I wouldn't put myself through three years of torture just because I like the suits. I take this seriously. Otherwise, why would I be helping you? It's not like you're the best company."

He stared, unable to counter her, and Violet haughtily turned back to her work. Ignoring his seething breathing next to her. "I was wrong about you," he finally muttered.

"Are you saying that to make me feel better or because you mean it?"

"I wouldn't lie to you. You'd see through it."

"Apology partially accepted."

"Partially?"

"You'll have to earn the rest."

"I look forward to it."

Violet didn't know what to make of that response. Her skin flushed under her cat pajamas, finding the cotton stifling, and the collar too tight around her neck. He may look forward to it, but Violet sure didn't.

Chapter Ten

The firm stayed closed, and Scott found himself at war with his superiors. The other lawyers seemed apprehensive about giving him information about the police's investigation. Someone smeared *BURN THE WITCH* in red paint over the entrance of the firm. Scott thought the warning stupid. There was no doubt in his or the other lawyers' minds that the break-in was about the witch they were defending. He expected Carl to tell him they no longer had a choice but to drop her. The gunman moved on from a targeted attack to now attacking the firm, but to Scott's surprise, Carl reacted quite the opposite.

"Are you still working on this case?" he asked. His face was so red Scott worried he might induce a stroke.

"Of course."

"Good, I want you to focus only on this case. Got it? No one is going to threaten our firm and get away with it." He was seething and biting the head off any associate that disagreed with him. Even though some threatened to quit. Scott didn't blame them for being angry with him, but it surprised him that Carl would stick by him.

Carl explained he still wanted only Scott's name to be attached, but if he needed extra resources, he would help. Scott was thankful, but it made his palms itch. Nobody knew about Violet's help, and he could only imagine the backlash he would receive from Carl if they found out.

Yet, as much as Scott wanted to pretend like he could do it all, even with the extra time from not sleeping, there was no way to get everything done on his own. Not to mention his lack of sleep was affecting him in strange ways.

He'd left a box of discovery in the fridge. He found a bird nest in his closet, and he was unsure how it got in and how long it had been munching on his houseplants. If he missed a few emails, he could understand that, but a whole nest? He brought grubs so the mama bird didn't have to go far for food, realizing that there were worse ways to be a father.

He needed Violet, and so he arrived for a week at her apartment, coffee and breakfast in hand. Violet no longer appeared in her ridiculous cat pajamas. Instead, she kept it casual, with jeans and an array of colorful sweaters. She wore her hair in a braid, her black hair thick behind her back.

Scott liked to observe Violet in her home. At work, she was often rude. She didn't know an insult or a backhanded compliment she didn't like to throw at him. But away from the others, isolated in her own home, she listened to his feedback and his critiques without an eye roll or an insult. When she disagreed with him, she defended her side with such passion that Scott was inclined to listen, finding it captivating instead of annoying.

But she hadn't changed completely. She would still insult his taste in music, although he had yet to play anything out loud. She continued to needle her way under his skin. He tried not to lose his temper. It was her home, after all. Still, he couldn't help but let his eyes linger on her.

They were together for long hours, spent sometimes in silence. He needed to concentrate on the work in front of him, but she was a little more than distracting. She sighed a lot, a high-pitched breath that would have annoyed him before, yet now he looked forward to the break from the silence. She often sat slumped on the couch, her back on the seat, her ass almost hanging in the air. How was that comfortable? Scott didn't understand it. But his eyes betrayed his disinterest, drawn to her without her having to do anything at all. Playing with her dark hair, biting her lips as she typed, or her fingers suspended hesitating over the keyboard.

None of these things were inherently interesting. Violet was comfortable enough around him to be herself. This authentic version of her that didn't show off to others or fight with him to exert some sort of upper hand over him at work. He liked this Violet, and now it was the only thing he wanted to focus on. It impeded his work, and it was during one of those distracted moments that he got caught.

"What?" asked Violet, catching him looking at her fingers as they typed on her keyboard. "Are you reading over my work?"

"No—I—I mean, yes, I was," he lied, turning away.

"God, you're annoying. Can't you wait!"

"Sorry, it's just a habit."

"Did you micromanage your exes, too?" Scott watched Violet turn bright red. She bit her lower lip as if to stop more words from tumbling out of her mouth.

"No, I didn't micromanage my girlfriends. I never lived with any of them, so there was nothing to manage." He fumed, and he picked up the red pen and crossed out an entire section of work Violet had written. He would pay for that later.

"Wait, you've never lived with any of your girlfriends?" she sat up straighter. Scott hated how interested she was in the topic.

"It's a big step to take in any relationship. I never felt compelled to take it."

"Scott," she said slowly. His heart skipped a beat. "How many girlfriends have you had?"

"This is an inappropriate conversation, Violet," he countered, hoping she would drop it.

"We're not in the office. Decorum doesn't matter here."

"It matters to me, and we're working. Work rules apply."

"So you've only had one girlfriend?"

Scott sighed, rubbing the bridge of his nose. Of course she wouldn't drop it. "No, I think I've had five."

"You *think* you've had five?"

"Well, it depends on what your definition of a relationship is. And in my definition, I've had five."

"How many were long distance?"

"All of them."

Violet, for once, didn't have a quick comeback. She sat with her mouth open, but a smile crept along the corners. "Do you only date on vacations? How did you end up in five long-distance relationships?"

"It wasn't on purpose. It just happened that way," he lied. He hated to lie, but she put him on the spot, and he wanted to defend himself.

"Did they never want to move in with you?"

Of course they had. All of them had wanted to, but Scott wouldn't let them. As soon as the conversation started, as soon as he realized that was where they were headed, he ran. Like a coward, but he wouldn't let Violet into that. "The conversation never came up. Usually, either I or they would want to break up before that happened."

"Well, you must have dated a ton of smart women then. Even they figured out you would be the most annoying live-in boyfriend."

"Does it not look good on me, then? That I dated smart women?" Scott's annoyance evaporated with a small chuckle as he fished for at least one small compliment.

"Maybe you have good taste in women," said Violet, rolling her eyes. As Scott smiled wider, she quickly added, "but it doesn't change the fact that you have serious issues."

"Does it not matter to you that I wanted to focus on school and on work, and I didn't want distractions like relationships in the way?"

"All that tells me is that you can't multi-task." Violet's phone rang, but before Scott could feel relieved that she might drop the conversation, she ignored the call from Margaret and stuck her phone in between two couch cushions. But luckily, she turned back to her laptop and started typing away.

The conversation appeared over, and Scott relaxed his hands. He didn't know when he had balled them up. Had the conversation about his exes really made him that uncomfortable? He needed to change the subject. She stopped typing, and he worried she was preparing for round two.

"What are you doing for Christmas break?" he asked.

"I'm staying here," she typed again and didn't elaborate.

Did he hit a nerve? She wouldn't drop anything like that with him. Why should he?

"What, you're not going to visit your parents?" he asked.

"I don't talk to my parents," she said. Her eyes didn't move from the laptop, but she stopped typing. Scott's guilt churned in his chest.

"I shouldn't have asked," he said.

"It was a normal question to ask," she countered, turning to him. He wanted to look away. She didn't look upset by it, but the fierce Violet he knew waned, replaced by a tender rawness that left him speechless.

"I... didn't know—"

"Why would you?" she interrupted. She started typing again, and the conversation seemed over. Scott wanted to apologize, but he wasn't sure exactly what he should apologize for.

"What about you?" she asked after a moment.

"What about me?"

"Any plans for the holidays?"

"I don't speak to my dad, and my mom's dead, so…"

"I see." She stayed quiet, and Scott was thankful for it. "What about the rest of your family?" she asked after a moment.

Her voice made Scott tense up again, his fists balling up of their own accord.

"I have a brother. I don't speak to him."

"I guess we have more in common than I realized. How fucked are we?"

"Are you saying I need therapy?"

"Maybe we both do," she smiled, turning to him. There was something in her eyes — an earnestness that Scott hadn't expected to see. It made him uncomfortable, and he wished the old Violet, who hated him, would return.

"What are your parents like?" He wasn't sure what made him ask, but he was curious. He noticed the lack of family photos in her apartment. There were a few photos of her and some friends on her fridge. She often texted her friends, but he never noticed her calling or texting her parents.

He had wondered about her life during the long nights of sleeplessness. He imagined her mother looking like an older version of her, and a sister just as biting. Although in some of these daydreams, he also saw himself meeting her parents. That normally freaked him out enough to stop. The curiosity lingered, but he thought it inappropriate to ask.

"My mom's a stay at home mom, and she was always taking care of me and my siblings. She doesn't have a selfish bone in her body. The church made sure of it. All she ever did was take care of us and take care of my dad. She was my favorite."

"Do you have any siblings?"

"Two brothers and two sisters. They don't talk to me either."

"What about your dad?"

"My dad was around. He always liked to point out how lucky we were, that we were growing up with a mother and a father. My dad didn't grow up with his father, and so I think for him, being there should have been enough. We weren't like all those 'fatherless' homes that the church and my parents always talked about. They loved to drone on and on about how everything that was wrong in society was because fathers were not in the house and mothers were out working." She rolled her eyes, and Scott could see that she wanted to cry.

"But it's funny. He was in the house, but I don't know my father. Not really. I can't tell you what he likes. What he did growing up or what he liked to do. He liked church, so we all had to like church. Even when I lived with them, he didn't really know me. But my mom knew me."

She stopped talking and looked distant again. Scott wanted her to continue. He wanted her to tell him everything, but he wouldn't push her. It was a strange sensation. He cared about the inner lives of his previous girlfriends. He knew more about them than they knew about him, but he had never had this feeling before, like curiosity, but more. As if finding out about this part of Violet meant something more to him. But what it meant, he had no clue.

"So you don't speak with them anymore?" he asked.

"No," she sighed. Scott watched her rub away her tears. A mixture of anger and surprise on her face. He wanted to reach out but kept his hands still by his side. "Last I heard, they were alive. But I haven't spoken to them since I was eighteen."

"If it makes you feel any better, I'm not in contact with my dad, too."

"What happened?" She didn't look at him. Her gaze was on the floor, which made things easier for him.

"My mom left us when I was ten. It was my brother, my dad, and me after that. He never told us why she left, but I always suspected it was something he did." He didn't want to continue.

A part of him wanted to tell her about coming home from school with his older brother and finding his mother's car gone. Scott wanted to tell Violet how they called for her and looked for her in every room. He even looked under his bed, as if he would find her beneath it like the monsters she used to scare away. He wanted to tell her how he had looked in her closet and found her clothes gone. Her drawers were empty, too. They were too young and had no clue what any of it meant. So when his father came home and asked why they hadn't called him, or why they hadn't called the cops, he placed all the blame on himself. They'd lost valuable time, and now his mother was miles and miles away, and they would never catch up.

"Did she ever come back?" asked Violet.

He wished she hadn't asked, but he couldn't lie to her about this.

"No, she didn't. I looked for her last year and found out she had died when I was sixteen. I told my dad about it, thinking that it would be news to him, but he knew. He found out the day it happened, and he never told my brother and I."

"Fuck."

"Yeah. Fuck," it was all he could say in front of her. The hurt he thought he'd dealt with in the past flooded his senses all the same.

But he used more choice words for his dad when he found out. Words that he didn't regret and would never take back. His relationship with his father was never the same, nor did he see a reason to fix it. He contemplated changing his phone number, since his dad had been calling every day since the shooting. However, his important contacts had this number, and he didn't want to deal with the hassle of changing it.

"I think I'm done for today," Scott said as he stood up. He felt sick. Normally, if he were to have dredged up old painful memories, he would have made sure he had a bottle of tequila next to him.

"I'm sorry," said Violet.

"For what? You did nothing wrong, Violet. Really," he added on seeing her worried expression.

"I shouldn't have brought up my parents," she said.

"I shouldn't have asked about your parents." They needed to focus on work. Not whatever this reminiscing thing they did. He reminded himself of the importance of professionalism, reinforcing the barrier he had created to avoid getting too close to her. He had no clue where it had gone during the conversation.

He started putting his laptop away in his backpack. Gathering what he needed, he noticed Violet staring at him. He couldn't pinpoint the look. Was it pity? Sadness?

"Honestly, Violet, I'm not mad. I'm just tired. That's all." He wasn't tired, but he felt sad. A sadness that crawled, enveloping him in a web, and what he needed was to be alone.

"I know you're not mad," she said. "I guess I shouldn't be so harsh with your relationships. I have no room to talk on that front."

"If you're not harsh with me, Violet, I would assume they kidnapped you and I was talking to a clone trying to take over your life." She chuckled at that, and he felt a little lighter.

He left quickly and drove home, going over the speed limit. He wanted to put as much space as possible between him and Violet, but more importantly, between him and the memories that were rushing back.

There was a reason he ended his relationships before they got too serious. Endings before the dissections. Before his girlfriends asked to meet his parents. Before they laid in bed together, exposing themselves to him, wishing he would be vulnerable and tell them one secret about him. The one thing he kept guarded so tightly that even the jaws of life couldn't separate it from his clutches. The one moment in his life that he could point to where he changed. He would never tell them, and the moment they asked, the moment they searched for that inkling of humanness from him, he sent them packing.

Piper had broken the one cardinal rule of their relationship. One rule that sure he'd never explicitly explained to her, but he hadn't expected her to dig so soon. They'd only been together for five months. How dare she contact his dad? Or his brother, who in the fight had taken his dad's side. Piper had exposed him, and the questions started. *'Why can't I call your dad? Why don't you talk to him? Why is it such a big deal?'*

Lying in bed, he went over the exact words he had told Violet. Ruminating over the words as if he could have changed her reaction to them if he had only chosen a different verb or adjective. He tossed in bed; the conversation with Violet not helping his insomnia. In his self-flagellation, from baring his secret open, he found an undercurrent of confusion. Why had he told her?

He thought of her. Her incessant quips. Her gray eyes which were in a constant state of rolling into the back of her head when he talked to her. He thought of the mole beneath her right eye. In his mind, he touched it, letting his finger graze it. He thought of her in those silly cat pajamas and with her braided hair. A question hung in the back of his mind, but he dared not touch it. If he let himself think of it, he couldn't stop whatever came next.

Chapter Eleven

Scott didn't return to Violet's apartment for two days. He sent her emails with elaborate instructions, but Violet didn't always understand what he meant. In person would be easier, but he couldn't bring himself to be around her, not yet, anyway. He knew he would eventually need to go back, especially since the firm stayed closed.

However, an unfamiliar voice in his head made the idea of reaching out again almost impossible. His skin crawled at the memory of his vulnerability. He convinced himself during his hours of sleeplessness that she wouldn't want to be around him anyway. Who would? He wouldn't deal with a person like that. Emotional, needy, with too much baggage. Why would she?

Scott got ready for his day after another night of restless sleep. He had stopped counting how many hours he got now, finding the amounts too depressing to acknowledge. The work he needed to finish piled up in his apartment and mind, so he swallowed his pride and asked Violet if he could come over. He waited for her answer. A small voice in his head told him she didn't want him to come back. Not after what he told her.

Her message came fifteen minutes later. She had classes during the day, but she would be free after six. Scott sighed; his plans for the day were already dashed. Perhaps it would be better if they met the next day; however, there was a deadline and neither of them slept much anymore, anyway. He messaged back, telling her he would be there.

He arrived a little later than he had promised. A long phone call with Carl had held him up. It seemed the police were nowhere near solving the case. They had narrowed their list of suspects to at least forty-five people who had been near the firm when it was broken into. Scott thought the police were truly nothing more than a blundering bunch of idiots. Yell 'Witch', and they would have arrested half the neighborhood, but someone being hunted for defending a witch and they now had to wait for due process.

He broke several traffic laws getting to her apartment. The urgency surprised him, but he convinced himself it was all the work they needed to finish. There could be no other reason.

Scott reached Violet's door, knocking once to alert her, but the force of his knock opened the door. The light from her living room spilled onto the hallway's concrete floor. Scott's heart started beating fast. Why was her door unlocked?

He pushed it open and looked through. From where he stood, the living room and kitchen appeared empty. Normally he could count on her studying on her couch, with a playlist playing on her TV. But Violet was nowhere in sight.

He walked in, locking the door behind him, preventing the trespasser from escaping. He kneeled and pulled out the baseball bat from under Violet's couch as his heart hammered painfully in his chest. While he had mocked it only a few nights before, he now appreciated its purpose.

Scott checked the kitchen first, opening the pantry and finding it empty. With the baseball bat poised over his head, ready to swing, he continued. There weren't many places an intruder could hide in her tiny apartment.

The sound of running water from the bathroom urged him forward. He turned the knob slowly, panic making his breath choke in his throat. He craned his neck through the door to peek. The fog in the room covered his sight, but a scream made him jump.

Scott raised his bat as Violet's head popped out from behind the shower curtain.

"WHAT'S WRONG WITH YOU?" she screeched.

"YOU LEFT THE DOOR UNLOCKED! I THOUGHT YOU WERE IN TROUBLE!"

"YEAH I AM IN TROUBLE! THERE'S AN IDIOT WITH A BASEBALL BAT IN MY BATHROOM!"

"IT'S YOUR BASEBALL BAT!"

"GET OUT!"

Scott rushed out of the bathroom. His adrenaline ran through his bloodstream. He massaged his chest to ease the uncomfortable drum of his heartbeat. But then, laughter replaced his shock. He couldn't help himself, as she popped into his head, holding the green shower curtain around her body. Her dark hair plastered to her face as she yelled at him. He laughed harder, doubling over to hold his stomach. He didn't want to provoke anymore of her wrath and turned to leave, when he noticed her bedroom door was ajar.

He'd been in every space of her small apartment except her room. Violet tolerated his presence, but the last thing she would do was give him a tour. What secrets could she hide in her bedroom, away from his prying eyes? Curiosity got the better of him, and with one quick glance behind him, towards the bathroom door, he entered her room.

It was cozy, with a queen-size bed taking up most of the space. She had a desk with all the contents of her backpack spilled on top of it. He didn't think she used her desk that often, since on her desk chair was a pile of her clothes. She'd hung prints in mismatched frames above her bed. Most of the artwork was colorful, and abstract to the point Scott wasn't sure what he was looking at. Her clothes spilled out of her closet, and several of her drawers were open, as if she's lost track of closing them mid-thought.

He looked through a small black bookshelf beneath her window. Her organization was as messy as she was. If they lived together, he would have to insist they alphabetize their books. He stopped himself. Why would he think that?

He coughed as if to clear the idea from his head. Her bed looked comfortable, inviting even. But he noticed a crowbar leaning against her bedside table. He wanted to lie down on her bed. The pink duvet and fluffy pillows looked soft. How long had he even slept the night before? Maybe three hours, maybe less. He heard the water from the shower turn off, and he had an idea. Well, she was mad anyway, and although the chances of her using the crowbar to bash him over the head weren't zero, his body craved sleep. What was one more thing?

Scott lay down and sank into the mattress. Her bed smelled like her, with a hint of vanilla. He resisted bringing one of her pillows into his chest. Although the thought of her perfume enveloping his senses brought him a strange comfort, he didn't dare explore it. He closed his eyes, not that it did any good, but he couldn't remember feeling this comfortable in a long time.

Violet's phone vibrated next to him. He peered over to see a picture of a younger Violet and another young girl pop up. He stared at the photo as Margaret's call rang out. Violet had a goofy big smile crinkling her face, a joy he had yet to witness, as she hugged her friend tightly. It was weird to think of her as a carefree teenager. None of the harshness had yet solidified. His softness was long gone.

The call went to voicemail, and Scott turned back to the ceiling, his eyes closing of their own accord. But the peace was short-lived.

"Wow, you really have lost your mind."

He opened his eyes to see Violet standing with a purple towel wrapped around her body. She wrapped her hair in a small towel on top of her head.

"Don't mind me," he said, smirking. It wasn't often that he made her as annoyed as she made him, and he planned on reveling in it for as long as he could. But he also didn't want to move. His muscles had turned to jelly. "You have a missed call, by the way, from Margaret."

"I'll call her later. Close your eyes," she said, scowling.

Scott obliged, but he didn't want to. He ignored the voice in his head that told him to peek. She shuffled around her room. The sound of drawers opening and closing broke the silence. He thought of her in that towel. Beads of water falling down her shoulders towards her breasts. Her skin erupted in goosebumps in the cold. *Tempting, if only she had dropped it.*

"You can open them," she said. She stood in front of him, cat pajamas and all. "Well?" she asked.

"I'm sorry for breaking in. But in my defense, I really thought that you were in trouble." Scott raised his hands, pleading for mercy.

Violet sighed and lay down next to him. Moving her soaking wet hair off to the side so it dangled off the bed. "I must have forgotten to lock it when I came in. I've just been so tired. I'm normally so careful."

They both stared up at her ceiling. Scott was more comfortable this way. Something about lying in the same bed together looking at each other would be a little too intimate. He tried to find patterns on the popcorn ceiling.

"How many hours did you sleep last night?" he asked. Violet raised a solitary finger into the air. "That's bad."

"I think it's getting worse," she said with another heavy sigh.

"You should go to a doctor."

"Have they helped you?"

"No," Scott admitted. "I ran out of sleeping pills."

"How did you run out of sleeping pills?"

"I was taking four a night."

"I'm pretty sure you're not supposed to do that."

"Yeah, well, I did. Only now I can't get a refill until the end of the month," Scott yawned.

"Was that a yawn?" teased Violet.

"I guess talking about sleep brought it on," he replied. Violet answered with her own long, drawn-out yawn. Scott started laughing. He wasn't sure whether it was because he was still laughing about scaring Violet, or because she really had had the most cartoonish yawn he'd ever heard. His laughter shook the bed, and Violet shifted next to him.

"How old are you, Scott?" asked Violet.

"Thirty." He sensed her eyes burrowing into him. He didn't dare look to confirm his suspicions.

"You don't look thirty."

"What's that supposed to mean?"

"You have crow's feet."

"Yeah, you get crow's feet when you smile a lot."

"I've never seen you smile. And anyway, if it was from you smiling, you would also have a wrinkle here." Her fingers brushed the side of his mouth.

Scott stopped breathing, wishing she would touch him again.

"You probably got the crow's feet from squinting at work all day," she continued.

"Are you saying I need glasses?" asked Scott, trying to snap himself out of it.

"I'm saying you need a skincare routine."

Violet shifted again, and Scott was afraid to turn his head. If he kept looking at the ceiling, he could still pretend that this was a normal conversation in an abnormal location. He wanted a glimpse of her, but he worried about what he would find. Would she be staring at him? Would her face be inches away from his? The urge to kiss her would be impossible then. He couldn't trust himself not to ruin everything.

Don't be stupid. Just look. He finally turned to her. Violet's eyes were closed, and she hugged a pillow to her chest.

"Are you sleeping?" he whispered.

"No, I'm resting my eyes. You should try it."

Scott didn't want to. He wanted to keep looking at her. He shouldn't be looking at her, not the way he was now. Her chest moved the pillow slightly up with every breath she took, and her lips were a little parted. Her skin was still flushed pink from her hot shower.

Since the night he had told her about his parents, he had been running from her. Running from the feelings that he felt swimming beneath his skin and begging to come out.

Okay, I like her. Now what?

"Close your eyes, Scott," she said.

It spooked him. How did she know?

He followed her orders and listened to her steady breathing. The bed only seemed to get softer, and he felt himself sinking further. He made a mental note to ask her where she got her mattress from. Violet yawned again, and he answered with his own. He drifted off to sleep, with visions of Violet in a towel flickering in his mind.

Chapter Twelve

Violet first noticed how heavy she felt. The idea of moving her limbs felt like an insurmountable task. Her eyelids were stuck together, and the sound around her came back muffled. Faint birdsong drifted from outside her window. She found it strange that the birds would sing at night. Perhaps they still weren't used to daylight savings either. She wondered how long she had napped, but it was the most rested she'd been in weeks.

When she stretched, something moved against her chest. She opened her eyes and, as they adjusted to the light, she thought it looked like dawn. The weak light cast a grayish-blue hue on her wall. But she didn't focus on the time for long, as she noticed the two arms wrapped around her chest in a vise.

She recognized them right away. She'd been secretly watching and admiring those arms for weeks. How did this happen? Why was he holding her? Her senses snapped awake, and panic set in. His steady breathing and small snores blew near her ear. His body enveloped hers from behind. He was warm and solid. So incredibly solid.

A million questions floated through her head, but she had no time to worry about that now. She needed to escape from his arms first and figure out the rest later. She shifted a little, moving her body away from his by no more than an inch. He responded in his sleep, pulling her closer into his chest and pushing his legs up to spoon her. His grip on her tightened. He breathed in her hair, and his lips pressed on the nape of her neck.

Was he still asleep? If he was, was this just his normal reaction? Violet tried to even her breathing, but with him even closer, his morning wood pressed behind her.

She hated to admit it, but she was comfortable. She felt safe, and a little turned on. And as much as she was trying to find a way out of this predicament, another side, the horny side, wanted her to stay put. Stay put and maybe encourage something else.

Get a grip, Vi, she thought, brushing her dirty thoughts away. He was a deep sleeper, and she needed to use that. She pulled away for the second time, trying to shimmy down instead of away. Violet realized it was a mistake right away. Her ass was now directly on his cock, and he settled in behind her again.

He scooted forward, bringing her even closer. She felt him hard against her ass, and she wanted to laugh. She sighed, frustrated that there was no way out of this. Not without waking Scott. But if waking up Scott was the only way to get out from under him, it was exactly what she was going to do.

She closed her eyes and pushed her ass back. She could feel him better. He was big. It wasn't like he needed more flaws, but she was mad about it. She ground against him, hoping it would be enough to wake him. He responded in his sleep, grinding back against her. Violet's heart quickened.

He's not supposed to be enjoying this.

She pushed back harder, and she got angrier the more he seemed to enjoy it. He kept snoring, but his body gripped her harder and his hips moved against hers. His hand squeezed her breast, and she bit her lips. She hated that a part of her enjoyed this, too.

She couldn't be gentle about it anymore, so she ground even harder, letting her ass rub back and forth. A soft groan erupted from behind her, and then it stopped.

Violet shut her eyes and slowed her breathing. She hoped her beating heart wouldn't give her away. His arms around her loosened, and he shifted away from her. She almost regretted it when she felt a chill on her back.

She pretended to stir awake, making a show of rubbing her eyes and sitting up. Scott got out of bed and walked towards her door, where there was a full-length mirror attached to the back. He looked at himself up and down as if not registering what he saw.

He turned and looked at her as if trying to work out what had just happened. Violet didn't move. She watched Scott, his work clothes wrinkled and his hair standing askew. He looked frazzled and confused, and she didn't know whether to laugh to make him feel better, or to make excuses and explain.

"What time is it?" he asked. His voice sounded much deeper in the morning.

Violet reached for her phone. "Shit, my phone's dead. I usually put it on the charger before bed, but I forgot."

"It looks like it's around six in the morning. That means we slept for..." Scott did the math in his head. "Twelve hours."

"There's no way," said Violet. She got out of bed and pushed her books to the side of her desk. She opened her laptop, which was thankfully charged. 6:12 a.m. "What time did you get here?"

"Some time after six."

"Shit, we fell asleep last night." Violet sat back on her bed, and Scott followed. The bed slumped under his weight, and Violet shifted aside to avoid falling towards him.

"Isn't that weird?" asked Scott.

"Weird how?" Of course, Violet thought it was weird, but not weird coincidence, weird magical. Something was happening. This wasn't normal, but then again, she had long stopped believing her insomnia was normal.

"I mean, it's just weird that our insomnia was cured at the same time." He rubbed his face. Violet noticed the bags under his eyes had improved. She wondered if she didn't have to wear as much concealer under her eyes now.

"Yeah, that's weird," she said. She didn't want him to continue along that train of thought.

She got up and walked to the bathroom. What more could she say? That it was weird to her, but she was also a witch and sometimes weird things were just the norm? She couldn't tell him she suspected in the beginning her insomnia was magic related, but she tried every magical remedy, and nothing worked. She couldn't explain how, after much deliberation, she concluded that her insomnia was trauma related and had made an appointment with a therapist recommended by Margaret. But now that she'd been able to sleep, next to Scott of all people, she wasn't sure what it meant.

She brushed her teeth and heard Scott shuffling about her apartment. The need to stall and come up with an explanation kept her in there longer. There was no explanation in the world that would make sense to Scott. Not without perhaps outing herself as a witch. The longer she stayed in the bathroom, the more suspicious she thought she looked, so she left to her kitchen. She found him there, fumbling around in her cabinets.

"Do you have any coffee?" he asked.

"Nope, sorry," she said. "I got rid of all the caffeine in the house a while ago. I thought it would help with the insomnia." She filled the kettle with water and set it on her stove.

"What are you going to make?"

"Tea, decaffeinated tea," she said.

"I need something stronger," he said.

"Why? You just slept twelve hours."

"It's a habit, I guess." Scott looked uneasy. He paced back and forth in her living room, as if unsure of what to do or say to her. Was this really about the sleep, or was it about how he woke up? Violet didn't want to know the answer.

She wondered whether he was catching on. Could he tell this was magical, too? No, not Scott. He was far too logical for that, Violet told herself. He was going to find a reason they'd fallen asleep together, and everything would go back to normal. Well, whatever this normal was.

"I should go," he blurted. He looked unnerved, running his hand over his messy hair over and over. She'd never seen him this disheveled before. It made him look almost human.

"Are you sure?" she asked. "We're behind on the case, and you came last night to work."

"Yeah, I'm sure. We'll catch up later." He went into her room and came out carrying his shoes. He sat down on her couch as he slipped them on.

She wanted to stop him, but her head swam with thoughts, too. She needed to be alone. As long as he stayed in her apartment, there were more and more questions flooding into her mind. She needed time to sort them. She needed him gone.

He grabbed his backpack and mumbled goodbye. The door slammed as he left.

Violet sat on her couch with her raspberry leaf tea steeping in her favorite pink mug. Guilt flooded her system as she remembered grinding against him. She shouldn't have. What if it weirded him out?

Things were strange with Scott since she'd told him about her parents. She didn't want to tell him. But something almost compelled her story out of her. As if her voice that night was not her own, but a benevolent ghost that just wanted her to open up had possessed her. She told the girls in the coven about it over the years. Margaret had been with her as she lived it. She trusted the coven, but she didn't know Scott well enough to determine what he would do with that piece of information. She hated that she had told him, but had to stop herself from dwelling on it because it made her cringe. It was too vulnerable. She shouldn't have said anything.

He was keeping his distance now, and she wondered if her story made him uncomfortable being around her. His own story didn't make her uncomfortable; quite the opposite. She understood him a little better now. But she couldn't be sure her story had given him any understanding of her. Maybe it did, but not knowing exactly what he thought made her chew her fingernails to the quick.

Now there was last night to deal with. There had to be a magical explanation. She just needed more information.

Violet sipped her tea, and the day grew darker as clouds started gathering. It was Saturday, and she had nowhere to be. She spent the rest of the day distracting herself with movies, books, and when those weren't enough, homework. All to rid herself of the swirling questions about Scott, but nothing helped.

When night came, she kept her phone by her, expecting a text from Scott. Although she wasn't sure why she wanted him to reach out. She had no better explanation about the night before. But as the hours passed and sleep eluded her, she pretended not to be disappointment when he didn't send a message.

CHAPTER THIRTEEN

The next morning, she was up by four. She hoped her one night with Scott cured whatever had caused her insomnia. At first she thought it worked, yawning around nine while she watched TV. She went to bed at ten, reading for twenty minutes until her eyelids closed mid-sentence. She put her book away and snuggled in, turning off the lights. And waited. Three hours later, she turned the lamp back on.

Nothing helped her sleep, and for a fleeting moment, she wondered what Scott was doing. Was he able to sleep? She imagined him in bed, lying awake like her. But then the image shifted to his lips on her neck. She found herself in an apartment she'd never seen, his body behind her, grinding his hips against her.

The daydream was too much for her, and she shot out of bed, deciding a shower would give her energy. But the visions of him wouldn't stop.

As the hot water ran down her body, she thought of Scott. Of the way his cock pressed behind her. Violet hated to admit it, but she wanted to touch it. She wanted to hold it, lick it, and put it inside her. She grew hot, imagining his lips pressing against the back of her neck. Was he conscious then? Or had he been dreaming? Dreaming of her? Her hands slipped in between her folds, her fingers finding her clit. She massaged it, the warmth of the water aiding in her arousal.

She imagined his muscular arms, the way they snaked across her body in the morning. His grip was firm as he squeezed her close. She imagined him lifting her up against the wall in her room, pushing his body in between her legs.

She would have taken it. Begged for it. Goddess, how she would have begged. She wished her shower head was detachable, but it didn't matter. Just imagining him made her so sensitive. There would be no shame as he pushed his cock against her. She didn't care. All she wanted was him. She would deal with the shame later.

As she finished her shower, her blood pounded in her ears. She tried to ignore the fact that Scott had caused her orgasm. Feeling almost embarrassed to admit it to herself.

The fresh layer of snow from the previous night covered the streets, and Violet wondered if she could use it as an excuse to miss the coven meeting later in the day at Lola's house. Violet assumed meeting again so soon was risky. The police had been tipped off before when too many women met together. Many a book club had been disrupted. But it was a new moon, and Violet had received the meeting time from Margaret. Molly seemed insistent, and even though Violet wished to crawl back into bed, she got ready.

A few hours later, she arrived at Molly's house, her anxiety making it hard for her to breathe. Lenore opened the door with a cheery greeting, but Violet couldn't return the same. The meeting changed last minute to Molly's house, and Violet's hands sweat as she walked through the threshold. Despite Molly giving her herbal tea to help her sleep, their relationship had remained unchanged in the past weeks. Violet hadn't stopped by Books & Beans in weeks, preferring to avoid any place Molly had the advantage. But at least today she had the entire coven and River as cover.

She found an opportunity to slip past Molly as she spoke to Ellie.

"This is a coven meeting, Ellie," said Molly. "I get that you're still a little new to all this, but normally it's coven members only. No offense, River," she added.

"No offense taken. I was telling Ellie..." River turned to Ellie, smiling.

"I told River that he is part of the coven."

"He's not a witch," said Rosie.

"Not a full witch, but he is psychic. And anyway, Violet told me we weren't doing anything special."

Rosie and Molly swiveled their heads towards Violet. She had almost cleared the living room into the kitchen.

"We don't do anything on new moons."

"That's not always true," said Molly.

"Well, how was I supposed to know this new moon was any different?"

"Should I go?" said River, smiling. He enjoyed the bickering a little too much, thought Violet.

"No, it's fine, but for future reference, we sometimes do work on the new moon. Just not tonight." Molly left to her kitchen with a huff.

"Ignore her," said Violet. "Goddess knows I do."

"She's not that bad," said River. He brought Ellie's hand to his lips, and Ellie had a smile so wide that Violet fought the urge to gag.

"God, you two haven't calmed down yet?" She couldn't take their blatant affection today.

Ellie laughed, standing on her tiptoes to kiss River.

Violet let out a heavy sigh and left the room. Ellie gave her a sympathetic look, and Violet realized she was lucky that Ellie laughed off her derision. She couldn't afford to lose anymore friends. Walking into the kitchen, she found Lola, Lenore, and Margaret already there, taking off the plastic lids on the takeout Indian food.

"Hey where were you? You were supposed to be here thirty minutes ago?" asked Margaret.

"Fell asleep," Violet answered.

"Are you sleeping again?" asked Lola. She had recently dyed her hair pink, but Violet preferred her previous purple hair.

"More or less."

"Uh oh, that doesn't really sound like it improved," said Lenore.

"It has. The other night I slept twelve hours."

"Really?" asked Margaret.

"Yup," said Violet, her cheeks flushing as she remembered Scott.

"How?" Molly asked behind her.

"I'm sure it was your tea that did it. That, or I might have just reached a new level of exhaustion." She didn't want to tell them about Scott. Not yet, not until she figured out if it was more than one fluke night.

"Have you slept since that twelve-hour night?"

"No."

"We'll figure something else out. Was it Rosie's book we were looking at the other day, Lola? Rosie's book has sleep spells, and she's translated the Farsi, but not all of it trans-lates well into English."

"Why were you looking at Rosie's book? Most of the spells are in Farsi?" asked Violet.

"We were looking for you," said Lola, handing Margaret a bowl to serve the food in. "We figured you still weren't sleeping, and it was the last book we needed to check."

"You guys were looking for sleep spells for me?" Violet looked at Molly, but her attention was on her phone.

"That looks so good," said River, walking into the kitchen with Ellie, changing the subject.

But Violet looked back at Molly. Her eyes were still on her phone, and she texted away, oblivious to Violet's stare. Maybe Molly wasn't as mad at her as she pretended to be?

They settled around the table in the kitchen. Violet sat next to Margaret, making a beeline towards the daal. They mostly ordered it for her anyway; only Lenore and she ate it.

The conversation was pleasant enough, but Violet stayed quiet, listening in. She stuffed herself with dosas, but she grew tired. The coven laughed and joked around her, but her mind wandered. She found it hard to join in, not that the rest of the coven seemed to notice. She wanted to excuse herself and go upstairs to the guest room, but Molly's house wasn't the best for sleepovers. The ghosts that haunted her house liked to invite themselves into people's rooms as they slept. They weren't all bad or scary. Lenore often joked about a woman from the 1940s who gave her makeup tips, but Violet didn't understand how Rosie and Lenore enjoyed living there. She wasn't sure who was worse — the ghosts or Molly.

"Are you falling asleep?" asked Margaret.

Violet snapped up, sitting straighter. "No, why?"

"You look like you're about to fall asleep."

"Too much food," said Violet, rubbing her stomach.

"Are you guys still not working at the law firm?" asked Rosie.

"We're going back on Monday," said Ellie.

"Are they any closer to figuring out who's behind all the attacks?" asked Molly. The atmosphere became heavier at the mention of the shooter.

"The police found a letter from the killer," said River.

"What?" asked Violet. She looked at Ellie, but she didn't look as surprised as Violet.

"Sometimes when the police come for the results of an autopsy or need information, we talk. Ellie told me about the attacks on the firm, so I asked about them. They told me they had found a letter in the middle of the floor. The person didn't address it to a specific person, but it said, 'I know you're in here.' They ran it for fingerprints and everything, but they haven't figured out who sent it."

"That's ominous," said Rosie, raising her eyebrows.

"Did someone tell Scott?" asked Violet.

"I don't know what information the police shared with him," said River.

"What can we do?" asked Violet.

"We?" asked Molly.

"Yes, we," said Violet, confused.

"We're not doing anything."

"What do you mean?"

"We're not getting involved."

"Why not?"

"It has nothing to do with us. This person, whoever it is, is after Scott, or after that mortal woman, not us. This isn't a magical issue." The rest of the coven was silent, watching the volley between Molly and Violet like a tennis game.

"I—I just thought..."

"You don't think, Violet. This is what I have always told you. You don't think, you act. You jump into these problems without thinking of the consequences."

"I don't jump, Molly."

"Yes, you do. You jumped with Derek, and now you want to risk our safety, your safety, for Scott?"

"You know what, Molly? Maybe I jump. Maybe I act first, but if I hadn't, Maggie would be dead. Ellie would be dead. And now Scott is in trouble, and I can't sit back and do nothing!" Violet stood. The weeks of ice between them finally cracked, and she couldn't stop herself.

"If you feel so inclined, you can do whatever you want to help Scott, but this isn't a coven issue!" The glasses on the table were shaking, and the coven members tried to grab the shaking tableware.

"We can vote on it?" A small squeak emerged from Margaret.

"Fine!" Molly turned to the rest, her eyes seemed to glow in her anger. "All those in favor of helping Scott, raise your hands!"

Only Margaret lifted her trembling hand.

"Fine," said Violet. She looked at the rest of the coven, their eyes downcast. *Cowards.* She turned away from Molly and the others and stormed out of the kitchen.

She grabbed her things in the living room, struggling to put her arms through her coat sleeves. Lola came to her before she finished grabbing her things.

"Don't, Lola," Violet said. She didn't want to be there anymore. She wanted to go home and sleep. If she could sleep.

"Listen, she means well."

"You know what, Lola? I'm not sure she does. This is a power trip for her. If we don't do what she says, when she says it, she hates it, she hates you, she hates everyone!" She screamed, and she knew Molly and the rest could hear her, but she no longer cared.

"You don't know Molly like I do. She does this out of love, to protect you, protect us," Lola kept her voice even.

"She doesn't need you to defend her, Lola. I don't care what she's been through. I don't care what her reasons are, this is not how you treat your sisters!" Violet clenched her fists to keep from shaking. Lola opened her mouth, probably to protest further, but Violet wouldn't hear it.

She left, the cold air blasting in her face. She ran to her car, shutting the door hard enough for the accumulated snow to shake off.

Chapter Fourteen

Violet sat back in her seat, trying to breathe through her nose to calm herself down. But her shaking wouldn't stop. She tried not to think about the others and whatever opinions they had of her. She didn't care. Molly had it coming. She deserved it. Everyone else was just too chicken to admit it too.

Her tears welled in her eyes, but she shut them tight. She wouldn't cry. She would never give Molly the satisfaction of knowing she had made her cry.

Scott was important to her now. Not that she'd told anyone, but shouldn't it have mattered that there were attacks at a firm where she and Ellie worked? If it didn't affect Molly, then it wasn't a problem.

Violet needed to get back home, and as she started her car, her phone chimed in her pocket. She was surprised to find a message from Scott asking to meet up. She wanted to tell him no, but she didn't want to be alone. Not after alienating herself from the coven.

Violet pulled into the parking lot of her apartment complex and found Scott inside his car. He came out with a soft smile on his face. He looked her over, his eyes lingering on her face. As much as she had tried not to cry on the drive over, she couldn't stop the tears once they fell. Self-control was hard when she was too focused on not skidding. They walked to her apartment in silence, and she opened the door, relishing the warmth of her home.

Scott said nothing. He looked a little worse for wear. He wore a casual tracksuit underneath a heavy jacket.

"Do you want some tea?" asked Violet, placing her coat away.

"No, thanks." He looked nervous. He massaged his thighs compulsively, and he looked like he was on the brink of saying more.

"Well, I'm having tea," said Violet, walking to the kitchen.

"Were you crying?" he asked.

"What? No."

"You look like you were crying," he said.

"It's just cold outside. That's why my nose is red. I didn't cry," she said, rubbing her face.

"Oh, okay," he said, but he didn't look convinced.

The silence that followed made Violet nervous. What was this about?

"I was wondering, did you sleep last night?" He asked after a moment.

"I didn't."

"I thought after that night my sleeping would go back to normal, but it hasn't."

"Mine either." The kettle finished boiling, and Violet grabbed the chamomile from her cupboard. How much did he know? She busied herself as she tried to come up with an excuse, but her mind came back blank.

"So what that night was a coincidence?" he asked.

"Maybe?"

"I've been thinking," started Scott. Violet didn't like the suggestive tone of his voice. "What if we tried it again?"

Violet remembered the morning, his arms around her, his cock pressed against her back. "Try it again?"

"Yes."

"So you think we should sleep together?"

"Yes."

"Do you think it would work?"

"I'm desperate enough to try again," he said.

Violet looked away. That hurt. She didn't know why, but it did. Her finals were coming up, and after everything that had happened in the past couple of weeks, the last thing she needed was to fail her classes for the semester. She really needed some rest, among other things. Her mind flickered with images of Scott's lips against her neck. *Not that*, she reminded herself.

"Why not?" she shrugged.

Scott smiled, a genuine smile that reached his eyes. It took Violet by surprise. "I'll be right back," he said, leaving her apartment.

While he was gone, Violet ran to her window. On the windowsill, she checked her protection charms. The tourmaline she had hidden behind a succulent and the sigil she had carved onto the window frame glowed under the street lamp. They were still intact. She ran to her room and checked the charm bag under her bed. If Scott stayed in her apartment, she could keep him safe. The coven wouldn't help, but she didn't need their help. She would protect them both.

Scott returned carrying a large bag. It looked like he wanted to stay a lot longer than one night.

"What's this?" asked Violet. She already felt better, the idea of a full night's sleep turning her mood around.

"My overnight bag," he unzipped it, pulling out black pajamas.

"You were so sure I was going to say yes?"

"I was hoping you would say yes," he said. He pulled out a toothbrush and a towel and left for her bathroom.

Violet took the chance to change into her pajamas once alone. The fight with Molly had drained whatever energy she had scrounged up. She needed a full night's rest, but she doubted Scott's theory. She imagined them lying together, waiting for sleep to come. Stiff and awkward, like corpses. Afraid that if she accidentally brushed against him, her fantasies from the morning would overpower her will.

She waited for him to finish using her bathroom before going in herself. The telltale signs of her crying were there. Her puffy eyes and her red nose were so obvious. No wonder Scott asked. It made her uncomfortable crying in front of people. But she hoped Scott wouldn't bring it up again.

She finished up and went to her room to find Scott already on her bed. She wanted nothing more than to cuddle against him. To feel his arms around her again, and to lay her head on his chest, listening to his heartbeat. She didn't do it. He didn't owe her comfort, no matter how much she craved it.

"Scott, can I ask you a question?" She asked as she climbed into bed. His heat warmed up her side of the bed a little.

"Sure," he said, stretching out.

"Do you always cuddle like that in the morning?"

"Yeah," he laughed. "Yeah, I do. I'm sorry about that."

"It just took me by surprise," she said, turning to him. His eyes were already closed. She wanted to reach out and touch him. He looked so peaceful like this, and not at all the annoying man she knew him to be.

"Why did it take you by surprise?" he asked.

"Well, you just don't seem like the cuddling type."

"What made you think that?"

"I mean, you told me that all your relationships were long distance?"

"That doesn't mean I didn't enjoy cuddling when we were together in person. Frankly, I could ask you the same question.

Do you always grind your ass like that when you're the little spoon?"

"Okay, forget I said anything." Violet's cheeks warmed.

"So you're allowed to poke and prod me to death when you know it makes me uncomfortable, but I can't do the same for you?"

"Forget it, Scott," she huffed, turning around.

"If it bothers you so much, maybe we should put a pillow in the middle."

"Great idea," snapped Violet, pulling a pillow out from underneath her head and putting it in between them. She settled onto her side, closing her eyes. Scott said nothing for a while, and Violet's body relaxed into the bed. She couldn't believe how comfortable she felt, or how quickly her body relaxed next to him.

"What happened to you today?" he asked.

"Nothing happened to me," she lied.

"You lied about crying. Did something happen with your parents?"

Violet sighed, turning back to face him. Even in the low light, she could read the worry in his eyes. "It wasn't my parents. It was my friends."

"Did you fight with them?"

"Just with one of them."

"Anything I can say to help?"

"No," said Violet.

"I wanted to tease you today, by the way, but you had a hard day," he tried to distract her; she could tell. She smiled in the dark.

"You wanted to tease me?"

"Tease you, make your skin crawl, the way you do for me."

"You can still do it, you know."

"It's no fun bringing you down when you're already upset."

"Do it. You can't get to me."

"Well, I was going to ask you about your boyfriends. It's not fair that you know about my exes, but you've never told me anything about yours."

"That's because I don't have any."

"What?" he asked.

"I've never had a boyfriend."

He didn't speak, and Violet wanted to laugh. "So... you're a virgin?"

"I am not."

"But you said—"

"That's not what I said. Since when do you need a boyfriend to have sex?"

He was quiet again, and the silence made Violet uncomfortable. She wished she could read his mind.

"How have you never had a boyfriend?" he finally asked after too long of a stretch.

"Have you met men? No offense, but it's slim pickings out there. Most men are gross, misogynistic, and wouldn't know how to find the clit if their life depended on it."

"You've never fallen in love?"

"No, I've never fallen in love. What about you?" She hated this topic now. She didn't want to know if he'd been in love or about his exes.

"I've never been in love either."

The statement hung there, thick in the dark. Violet never cared that she hadn't had a boyfriend. She never cared that she had never been in love before. She often joked with Margaret, who had also never had a boyfriend, that they would end up together. Two little old ladies living in a haunted home and scaring the neighbors. Margaret hated that, but Violet thought it was the best outcome. She could count on Margaret being there until the end, but she couldn't count on a random man. Margaret believed in true love. Violet had given up on the idea a long time ago.

"You've had five long-distance girlfriends but you've never fallen in love?"

"You'll never let the long-distance thing go, will you?"

"Nope. Answer the question."

He sighed. "It's hard to fall in love with someone you only see once in a while, don't you think?"

"So, did you do that on purpose?"

"I'm not answering that."

"Oh, come on," Violet fought off the exhaustion as she leaned up on her elbows. She peered over the pillow, her hair brushing his chin. "I answered all your questions."

"I didn't do it on purpose." His fingers grabbed the ends of her hair, running his fingertips over it.

"Even if you had, I get it." Scott had no response to that, and Violet flopped back on her side.

As the conversation finished, Violet realized her body relaxed faster and faster with each breath. Her eyes closed of their own accord, and she snuggled into her pillow.

"Do you feel that?" asked Scott, his whispered voice startled her.

Violet sighed, a yawn making it difficult to answer. "Yes."

Chapter Fifteen

S cott felt something warm against his body, a steady heartbeat against his chest, and a soft breath blowing on his neck. He sighed, letting himself indulge in Violet's warmth.

He had no clue where the pillow had gone during the night, but he didn't care. Her heat warmed him through his shirt. He would have slept shirtless, but thought it best not to make things more uncomfortable than they already were.

The sweet vanilla that permeated her hair and body enveloped him. He smelled it on his skin and clothes when he wasn't around her. Even a shower did little to rid him of her scent. Her fragrance clung to him, and the feel of her body in the morning was imprinted on his body. All of his senses craved more, prayed for more, but he had no hope she would ever give him more than the few crumbs she doled out. The logical part of his brain reminded him he shouldn't need or want more. However, in her bed, that logical voice was nowhere to be found.

She stirred in her sleep, and he held her closer, wrapping his arms around her. He didn't want her to wake up, but wanted to keep her there against his chest. Questions and accusations bounced around in his head. If she really didn't matter to him, why was he holding on as tightly as he was?

When she finally did wake up, he wondered what she would say. Probably a snide remark to annoy him again. He shifted, trying to move his erection away from her. This close to her, his body wanted more. At least he told himself it was just his body, because admitting that more of him wanted her was out of the question. He tried not to dwell on it, but he couldn't deny his cock hardening in his underwear.

His thoughts would dwell on her touch for hours. Even though she kept her distance most days, the few times he counted in his head stayed embedded in his memory. An overwhelming urge came over him to kiss her. Well, more than kiss her, but he didn't want to think of that now. Not while Violet lay on top of him. Not when all it would take to fuck her would be to slip off her cat pajamas and shift her a little lower so her hips were in line with his.

Chaste thoughts, he reminded himself. He thought about work. Nothing would make him lose an erection faster than thinking of his to-do list.

There wouldn't be a trial this close to the holidays. The courts would push back the trial date until January. He needed to respond to the latest motions by the prosecution. They wanted to allow into evidence his client's history of drug use, as if that mattered. He needed to check his email and try to make a dent in the correspondence.

Violet sighed into his neck. She shifted a little, and Scott was sorry for it. Her eyelashes fluttered, tickling his jaw.

"Shit." She pulled away, and Scott loosened his arms around her. "So much for the pillow," she mumbled. Her groggy voice was kind of cute.

"So," he said, switching on his phone and checking the time. "It's six in the morning. We slept for eight hours."

"Much more respectable than twelve," said Violet.

"So it wasn't a fluke, then?"

"I guess not," she said. She looked worried, her eyebrows furrowed. She got up and left the room without another word.

Was she that upset about it? Scott was elated. He had figured it out; he had found the cure for his insomnia. Sure, it meant that he would have to sleep next to Violet, but that wasn't so bad. Better than abusing his sleep medication. Of course it was strange, but he was so desperate for sleep, he didn't want to question it further. He followed her out to her kitchen.

"Are you not happy about this?" he asked. If she was that uncomfortable, he wouldn't push it. Regardless of the sleep, he didn't want to do anything to make her uneasy. He already understood how bad this would look to his coworkers and to Carl if anyone were to find out.

"I... I don't know. I'm happy that I'm sleeping, and you're sleeping. And sure, it's a little weird, but..." she looked at him, and Scott thought she was waiting for him to say something, something specific. It was the same look that some of his exes had given him when he had forgotten something important about them. Anniversary dates, birthdays, an interest they had told him months before but that he had forgotten about. He was as lost now as he had been then.

"I know it's weird." Maybe she needed some reassurance. "It's weird for me, too. I've never had this happen, but we found a solution. It might not be like this forever, but it's enough, at least for now."

"For now," she repeated. "Right, for now. Okay. So what do we do?"

"What do you mean?" he asked, confused.

"Well, we have to go back to the office today. How do we keep it a secret? They're going to think we're *sleeping* together."

"We take two cars. We can sleep at my place some nights—"

"Absolutely not. We sleep at my place."

"What's wrong with my place?"

"My place is closer to school."

"My place is closer to work."

"My place is cleaner."

"You've never been to my place. I'm not a slob!"

"My place is better," she said.

"Violet, you live in a terrible neighborhood."

"What's that supposed to mean?"

"You have a baseball bat under your couch! There's a crowbar by your bedside table! Somebody stole your neighbor's tires the other day! Their car was on cinder blocks!"

"We sleep at my place," she said firmly, crossing her arms over her chest.

He needed to compromise, but that wasn't an easy thing to do when he had spent most of his life doing what he wanted. "Fine," he conceded.

"We keep our distance at the office, like we normally do."

"That's a given."

"Then we should be fine."

"We should be fine," repeated Scott. He started building a to-do list in his brain. He would have to bring over clothes, more toiletries, and coffee. He needed to check the water pressure in her shower because he was sure it sucked.

Scott looked up and saw Violet staring at him. "What?" he asked. Her eyes were bewitching, holding on to his gaze, trying to compel him forward.

In his mind, he saw his next steps. He would move towards her, his arm would wrap around her waist, and he would dip her back, his lips pressed against hers. He would push her against her countertop. Push his hardening cock against her and feel her through the fabric of her pajamas.

"I'm just happy we're sleeping again," Violet's voice broke through his daydream.

"Me too," he smiled, and he mentally started running through his to-do list again.

Chapter Sixteen

"Scott's looking cuter, don't you think?"

Violet turned to Beth as she stared at Scott as he passed by. Her green eyes stayed glued to Scott's back as he walked to his office. Her head tilted, and she giggled as she probably imagined a version of Scott that was a lot more romantic than he actually was.

Ellie and Violet didn't react. It was always better not to pay attention to some of the outlandish things Beth liked to say. She enjoyed making people feel uncomfortable.

"I mean, he looks no different to me than before," said Violet, spinning back to her laptop.

"I don't know. He's looking hotter. I didn't think that was possible, but he is," said Beth, biting her lips.

Violet tried not to mention it was because he had slept the past five days with her at her apartment. Five days that Violet slept more soundly than she had in years. Five days of finding herself wrapped in his arms.

"The only hot thing about Scott is his disgusting breath," said Violet. Beth giggled, and Violet hoped she would drop the conversation and move on.

Since making their deal, Violet's nerves were on edge at the office. She had never observed just how many interactions she had daily with him. She never had a reason to count them. But now that they spent every night together, she couldn't help but notice how many times they walked by each other or shared glances in the hallway.

There was no way they were going to get away with this.

"Come on, Violet. You're telling me if you were stuck in a conference room with all six feet of him, you wouldn't try it?"

"She wouldn't. Violet hates Scott," said Ellie, defending her.

"I don't hate him. I would just rather kiss the devil before I kissed Scott."

Liar.

"Well, if the devil looked half as good as him, then I would too," smirked Beth.

"Can we move on?" asked Violet, standing up from her desk. "Does anyone need copies or something?"

"Or something," giggled Beth.

"Forget it." Violet left her desk and got as far away from Beth as possible.

Violet's attention had improved since they had started sleeping together. With that renewed attention came more awareness of just how wild their plan was. There was no doubt in her mind now that the insomnia was magical, but magic involving Scott was strange. Her sleep after weeks of insomnia felt great, but was it worth it for all the worry?

Not to mention she found herself on top of him every morning, and disentangling herself from him hadn't gotten any less awkward. Although, a part of her kind of enjoyed her mornings now. His arms felt so steady and warm. Their alarms forced them out of bed by six, but no matter how much she tried to deny it, she would have preferred stayed in his arms a little longer.

After making the copies she needed, she realized she had no other excuse not to return to Ellie and Beth. Sighing, she made her way back, passing by Scott's office door, which was thankfully closed. She imagined what he was doing in there. He would be working, tousling that dark hair of his back when he grew frustrated. Or rubbing the bridge of his nose when he wrote his emails. He flexed his hands before he typed, and she couldn't help but stare at them, remembering those strong hands cupping her breasts while he slept.

"Hey," said Ellie when she came back. "Do you have the homework from Bennett last night?"

Violet nodded, happy that everyone seemed to have moved on from all the Scott talk. "I'll send it to you."

Violet was halfway through emailing Ellie the worksheet when Scott's cologne flooded her senses. He was too close if she could smell the crisp wooden scent she'd grown accustomed to. Her pillows at home smelled like him now.

"Violet," his voice would have made her turn at home, but she continued to ignore him. "Violet," he called again, and she finally looked up. "Congratulations on the publication."

"Thanks," she replied curtly. Scott said nothing else and walked away. Violet grew hot under her sweater.

"Oh my God," said Beth in her ear. "Looks like someone has been kissing the devil. What was that about?"

"I don't know what you're talking about," said Violet, turning to Ellie for help, but she only stared back, perplexed.

"Does he like you?" asked Beth.

"What? No, of course not! He's probably sick or high right now. There could be no other reason."

"He's never said I did a great job on anything," said Beth.

"I'm sure he's told Ellie that before," said Violet, hoping she would read between the lines.

"He's never said anything remotely positive to me."

Violet glared at Ellie, but she still wasn't getting the message. "I'm sure I'm not the only person in this entire office who's gotten a compliment from Scott," she said through gritted teeth.

"The only person I've seen with my own eyes," said Beth with a smirk.

Violet ignored her and got back to work, but she rewrote the same sentence over and over. Ellie and Beth returned to their tasks eventually, but Violet was sure they were still thinking about what had happened. This plan would never work if Scott couldn't keep up the charade.

After a few minutes, Violet got up from her seat and left her desk. She glanced behind her, making sure no one followed, and hid in the lounge. Luckily, it was empty, and she waited. It would only be a matter of time until Scott came back to get another coffee refill. The man sure loved a routine.

Sure enough, about five minutes later, Scott walked out of his office, mug in hand. But before Scott could step foot into the lounge, Violet grabbed his shirt and dragged him in.

"What the fuck?" he asked as coffee spilled on his pants. "Violet—"

"What the hell was that?" she whispered.

"What are you talking about?"

"*Congratulations on the publication?*" She mimicked, and Scott breathed hard, already growing angry at her tone.

"I don't have time for this, Violet."

"Yes, you do. You're going to get us caught. What the hell were you thinking?"

"I was thinking I need to give Beatrice a message, and on the way back I saw you and I thought I would compliment you. I heard they accepted your article."

"So you decided today of all days you were going to be nice to me?"

Scott sighed, rubbing his head. "I can't win."

"Beth and Ellie are suspicious now."

"Beth walks into doors every day while she's texting. I'm not worried about her."

"But Ellie?"

"Ellie is your friend. Can't you just tell her not to talk?"

"I'm not telling my friends about what's going on; it's too..." she didn't know how to finish that sentence. Too awkward? Too magical? She was sure the coven would have a vested interest in figuring out why he cured her insomnia if they knew. But she didn't want anyone finding out, not after her fight with Molly.

"I'm sorry I complimented you. Never thought I would have to apologize for a compliment."

"Look, I know you meant nothing by it. But I need you to be meaner to me."

"Meaner?"

"Yes, like your old self."

"I was mean to you?"

Violet paused; Scott looked genuinely surprised. Did he never see it? Did he never pay attention to the interns he made question their decision to be lawyers, or notice just how harsh his critiques were?

"You could be...difficult." She wasn't sure what made her couch the truth. It wasn't like he would do the same for her.

"Right...difficult."

"Just be more careful. I don't want this to ruin my future."

"I wouldn't let it, Violet. I promise."

Violet hadn't realized how close he'd gotten during the argument. Sure, she'd been whispering, but he stood so close she breathed in his cologne again. The scent made her head swirl, and she remembered just how she had woken up that morning. Draped over his body, hearing the steady thrum of his heart under her ear. No matter how hard she tried, she always found herself intertwined with him.

"Do you want to leave first, or should I?" asked Scott, pulling her from the memories.

"I will," she said.

Violet looked out the door, and finding no one in the hallway, she slipped out. She hurried back to her desk and tamped down the part of her that missed him.

She would see him later that night anyway.

Chapter Seventeen

They settled into a routine; it would always start by cuddling. They tried the pillow for a few more nights before realizing that it didn't work. No matter how many times Scott assured Violet he wasn't cuddling on purpose, he still found himself in some twisted configuration with her body in the morning. Scott reveled in it, finding comfort in her warmth, enjoying her body against his cock, and grinding back into her when she rubbed her ass on him. He pretended to be asleep then, and he didn't know for sure, but he sometimes thought she was awake too.

He grew accustomed to her. He knew what she sounded like when she was in a deep sleep, versus lightly asleep, versus awake but pretending to be asleep. She liked to watch cooking shows while she cooked, preferred to study on her couch, and she liked to read for at least an hour before bed. He learned she stress-ate when studying and she hung out with her friends every weekend. She hated legacy students at her school, and people who gave customer service a hard time.

Violet told him about her friends and her relationship with them all. He got the sense that her relationship with Molly had problems, but she wouldn't explain further. Some of her stories had holes, but Scott knew when to stop asking follow-ups, although his lawyer training had taught him otherwise.

He realized their relationship was nebulous. Everything needed to be assessed to maintain its precarious balance. When she told him something about her life, her friends, her dreams, her experiences, she needed him to do the same. So he did.

He told her about his childhood friends. About the frat he was in college, but almost got kicked out because he hated the partying and hazing, and had only wanted to join for the connections he could make. He had wanted to be an astronaut when he was growing up but got scared when the Columbia shuttle exploded when coming back from space. He told her about his favorite shows, movies, and books. He finally told her what music he listened to, but it had the opposite reaction that he wanted.

"Beethoven?" she asked, her mouth wide. "Are you three hundred years old?"

"It's good! In fact, it's great! There's a reason the classics have survived until now. They're not as boring as you think they are."

"I can't believe it. I think I would have preferred the ska."

"You'll see. Next time the symphony plays his music, I'll take you."

"I'll fall asleep in the theater!"

"Oh trust me," his voice lowered, "I can keep you awake."

Violet blushed, her mouth falling agape again. Scott hadn't meant for it to sound flirty, but then again, he didn't mind the implication. The idea of it wouldn't leave his mind for the rest of the week, and he looked at the symphony's schedule. With images of his fingers in her underwear as the music swelled around them. Her eyes fluttered closed the closer her orgasm came. They would need a box.

With every confession, every story, Violet let him in, and he would do the same. Their stories were surface level. Scott knew Violet had stopped herself from letting him in too much. He did the same. They shared grains of stories that were enough to satiate their shared curiosity, but kept each other at arm's length. Scott had never slept so well, even before the shooting. He wouldn't pry further; he wouldn't ruin the good thing between them.

Scott loved the routine. The domesticity of cooking in the evenings and choosing a show to watch together. The irony wasn't lost on him. He had lived his entire adulthood avoiding moving in with all his exes, and now he lived the domesticated dream that his exes must have been praying for. He liked the companionship. Perhaps they were right after all. It was nice to come home to someone. Someone he could share his day with and talk to. He had never thought of himself as lonely before, but on the days when she stayed out late to study or hang out with her friends, he glanced at the door periodically, waiting for her to come home.

It was almost perfect, except for the *not* sleeping together. It hadn't gotten any easier. Every morning, he resisted the urge to take it too far. A kiss, a grind — all of it was dangerous. So he had another routine now, of running through his to-do list every morning, as he ignored the massive boner in his pajamas and Violet's body on his. He had had quick wanks in her shower, remembering the contours of her body, the smell of her skin, the warmth of her pussy on his thigh when she used it like a pillow.

Afterwards, he would dry his hair on a towel, watching Violet in her home, wondering if she maybe felt an inkling of the hunger he felt for her. She didn't like him; he reminded himself. Even if her teasing had lessened, even if she knew him better now, she was using him just as he was using her for sleep.

"What are you staring at?" she asked when she caught him.

"Nothing, it's just that your hair is clogging up the drain."

She raised an eyebrow, not quite believing him. "What does that have to do with you staring at me?"

"I was just wondering how you still have so much hair, even after it falls everywhere."

"It's not everywhere," she said, rolling her eyes.

Scott opened the box filled with discovery and removed one long strand of dark hair.

"Well, that will be hard to explain at work," she laughed.

But their secret was easy enough to hide from the office after that first slip-up. They arrived in separate cars, wouldn't speak to each other, and Violet would always mock his shoes, clothes, or attitude, loud enough for the others to notice. Scott would criticize her work a little more harshly than necessary. Sometimes he wondered whether they were laying it on a little too thick. But no one told him of their suspicions, if there were any, and Carl made sure Violet wasn't on any cases with Scott.

Still, Scott found himself nervous, thinking that somebody would eventually figure it out. He looked forward to the holidays. The office would be on a break for two weeks. Violet had passed her finals and wouldn't have school until January. Neither of them were going home for Christmas, and Scott daydreamed of their break together. Long, dark nights spent together talking and hanging out. His daydreams were quick to dive into fantasy. He wanted to fuck her on every surface of her apartment, every surface of his. They could take a trip somewhere, rent a cabin where they could be as loud as they wanted. She would scream his name; he would make sure of it.

"Scott."

No, it would have to be louder than that, thought Scott.

"Scott!" he turned around, startled to see Beatrice standing in the doorway of his office. "You didn't hear me calling?" She asked as she approached his desk.

"I didn't. I'm sorry," he said.

"You've been very distracted lately. Are you stressed, honey?"

"Just tired."

She placed a stack of new motions on his desk. Scott sighed, leafing through it. "Don't look at it now," said Beatrice, taking them away. "Take a break, sweetheart. It's Christmas."

He had always liked Beatrice. He found her calm demeanor in the office comforting. Nothing ever seemed to faze her, not even stressed out over-caffeinated lawyers. "I'll take a break. I promise," he said, putting his hand on his chest.

"Go home early," she insisted.

"Can I have the motions?" he asked.

"I'll give them to you if you promise to go home early today and take an actual break during Christmas."

"I promise," he said, hand on his chest. She handed them over, and he put them in his messenger bag.

"Good, and while you're at it, you can give Violet a ride home," she said.

Scott's heart raced. "What? Why would I give her a ride?"

"Well, seeing as you've been on a nice kick lately, I thought you could help. She's outside trying to get her car started. Poor thing is out in the snow."

"What do you mean by nice?" asked Scott, trying to change the subject.

"Beth forgot the cover pages for the exhibits, and you didn't even yell at her. You seem less stressed than usual."

"You noticed that?"

"I notice everything." Her tone sounded pointed, and Scott cleared his throat.

"I'll go check up on her." He stood up, grabbing his jacket and messenger bag. As he left, he could swear Beatrice gave him a knowing look. She must have figured it out. He had no clue how she did. He thought they had been careful enough.

As he left the office, a gust of icy wind hit his face. Little flurries of snowflakes fell on his eyelashes. He saw Violet at the end of the parking lot and heard the whine of her car carried through the wind.

He knocked on her window, and Violet jumped in her seat. She opened the door, hand on her chest.

"You scared me," she said.

"Sorry, I heard you had car trouble."

"I don't know why it's not starting." She turned the key again, and a horrible grating noise emanated from the hood of her car.

"Is it a battery issue?"

"I don't know," she replied.

Scott was out of ideas. He was not a car guy. He had used up the extent of his car troubleshooting knowledge that he possessed. "Listen, I can give you a ride to Books & Beans." Violet had told him earlier that she was going to hang out with her friends that evening. He hid his disappointment from her. Even though he had wished to spend the night with her alone again.

"No, don't bother. I'll just catch the bus," said Violet.

"Come on, Violet. You're shivering; it's too cold. Let me take you."

Violet glanced towards the office. He figured she was trying to see who in the office might be looking. There weren't many people left, but Scott assumed Beatrice probably watched.

"We would already be halfway there if you said yes," he singsonged.

"No, we wouldn't," said Violet.

"You're going to be late."

"Fine."

She followed him to his car, and he opened the door for her. Violet rolled her eyes as she sat inside. It made Scott smile, but he stopped, reminding himself that Beatrice might be watching.

Scott turned on his car, and Violet settled in. He drove carefully as the snow came down harder.

"Do you need me to pick you up after?" he asked.

"Don't worry about it. I can get a ride with Margaret."

"What are you guys doing today anyway?" he asked, trying to make conversation.

"We're just hanging out, exchanging Christmas presents, those sorts of things," said Violet quickly, as if she wanted to change the subject.

"Will I ever meet your friends?"

"Why would you meet my friends?"

"Right—I—I just meant, do you tell them we spend all this time together?"

"No, do you tell your friends?" Scott had two friends. Omar, who he met in college, and Frankie, his friend from elementary school. Both were married; both had kids. It was hard for them sometimes to make the time to see each other. The last time Scott had spent more than an afternoon with them was during their bachelor parties.

"No, I haven't told my friends about you either. So, it's a Christmas party," he said, changing the subject. Embarrassed that he had asked to be introduced.

"Yeah... Christmas." The way she said it made him think it wasn't. Hanukkah had passed? What else would they be celebrating?

They reached their destination soon enough. Scott had a hard time finding parking. The square was packed with last-minute holiday shoppers. Violet's smile caught him off guard as she turned to him.

"Sorry, I was rude. You didn't deserve that. I'm just a little on edge."

"Why?" he asked.

"I'm going into enemy territory," she said, squinting her eyes. Of course, Molly owned Books & Beans.

"You could skip it. We can go home," he said.

"No, I have to be there today."

"You'll be fine," he said. "Just be your usual obnoxious self. I'm sure she'll hate it." Violet laughed, and it made him happy to see her smile.

"Thanks for the ride," she said as she opened her car door. She had stepped one foot out when suddenly the glass on her car window shattered.

The world slowed down for Scott. He reached for Violet, pulling her back by the collar of her coat. Violet fell back against him. Her spine was on the middle console. More shots rang out. This time it hit his front window. Splintering spiderwebs of glass shattered around them.

Scott folded himself over Violet, but the sharp clink of bullets hitting his car continued. He waited for it. He waited for the burning pain of a bullet again. Waited for the startling warmth of blood rushing down his body, but none came.

Then it stopped. The sound came back first. The sounds of screaming and running. Then sirens. He raised himself and inspected Violet. She sat up, her hair messy around her face. He looked her up and down, looking for blood. She was fine. She was okay. He realized she was doing the same to him. Her eyes searched his body all over. They met in the middle, their eyes fixed on each other's.

Scott opened his mouth to say something, but nothing would come out. Violet reached out to him, her hands finding his. How long had he been shaking? Her hands weren't trembling.

"Scott?" her voice sounded far away, muffled, as if under a pillow. "Scott?" he heard again.

CHAPTER EIGHTEEN

The memory had an edge to it. A sliver of cliff that Scott tumbled from, unable to grasp onto anything solid. They were in the library.

His body felt icy but also hot at the same time. He stared into the water stained fissured ceiling tiles above him. This was it. This would be the last thing he saw before he died — a gross ceiling.

"Shhh," he heard next to him. "Please Scott. You have to be quiet." He hadn't said anything. Warm hands pressed on his face. His eyes met Violet's eyes. Her cheeks were tear-stained. A river of melted mascara smeared her lovely face. Her eyes locked onto his. He needed to keep looking at them. If he looked at them, he would live. He wasn't sure where this thought had come from. But he knew it was true. As true as his name was Scott Pruitt.

She wouldn't look away either. Her eyes were pleading with him to hold on. For those eyes, he would. They were the anchor to this life. As cold, painful, and full of suffering that it was, he would stay. For those eyes.

For her.

Then he heard something new. Heavy shuffling footsteps. The sharp mechanical clicks of a gun. Her eyes moved away from him. Scott wanted them back. No, he needed them back. He would fall without them. He would die without them.

His eyes followed her gaze, and he saw a man standing in the doorway. Only the man's legs were in his eyeline. Wide as trunks, strong and unmoving. Wrinkled pants and tactical armor. Scott was unsure how long he had stood there.

Scott didn't care for this man; he needed him gone. He took away the eyes that Scott needed. If this man didn't leave, Scott would die.

The man sauntered out. Scott thought the asshole dragged his feet on purpose. When the man left, her eyes came back. Scott's eyes, for he had taken ownership of them. Those eyes belonged to him. Violet belonged to him.

"Scott," he heard.

"Violet," he said out loud. His voice was a foreign note in the silent library.

A hand cradled his cheek. "Scott," repeated Violet.

His vision cleared. The darkness lifted, and in its place was Violet. Her warm hand pressed against his cheek. Her dark hair fell on either side of her face as she leaned over him. He glanced up at the ceiling. It wasn't the water-stained ceiling of the library. This ceiling was gray and bare, industrial-looking.

He looked around him. There were old leather armchairs strewn around the shop, books lined the walls, and an espresso machine whirred behind a wooden counter. The place smelled of coffee and pastries. Christmas music played in the background. He wasn't in the library.

"You're awake," sighed Violet in relief.

He had passed out? He didn't remember when.

"Hey don't get up!" said Violet, pushing his head back on the worn leather couch. "Just stay put for a bit."

He couldn't. Time caught up with him again, and he remembered the car.

"Are you okay?" he said, sitting up. He regretted it instantly. His head spun, but he ignored the pain as his eyes scanned her body. "Are you hurt?" His hands headed to her waist, but Violet pushed them away.

"I'm fine. I promise." She locked eyes with him, begging him to stop.

He looked around to find a group of people staring at him. There were four police officers and a few other people he didn't recognize.

"How long was I out?" he asked.

"A while." Violet looked nervous. Scott could understand why after being targeted again.

"How are you feeling, son?" He looked up to see a police officer near him. The man had watery blue eyes and a comb-over with wisps of brown hair covering his balding head. He stared at Scott with disgust, as if he already had a problem with him. Scott glanced at his badge, noting his last name: Wharton. Violet stood aside.

"Never better," he lied.

"We wanted to ask you a few questions, if you're up to it."

"Can't you wait?" asked Violet.

"If we wait, we'll lose valuable time to catch the guy who did this," the police officer answered bluntly.

"He's not in any condition to answer your questions. I doubt he saw anything. I already told you the shots came from behind us."

"Violet, it's fine. I'll do it."

Violet looked at the cop one more time before she left to join her friends. Scott had no clue what her face looked like, but it couldn't have been good because the officer looked pissed about it.

Scott gave perfunctory answers. No, he hadn't seen the assailant. No, he didn't know this was going to happen. Yes, he was the guy who got shot at the library. He didn't think the statement would do any good. He wanted the cops gone.

"So, after you arrived, did you notice anything out of the ordinary?" asked Officer Wharton.

"No."

"Really?"

"I said no, didn't I?"

"Tell me, Mr. Pruitt, is your car made of armored steel?"

"No."

"Are your seats lined with some bulletproof material?"

"No."

"I didn't think it was, since the entire body is covered in bullet holes, as are the seats, and the windows are blown. And yet you and Ms. Caldwell here are completely fine. Not a single scratch on either of you."

"Is that a question?"

"Do you find that odd, Mr. Pruitt?"

"I don't see how that is relevant to finding the shooter."

Officer Wharton pursed his lips in contempt. "It's relevant to me, Mr. Pruitt."

"Not to me. I won't answer any further questions without my lawyer present." Officer Wharton's face reddened, but cops didn't intimidate Scott. But he had already broken one of his key rules. Never talk to cops without a lawyer. And his incoming pounding headache made him cut his statement short.

The police left soon after getting his statement. There were only a few people left in the coffee shop. He saw Ellie as she leaned into the arms of the only other man in the shop. Violet talked to a girl with red hair, and from her stories, he knew it was Margaret. There was another woman behind the counter of the coffee shop with dark, tight curls framing her strikingly beautiful face. She stared at the cops as they left, Molly, he figured. Violet approached him once the cops had left. She looked shaken, and he doubted she would use this moment to introduce him to her friends.

"Margaret's going to take us to my apartment," said Violet. Scott nodded, too exhausted to answer, but he couldn't fathom sleeping tonight, even with Violet there next to him.

He didn't bother saying goodbye to the rest as they left. He shuffled into the back seat of Margaret's car. As they drove out, he saw what was left of his car. Yellow tape roped it off from the empty slots next to it. He saw the shattered glass around it and the deep dents in the body. No wonder the cops were suspicious. He had no clue how they had survived. He would have to call his insurance. Add it to the to-do list.

He didn't want to dwell on the shooting, but as they drove to Violet's apartment, his mind wandered into the library. He wasn't sure whether it was a memory or a dream. All he remembered were Violet's eyes. The eyes, he was convinced, kept him alive. She would probably roll them to the back of her head if he told her.

The worst part of the memory came back too. The part that made his heart beat faster and his hands get clammy. They had all been in the same room. But it could have been a dream. Why else would the shooter not finish the job?

They reached her apartment, and Scott broke out of his downward spiral. He thanked Margaret, and she returned a tight smile. Violet shook off her coat once inside and walked into her bedroom. Scott followed her there, unable to be far from her. She looked through the drawers and picked out her pajamas and underwear.

"I'm going to take a shower," she told him. "Are you going to be okay?" she asked.

"I'm going to be fine, Violet." A lie. He was one more surprise away from a nervous breakdown. He watched her leave to her bathroom and went into her closet and pulled out his overnight bag. Once dressed, he lay down on her bed and waited.

His body shook under the covers, and he placed his hands under his body to stop them from trembling. Violet needed to hurry. The memories of the day crept into his brain, intruding on the shaky control over his nerves. He needed the peaceful oblivion that Violet gave him when she lay cradled against him.

She came into her room a while later. Her face was puffy and red from crying. He didn't have to ask why she cried. She settled in next to him and turned off her lamp. Scott wanted nothing more than to reach out and hold her close. He wanted the tickle of her breath on his neck, and the heat radiating from her body. He wanted to tell her he would keep her safe even though he had been so bad at it, but he didn't push. Instead, he waited for sleep, and it thankfully engulfed him in a matter of minutes.

CHAPTER NINETEEN

Scott's fingers brushed over the worn books. He went alphabetically, seeing HAZ, HE, HEC, HU. He needed Humble. The last name was Humble. He remembered thinking it was a funny last name.

Shots rang out through the library. Dread flooded his nervous system.

Oh no, please. Not again.

Violet. He needed to find her. He ran through each aisle, a quick cursory glance coming up empty every time. Someone screamed in the distance. *No, no, no, no.* It didn't matter how often he repeated it. The scream belonged to Violet. He knew it did.

He found her near the entrance. Her eyes were open, horrified, pleading. Her hands were around her waist. Blood flowed out, like water through a stream, like it was meant to do that. He fell to his knees. He needed to staunch the blood, or she would bleed out.

Her slick fingers wound around his own hands. She had a look in her eyes, a look that begged him to leave her. No, he would never do it. He would stay and keep her safe, like she had done for him.

A familiar sound pulled him away from her. The same heavy shuffling footsteps. He scanned their surroundings and realized they were too exposed. He couldn't move her without hurting her more.

"Leave," she said.

No.

He meant to say it out loud, but his lips wouldn't part. The footsteps got closer. He had no choice. He leaned down and lifted her up. She winced in pain as he started running. The aisles disappeared as he ran through the building. Office doors around them dissolved. Their doorknobs rattled against the floor. The faster he ran, the faster the escape routes disappeared. They had nowhere to go. Nowhere to hide. The footsteps were behind them. Scott turned around and met a faceless man. He raised his gun, pointed not at Scott but at Violet.

"NO!" his dream and real self yelled.

Scott sat up, his heart hammering. It was a dream. Just a stupid dream.

"Scott?" Violet's groggy voice sounded far away.

Her arms wrapped around him, holding him close. Violet held him, and for whatever reason, it made it worse. He couldn't stop the panic. His breath came in faster, like there was no air left in the room.

"You're okay. You're safe." Violet grabbed his hand and placed it over her chest, under her collar. He followed the soft, undulating heartbeat beneath her skin. "You're safe," she repeated, her voice a faint whisper next to his ear.

His heart rate slowed, and he forced his attention onto her skin. So soft and warm beneath his cold, clammy flesh. He swore he felt her blood rushing beneath her skin. Her voice was a beacon of light amidst his fear, pulling him further away from the dream.

The full moon bathed the room in light and illuminated her. He found her staring back.

Her eyes, the one thing that pulled him through once before. She didn't know that. She saved his life, but not in the way she thought. Not by stifling the blood, or hiding him away. Her eyes were the answer. How couldn't he have seen it before?

Scott wrapped his hand around her cheek, his fingers brushing her lips. Violet stood still, almost not breathing, watching to see what he would do next. He leaned in and kissed her, his lips caressing against hers lightly. Her lips didn't respond at first, taken by surprise, but he kissed her harder, pushing her lips apart for him. He wanted her tongue on his. Wanted to feel every part of her now that he had crossed the line he had wanted to cross for weeks.

She responded, opening her mouth, kissing him back. His erection swelled, every kiss rushing more and more blood into it. He needed her now. He needed to feel every inch of her skin. His hands grasped anything they could get hold of. Her nape, her back, her ass, her breasts. Roving and squeezing all that he could before his brain could tell him it was a bad idea.

Violet's hands stayed locked on his face, gripping him to her. Making sure that his lips stayed pressed on hers. He pushed forward, her back hitting the bed. He raised himself above her, trying hard not to break the kiss. Fear swirled in his brain, questioning him every time he kissed her back or pulled her closer. But her hips wriggled beneath him, responding to his sucking on her bottom lip, and the fear and apprehension fell away. Scott ground his swelling erection against her and groaned at the feel of her through his boxers. She pushed her hips up, rubbing her core against him.

They stayed like that for a moment, rubbing against one another, almost afraid to take it further. Doubt crept in again. What did it mean if he did this? If they did this? Nothing would be the same again. But Scott heard Violet's pitched breaths coming in faster and faster. Her hips unrelenting as she pushed her pussy against his cock, and the overwhelming need to have her around him won out over his hesitations.

Scott reached down and slid his hand beneath the waistband of her pajamas. He hesitated, but Violet didn't, pushing his hand down to cup her pussy. Her underwear was soaked, and as he massaged her clit over her underwear, he knew she wanted him just as much as he did. He stayed there a moment, letting her hips rub against his palm, the insistent pull of her hands on his neck as he pressed his tongue into her mouth.

He removed his hand, and a gasp replaced a soft whine as he yanked her pajamas off her. She hastily kicked them down as Scott ripped her underwear off of her. Violet didn't seem to care, as her hands grabbed at his face, bringing him back for a kiss. Her legs wrapped around him, and he felt her warm, wet pussy on his cock.

The dream played again in his mind, and he pushed back the thoughts of her blood gushing through her sweater. Violet was alive. Here beneath him. Moaning as he ground his hips into hers.

"Inside," she gasped as he slowed to feel her better. She felt too good to him for him to stop. "I... need you inside. Now."

That was all he needed to hear. Scott pulled down his pajama bottoms, only successful enough to take them off one leg. Her hands reached for his cock, guiding it to her opening.

He pushed in quickly. A gasp punctuated Violet's shock. Scott groaned. She was so warm and slick. Her walls pulsed around his cock, craving and begging for more. He started thrusting, keeping her face close to his. There was no time for gentleness; each thrust was hard and fast.

He had waited for this. Dreamed of this. He would have made a show of it. Made her squirm and gasp for hours, making her beg him for a release. There was none of that now. Only a quiet need that rang through the room.

Violet moaned and whimpered against him. Her gasps became quicker, her walls squeezing him tighter. She was getting close. He didn't know what she wanted, what she needed. He kept the pace. But he was going to come so fast. She felt too good.

"Violet," he choked out. "Are you close?" he needed to make sure.

She could only nod, her eyes rolling to the back of her head. She shuddered around him. Her back arching. He couldn't continue. He came quickly, with her walls clenching around his cock, unable to pull out in time.

Scott fell back on the other side of the bed. He tried to catch his breath, and Violet did the same. Their breaths were the only sound in an otherwise quiet room. Nothing more needed to be said.

He wanted her to reach for him. Pull him into her arms, but she didn't. He followed her breathing, matching it. Sleep came soon, and he didn't have another dream for the rest of the night.

Chapter Twenty

The shadows in the bedroom appeared harsher in the morning light. Scott's body pressed behind her, his arms wrapped around her tightly, and his face burrowed in the tangle of hair behind her neck.

She had grown accustomed to this. Accustomed to the body in her bed and her heart fluttering with glee when she found herself entangled with him. But today was different.

She replayed the night's events in her head. He'd been screaming so loud it startled her awake. For a fleeting moment, she thought the attacker had broken in. Her protection spells useless against an entity she knew nothing about.

Scott bolted up, and without thinking, she draped her arms around him like a cloak. Her only concern was to help him wake up and make him realize they were safe. She hadn't expected what happened next.

The pressure of his lips on hers. The forceful desperation of his kisses, and the hard grip of his hands on her body, as if she would disappear if he didn't hold on to her tightly enough. His tongue had pried her lips open, and Violet didn't fight it. She wanted to taste him, too. Feel his lips and so much more on her body. They hadn't bothered undressing fully. There was no time. She wanted him more than she had ever wanted anyone else. The want left her hungry and embarrassed. But she pushed it away. Any lingering shame could wait till morning.

But even now, as the lazy winter sun peeked through the curtains, shame didn't cross her mind. Instead, she thought of her body comfortably full as he moved in and out of her. His hips were unrelenting as he thrust into her. Unable to feel anything but pleasure. Their horrible day pushed far from her mind with each kiss and push of his hips. Remembering it now, remembering his arms flexed on either side of her face, as he grabbed the sheets for stability as he moved, made her squeeze her thighs tight.

He stirred behind her, and Violet dreaded what would come next. She took a deep breath. They would have to talk about it, eventually. There was no use in hiding. She turned to face him and met a regretful face.

She waited for him to say something. His dark hair hung tousled around his face, and he pushed it back, as if it gave him something to do. His lips stayed stuck together, and Violet couldn't handle the awkwardness for a second longer and stood up. She pulled the sheet off the bed and held it against her naked lower body.

"Violet, wait." Scott stood up. The sheet fell away, exposing him. He reached down to find his pajama bottoms and dressed hastily. "I'm sorry."

"What for?" asked Violet.

"We shouldn't have done that last night. I shouldn't have done that," he corrected. "I wasn't in the right state of mind. I wasn't thinking. I understand if you want me to never come over again." He rambled on, and Violet tuned him out. He was sorry for it? "Listen, it was completely out of line and—"

"Stop! Please, just stop! I wanted to."

The truth hung between them. She had wanted him for weeks. No matter how much she tried to deny it or lie to herself, last night had been everything she wanted. She couldn't explain it, but he fit. They fit. Yet, looking at Scott's remorseful face, she couldn't figure out if it meant anything more to him.

She rushed to the bathroom and turned on the shower. She let the hot water fall on her body, and she scrubbed off the dried cum on her thighs. Her anger at the situation dissipated for disgust with herself for wishing he would join her in the shower.

When she finished, she wrapped the towel around her and left the bathroom. She expected to find him gone, but Scott sat on her couch. He still wore his pajamas, with her favorite mug in his hands. He held up the mug for her, but she only stared at it as if he had poisoned it.

She ignored him and left to her room. He didn't follow, and she shoved away the hope he would come to her. Both frustration and anger coursed through her, for even wanting him to follow her. That's not what she should want. She should want him to leave immediately. Leave and never contact her again, and she would forget she ever knew him.

She dressed fast and found her phone, noticing she had one missed call and text from Margaret.

Maggie: Meeting at Lola's. It's an emergency.

She texted Margaret to pick her up before turning to the door, trying to psych herself up to face Scott again. Last night had been a mess. Chaotic from start to finish, she didn't even want to untangle the knot. Scott would have to wait. She needed to talk to the coven first. What would she tell them? What would they say if she told them she was sleeping with Scott? *Well, sleeping and now fucking*, she reminded herself.

She came out of her room, and Scott looked perplexed, staring at her outfit.

"Where are you going?" he asked.

"I'm going out with Maggie."

"Can't it wait?"

"No, it can't."

"We need to talk about this, Violet."

"About what?"

"What do you mean 'about what'? About last night? About me and you—"

"Fucking?"

"You don't have to be so crass about it," he scowled.

"I don't want to talk about it, Scott. There's nothing to talk about. I already know you're *sorry* for it."

"That's not what I meant."

"What did you mean then?"

"I meant sleeping with you was not what I wanted to do last night. It just happened, and I was worried that you regretted it. Or that I crossed a line with you that you never wanted me to cross. I would hate myself if I ever did that to you."

Violet stayed silent, the air charged around them. She hesitated, afraid to ask the one question stuck in her mind. She wasn't sure which answer would be worse. "You don't regret it?" she asked.

"No, I don't," he said. "Do you?"

"I—" she started, but she stopped, hearing a honk. "That's Maggie."

"Violet, you can't leave me hanging," he pleaded. "I won't be able to do anything all day. I need to know."

"So, this is about work," she smirked, but it hurt. It shouldn't hurt. He meant nothing to her. Last night meant nothing.

He reached for her, his firm hands wrapping around her arms, pulling her in closer. Her heart beat faster, his face inches away from hers. "Violet," he whispered.

The consequences of what she wanted to do were pushed far from her mind. She stood on her tiptoes and kissed him. His arms wrapped around her, pulling her into his chest. Her heart skipped a beat as his hands roved over her body, gripping her hard enough to hurt. It didn't take away the pain or the hunger flowing beneath her skin. Nor did it settle her like she wished it would, but as his lips pressed against hers, she realized a long-neglected part of her ignited. A part she thought she buried long ago. The part of her that wanted to be loved.

Margaret's horn blared again, and Violet pulled away. Scott didn't unwrap his arms. He held her in place against him.

"I need to go," whispered Violet, but she dared not move. She was sure her legs would fail her, and she didn't want him to know how he affected her.

He nodded, but he looked pained as he let her go. Violet grabbed her coat and headed out.

The entire coven sat at Lola's kitchen table. The kitchen's butter-yellow paint was a little too cheery for everyone's somber faces. Violet realized no one had slept easily last night. It was like she walked into court, only now she was on trial.

"How are you feeling?" asked Molly.

"Better," said Violet, surprised the first question wasn't a lecture.

She understood just how lucky she and Scott had been last night. The coven's intervention prevented the bullets from hitting their intended target, and the police's confusion had fooled them enough to not ask questions Violet couldn't answer. Until Officer Wharton, of course, interrogated Scott. The other police officers hesitated in accusing them of witchcraft outright, but Officer Wharton had no such qualms.

It wasn't the winter solstice celebration they had meant to have. The police officers' presence in Books & Beans put them all on edge. Lola, Lenore, and Violet had struggled to bring

Scott's unconscious body into Books & Beans. Violet had tried not to remember the day in the library, but seeing Scott unconscious again brought back the flood of memories she had tried to get rid of. Molly had ordered Lenore, Rosie, and Lola to leave through the back door before the police arrived. They couldn't be seen together, not on the solstice of all nights.

"What about Scott?" asked Molly, bringing Violet back.

"He's fine too." Violet waited for the dreaded next question. The one she wanted to stop.

"Be honest, Violet. What's going on between you and Scott?"

Violet sighed, and the others waited. She'd been avoiding this for far too long. She started with the beginning, the shooting, the lack of sleep. Letting everything spill out except for last night. She didn't want to tell them about that yet, not until she figured out what it meant to her. The others listened, not interrupting her. The truth relaxed her, unburdening her of all the secrets she had carried for weeks. When she finished, she waited for the lecture from Molly, but it never came.

"So this insomnia," said Rosie, playing with a strand of her black hair. "It's magical then?"

"Well, obviously, if they can only sleep while they're physically together," replied Lenore.

"But how did that happen?" asked Rosie. "I've never heard of anything like it."

"Unless," started Ellie. "Unless you bound yourself to him somehow?"

"Wait what? Like bound his soul to mine? The way you did to Derek and River?" asked Violet.

"He was near death, was he not?" asked Lola.

"Yeah, but I didn't cast. The help I gave was first aid. It wasn't magical!" She turned to Margaret for help, but found her staring at the mug in her hands.

"I don't think you bound his soul in the same way that River and Ellie are bound," said Molly. "But there could be something to this. Your insomnia wasn't normal. The solution is less so."

"How? I only cared about surviving in that library. I don't even like him!"

"I'm not sure, but it's something you did in that library. It might've been an accident, but you and Scott may be bound now."

"Is there a way to undo it? Would he die if I did?"

"His healing wasn't contingent on your binding, so I think he would be fine," said Lola. "That is, if he is bound to you in the first place, because without proof this is all a guess. You might not be bound to him at all."

"Is there a way to check for sure?" asked Violet.

"We would have to check the books, but there is probably a way," said Molly.

Violet didn't know what to think. Being bound to Scott had never crossed her mind. Besides the invisibility spell, she had cast no other spells in the library. If they were bound, it complicated things further in Violet's mind. She couldn't trust her feelings or his. Her accidental binding could be compelling them both.

"There is another matter regarding Scott we need to discuss," said Molly. "His attacker put all of us in jeopardy last night. Those cops suspected us, especially with it being the winter solstice. They might have been on the lookout for big gatherings like ours."

"Did they see all of us?" asked Ellie.

"Well, one asked about the girl with pink hair that helped at the scene of the crime," said Molly.

"Crap," said Lola, combing her fingers through her colorful hair.

"Yeah, not the most subtle color you've had, Lola," said Rosie.

"Do you think the cops are keeping tabs on us now?" asked Lenore worried. She looked out the window as if expecting to see a police officer staking out Lola's house.

"We're safe here," said Lola, reaching out to Lenore. "The amount of protections and wards around this home will keep them away. Trust me, even if they got the idea to check, as soon as they turned the corner, they would lose their train of thought and leave."

"We might be safe in our own homes, but I'm not sure about Books & Beans anymore. They may very well decide to keep tabs on the ones they saw that night. Which is why it's more important than ever that we do nothing rash. Agreed?" said Molly.

Molly meant the last point for Violet. She would have been angry in the past, but she was too exhausted to fight.

"Agreed," said Violet. She glanced at Margaret, but she sat silently staring at the wall above Lenore's head. Something was up with her.

"There's one last thing." Molly reached into her bag and pulled out a plastic bag zipped tight with a small object inside.

"Is that a bullet?" asked Violet. The metal gleamed in the light, but its tip had turned black.

"I stole it from the car before the police arrived." She handed the bag to Rosie. "We need to see who this person is. Can you get anything from it?"

Rosie reached into the bag, pulling out the squished bullet. Bile rose in Violet's throat, looking at it.

"Did you touch it?" Rosie asked Molly.

"No, I was careful."

Rosie closed her eyes, and the room became silent. Violet watched as Rosie closed her fist over the bullet. Rosie's eyes moved beneath the thin skin of her eyelids. Would they finally be able to find out who was after Scott? The longer Violet waited for Rosie's answer, the more anxious she became.

Suddenly, Rosie cried out with a shout, making everyone jump. She opened her palm, dropping the bullet.

"It burned me!" she yelled.

"What?" asked Molly. The bullet rolled onto the floor; the rest jumped away, too scared to touch it.

"It burned me!" The flesh on Rosie's palm bubbled and singed. Lola grabbed her by the wrist and they ran to the sink.

Violet and the rest followed as Lola ran water from the tap onto Rosie's palm.

"Rosie, are you okay?" asked Lenore.

"No! But the water is helping."

"Has that ever happened before?" asked Lenore, worry etched on her face.

"Never."

"What did you see?" asked Molly.

"I didn't see anything, but I felt something. A hate. A really horrible hatred. I've never felt such hate and anger before. Not even from Ellie's evil ex-boyfriend," said Rosie.

"Okay," said Molly. Her hand rested on Rosie's shoulder, rubbing it back and forth. "Lola, do you have aloe or calendula?"

"I have calendula," she instructed Rosie to keep her hand in the running water as she ran to her cabinets to check.

"Somebody grab the bullet, but be careful not to touch it," said Molly.

Violet returned to the dining room and looked under the table. The bullet sat still next to one of the table legs. She found the plastic bag and used a fork to push it inside.

"What should we do with it?" asked Violet, holding up the bag.

"We keep it. We need to figure out what's going on," said Molly.

Molly made tea, steeping the calendula before rubbing it into Rosie's palm. Rosie sucked in her breath as Molly's fingers touched her burn.

"I have aloe at home," said Molly, "but this will do for now." Molly turned to the rest of the coven as they stood back, watching. "Whatever is happening, we have to be careful. Violet, are you still okay with Scott staying at your home?"

"I'm not in any danger at home. I've protected my apartment well," she said. "And Scott is safe with me. If you guys weren't there yesterday, he for sure would have gotten hit by one of those bullets."

"Fine, he stays with you. But at any sign of trouble, Violet, you need to tell us. You can't keep these secrets anymore. It could put us all in danger. Do you understand?"

"Yes," she said, crossing her fingers behind her back.

CHAPTER TWENTY-ONE

T he coven had its instructions, and Violet hugged Lola goodbye as she left her house. Violet followed Margaret to her car, still uneasy from everything. Margaret wasn't acting like her usual self. She hadn't said a word since they had arrived at Molly's house. Margaret was shy with others, even with the coven she'd been in for years, but never with Violet.

Violet couldn't take the silence for much longer, but coming at her strong would only make her retreat farther back into her shell. Normally she had more restraint, but the events over the past twenty-four hours made her patience wear thin.

"Maggie, are you okay?" Violet asked.

"I'm fine," she replied. She was not fine. Margaret's green eyes filled with tears, and her voice was shaky.

"You're a shit liar," said Violet, leaning back into her seat.

"Well, what do you want me to say, Violet? You lied to me!"

"About what?"

"About Scott! You didn't tell me anything about him. You didn't tell me you had fixed your insomnia, or that you two were basically living together! I mean, I knew something was up.

You've spent less time with me over the past couple of weeks. And I told myself it was because you had finals, and maybe you were just stressed out, but I didn't realize you had replaced me."

"Woah, woah, I didn't replace you, Maggie. I would never replace you! I had no clue how to tell you about Scott and what was happening!"

"You could have tried to tell me something! I looked like such an idiot. Rosie and Lenore kept glancing at me like I had betrayed the trust of the coven for not telling them, as if I knew what was happening! But of course they assumed that because we're supposed to be close and they assumed you told me everything! But you didn't, and I'm not sure why," Margaret's voice warbled.

"Pull over, Maggie," pleaded Violet.

"No, I'm taking you home to *Scott*." She spat out his name with more venom than Violet thought she was capable of.

"Just pull over, okay?"

Margaret pulled into the parking lot of a grocery store after a moment. Violet expected her to be more stubborn, but thought her tears clouding her vision made her do it faster.

"I'm sorry I didn't tell you," Violet said once Margaret shut off the car.

"Why didn't you tell me?" she asked.

"Because... I wasn't sure how to explain that I think I like him. And I'm pretty sure the feeling isn't mutual, at least not exactly like mine. And I'm not sure what to do about it." Coming clean hurt. It didn't make her feel lighter or freer. If anything, the weight of her confession squished her chest tight.

"He probably likes you," said Margaret in a small voice.

"He's just grateful because I saved his life, and now he can sleep when we're together. Being grateful isn't the same as liking somebody." It saddened her to say it.

"Do you love him?" asked Margaret.

She shook her head. "No... at least, I'm not sure. I don't know what it's supposed to feel like, Maggie." She leaned back in her seat, rubbing her eyes.

"Well, I can't help you there," said Margaret with a small laugh. "I've never been in love either."

"I love you," said Violet, reaching for Margaret's hand.

Margaret had been there for her when no one else had been. When her parents had kicked her out after everything that had happened at church, it was Margaret and her family that took her in. Margaret, who'd spent nights listening to her cry about her parents and taught her everything about magic. Distinguishing the love for Margaret was easy. Love was late-night phone calls, midnight pancakes during sleepovers, and a shoulder to cry on after a breakdown. Romantic love, on the other hand, seemed empty to her. Even familial love made no sense to her, after everything with her parents. She had only Maggie.

"I love you too," said Margaret, smiling, "but it's not the same love you might have for Scott."

"Shouldn't it be? Shouldn't all love feel the same?"

"I don't think it does."

"I also wasn't sure how to tell you because I know how much you want to experience having a boyfriend, and falling in love and all that shit. And I'm... me. Goddess knows I don't deserve it," said Violet.

"So you thought I would be jealous or mad?"

"I thought it might hurt you," said Violet.

"Vi, if you're happy, then I'm happy. It hurts a little, but not for the reasons you expect."

"I wish I had told you sooner," said Violet. She should have known that her closest friend would understand, and she felt guilty for thinking anything different. "Also, I didn't tell you because I was still in denial about how I felt about him. If I didn't tell you, then it wasn't real."

"But it's real now?"

"Yeah, it is. Very real... I slept with him last night."

"Like fall asleep?"

"No, like I had sex with him."

"What?" Her eyes widened in surprise. Margaret's eyes already took up most of the space on her face, but now she looked like an owl.

"It was an accident."

"What? Like he tripped and—"

"No, absolutely not like that!" Violet nudged Margaret, making a chuckle escape from her best friend's lips. "He woke up from a nightmare, and he kissed me. And then, well..."

"Yeah, don't tell me the details," said Margaret, covering her ears.

"Don't tell the others," said Violet, pulling her hands away from her ears. "I don't want to hear it from Molly."

"I wouldn't," said Margaret, and Violet didn't worry or doubt it. "So, what are you going to do? Are you going to tell him you like him?"

"No, no, I can't. Things got more complicated last night, and if I tell him, I'm afraid that I'm just going to push him away."

"So you don't want to push him away?"

"Not if it means putting him in danger. Out there, he'll be a sitting duck for the shooter. At least when he's at my apartment, he's safe. Plus, I need him near me to sleep."

Margaret was quiet for a moment, her green eyes interrogating without a word. Violet wasn't sure Margaret believed her. Violet barely believed what came out of her mouth.

"So, what now? You pretend like you don't like him? Like last night didn't happen?"

"I don't think I can. I kissed him this morning."

"Did he kiss you back?"

"Of course he did, but he's a guy, Maggie. He would kiss a corpse."

"Ew, you have better taste in men than that!"

Violet raised an eyebrow. "You're kidding, right? This is me we're talking about. I only go for assholes."

"But you wouldn't fall in love with an asshole."

"Are you so sure?"

Margaret smiled. "Yes. I know you. And I already know what you're going to do."

"Well, can you enlighten me and tell me?"

"No. I trust you not to fuck it up."

Violet rolled her eyes. "You can be really annoying some-times."

"That's why you love me," said Margaret with an enormous smile on her face, and Violet didn't have the heart in her to ask further questions.

If only she trusted herself half as much as Margaret did, maybe then her life wouldn't be as complicated.

CHAPTER TWENTY-TWO

Margaret dropped her off, and Violet entered her empty apartment. She expected to find him there, sitting on her couch, laptop open, his brow furrowed as he reviewed the exhibits. He would look up, a smile on his lips, not mischievous like usual but warm, and relieved to see her at home. The vision made her miss him, and she cringed.

She had no clue where Scott had gone to and, checking her phone, saw no messages from him. It didn't matter; he would show up eventually. She sprawled out on her couch, and although she had slept all night, she yawned.

Violet felt unsettled. She exposed her secrets to Margaret, and she couldn't hide from the truth anymore. She liked Scott. A part of her—a small part she pushed and pushed away—was falling in love with him. Her body shivered, cringing at the thought. Even though she had told Margaret, she still struggled to come to terms with it.

Violet rubbed her eyes hard until colorful spots appeared. She couldn't fall in love with Scott, not after maybe binding herself to him. She couldn't trust her feelings or his. What if they slept together because of a spell she hadn't realized she'd cast?

It wasn't fair. She thought of Ellie and River. They liked each other before they were bound. It wasn't the binding itself that caused them to love each other. Could Violet say the same thing about her and Scott? Would they have spent as much time together if it hadn't been for the sleep deprivation? She had still hated him after the shooting. It was only now, after weeks of being stuck together in her apartment, that she could admit to herself that she didn't *dislike* him. But love? Love was suspicious.

The day dragged on, and Violet found herself with nothing to do. Her mind wandered back to the predicament. No matter what she did, or how hard she forced herself to think of something else, Scott would float back into her mind. His eyes, the feel of him inside her, the kiss from the morning. She wanted him, and she hated herself for it.

A weak ping from her phone had her scrambling off the couch to see the message.

SCOTT: I'll be home soon.

Home? Their home? Violet groaned, frustrated. Magic hadn't always been this complicated. She found religion to be complicated. Its rules, its contradictions, its hypocrisies. She counted on magic more than she had on her religion. It always came with a simple cause and effect. Cast and the results would follow. Whether the results were good or bad was another story. But she didn't know what to do now.

Violet realized she had two choices. One: ignore her growing feelings. Let Scott sleep over and maybe they would have sex again, but turn off her feelings. She didn't trust herself anymore. She didn't trust Scott.

Or the second choice: let herself fall in love. Love spell or not.

The second choice made her skin crawl and her heart beat anxiously. The images swirled in her mind's eye before she could stop them. Scott and her, alone somewhere. A home she'd never seen. A comfort she had never experienced with a man before. Her skin burned.

No, she couldn't do option two.

Scott would be home soon, and she needed to make her choice. She got ready and looked through her drawers for her silky pajamas. Dark blue silk with an open crotch. Violet laughed, thinking of what he would think.

She wouldn't fall in love. She had freewill. Magic had offered her more free will than her church ever did. She wasn't bound by a spell she didn't cast, and Scott for sure wasn't. She would enjoy this, have fun, and move on when the threat was gone.

The distinct sound of keys rattling on the door made her jump. Scott opened the door to her apartment, but Violet stayed in her room, taking shaky breaths. A voice in her head screamed at her to choose differently. She tuned it out.

"Violet?" he called out.

Violet strode out of her room, her nerves simmering as she caught sight of him in the doorway. His coat hung half-way off, but he stopped shrugging it off as he stared.

Violet's skin burned hot, as a shyness she was unfamiliar with took hold. She grew frustrated with herself. Why did she care about Scott's approval suddenly?

"Are you going to shut the door? You're letting the cold in." As she said that, she noticed his eyes focused on her perky nipples. He closed the door and cleared his throat.

"Violet?" his voice was harsh. His eyes roamed over her body, taking in every inch of her.

She walked towards him, each step steadier than the last. His hands reached out to her, bringing her in closer. He wouldn't waste the moment. He leaned down and kissed her.

Whatever agonized wanting existed between them in the morning multiplied. His lips were urgent. Each kiss was forceful against her lips. His hands drifted across her body, gripping her flesh to the point she thought would leave bruises.

He tried to lead her to the room, but she stopped him. No, she wouldn't let him control this. She pushed him down on the couch, breaking the kiss as he sat down.

"Violet," he said again.

She loved when he said her name like that. An urgent plea for more. It reminded her of that day in the library, calling out her name over and over. Her name seemed eternally poised on his tongue, ready to be said in exasperation, anger, and now lust. But she didn't want to think of the library. She didn't want to think anything at all. She straddled him, his arms wrapping around her.

He wore far too many clothes, and she wanted to be closer to him. She peeled off his coat and threw it on the floor. Scott helped her take off his sweater and undershirt. She smirked as her eyes caught sight of his chest, and he paused.

"What is it?" he asked.

"A gym membership," she said, laughing, running her hands over his well-defined abs.

"What?" he asked with a raised eyebrow.

"Don't ask."

Along the side of his abdomen, Violet caught sight of a scar. Small, although it hadn't seemed small in the library. Still a little red, even after it healed. She ran her fingers over it, and he shuddered under her touch. Neither of them had left that library untouched, she realized. Only Scott bore the physical mark of it.

He kissed her, bringing his face up to hers, and pulling her from her memories. His hands wandered down to her shirt, and they went under it. She shivered from the cold still clinging to his hands. Finding her breasts, he squeezed them, making her shudder, his thumbs grazing her erect nipples. His fingers tried to lift off her shirt, and she pushed his hands away.

"Please, Violet."

"Did you earn it?" she asked. He groaned and placed his hands under her shirt again. Teasing him made him squeeze her breasts harder. It took everything in her power not to just throw the shirt on the ground.

"How do I earn it?" he asked.

She grabbed his wrist and moved it down towards her silky bottoms. He started pulling the waistband, but she shook her head. She led him lower and slipped his finger into the warmth of her waiting center. He smirked at the surprise.

"You were ready for this," he breathed, his lips finding hers again.

She lifted herself from his lap as his fingers dove, ready to explore. Last night had been quick and desperate. Scott was in no hurry today. His fingers rubbed her clit in slow circles, and she had to break the kiss to breathe. She moaned against his neck, unable to contain herself as he applied more pressure to her clit.

"You're soft everywhere," he whispered into her ear.

Violet couldn't answer. As soon as she opened her mouth, another moan spilled from her lips. She didn't trust herself to not say something foolish. Every touch burned through the confusion of her feelings. She liked him. She more than liked him. But she wouldn't say the next part. She couldn't.

His fingers moved faster, finding a rhythm that seemed to satisfy her. She wanted to pull his fingers away; she wanted him inside her, but she didn't move as her climax ripped through her. Scott didn't move his fingers as she fell against him. He waited, kissing her neck, as her fingers slackened on his arm.

"Did I earn it?" Scott's voice pierced the cloudiness in her head. She smiled against his neck and raised herself up. His hands moved to her stomach, as if to urge her to take off her shirt faster. The silk brushed against her nipples as she slipped it off.

She fought the urge to hide her breasts and cover herself up. She wanted him to look, and he did. His thumb grazed her nipples, and he stared in fascination as they budded on his fingertips.

He smiled and reached up to pull her head down for another kiss. "You're absolutely perfect," he whispered as he pulled her in. She wasn't used to this many compliments from him. A million self-deprecating quips ran through her head, but she kept her lips locked.

Scott kissed her again, as if knowing that if he waited too long, she would crack a joke and ruin the moment. He lifted her up, not breaking the kiss, and she wrapped her legs around his waist as he walked to her room.

Scott placed her on the bed with a gentleness that surprised her. Violet's eyes wandered to his pants. She couldn't wait anymore and undid his buttons. He pulled her hands away, and she fought him, her fingers grazing his length in his underwear. He groaned a little, but pulled her hands away.

"Have you earned it?" he asked, his smile mischievous.

"Fuck you," she said.

"You will, but you have to earn it." He slipped his fingers beneath the waistband of her bottoms, and she raised her hips to help him slide them off. She really had to fight the urge to hide herself now. His eyes scanned her, stopping at her eyes and making her blush. More than her body seemed bare, but Violet ignored the thought.

"Touch yourself," he instructed.

"Excuse me?" she asked; her heart rate quickened.

He lay down next to her, stretching out like a python.

"Touch yourself," he said again. He grabbed her wrist and raised it to her nipple. She squeezed and rolled her nipple between her fingertips. Scott's eyes darkened as he watched her. "I want to watch," he whispered. "I want to watch you do what I know you've been doing in the shower every night."

Violet blushed, turning away from him. His fingers gripped her chin, forcing her head back to him.

"You think I didn't know? You're not quiet, Violet. It's been torture," his voice strained. "Hearing you coming in the shower, only being able to imagine what you looked like naked. Trying to piece together what your pussy would feel like, what it would taste like." He grabbed her wrist again, moving it down her stomach and down between her legs. Violet slipped her index finger onto her clit. She was already sensitive. Every small touch seemed poised to push her closer to her orgasm.

Scott, as promised, watched. His breath hitched with hers, his eyes wandered down to her hands, and he pulled them away from her clit. "Fuck yourself," he said. She didn't want to fight him anymore. She slipped two fingers inside herself. It felt inadequate. She did as she was told, sliding them in and out, but wanting more.

Her breath got caught in her throat with the pace. Scott looked up and caught her gaze. His eyes burned with lust, and more; there was something more. It took Violet by surprise, and she stopped.

"Who said you could stop?" He pulled her fingers away from her pussy and slid them into his mouth, and sucked them.

He slipped the fingers back inside her and moved them. She curled her fingers and let the orgasm come, no longer caring about any lingering embarrassment. Her back arched, her breasts into his waiting mouth. She couldn't focus on the feeling of his mouth on her, not while her body continued to shake with her orgasm. She giggled, finding herself not dragged down by the doubt that plagued her all day. He pulled her hand away slowly from her soaked core. Her eyes snapped open at the sound of him unbuckling his belt.

He lifted himself up over her, and the weight of him on top of her made her heart skip a beat. There was comfort in the feel of his body on hers. Weeks of finding herself twisted with his body every morning abated some of her nervousness now. She knew this body. Every morning, she would feel the pressure of his cock on her back and the weight of his arms around her chest. She had woken up with her lips pressed on the mole at the base of his neck, and his legs wound around hers like a trap. And the night before, she had opened her legs for him to glide in.

Before he lowered himself down; she glanced down at his cock. She wanted to slip into her mouth and suck it for him, but he had other plans. It would have to wait until another day. And there would be another day. Violet would make sure of it.

His first thrust was unceremonious, giving her no warning and sheathing his full length in the warmth of her. She arched her back, but his hand pushed her hips down, and he hastened his movements. She held onto his shoulders, digging her nails into the flesh.

"Fuck," he gasped, "you feel so good."

He moved in and out, and with each thrust, she tightened around him. She couldn't control it. She wanted him to keep moving. The force of his thrusts moved her body upwards, closer and closer to the headboard. She gasped, her orgasm coming fast. Scott slipped his tongue into her open mouth, finding the opportunity to kiss her as she came. Violet moaned, louder than she had all night, as her body shook with the waves of pleasure of her orgasm.

Was it the spell that made it so powerful? That made him fit so well and made every touch almost electric? She didn't want to think of it, and luckily Scott wouldn't let her.

"That's it," said Scott. "That's the sound you make in the shower. I wanted to make you make that sound for so long." Scott stopped, kissing her neck as he waited for her to be ready again.

Violet wasn't sure if she could take anymore, but she didn't want him to stop. She wanted more, much more. Spell or no spell, she loved this. She raised her head to bite his neck, and Scott hissed and laughed.

He moved again. Slow at first, letting the head of his penis slip in and out. Violet rolled her hips to take him in deeper, and he gasped at the suddenness of it. He moved faster, and Violet held on, her already sensitive core riding the sensation.

Scott moaned near her ear, and he quickened his pace. Violet felt him shatter inside her, as waves of pleasure throbbed through her again. He continued pumping his hips after his climax until Violet dropped her hands from his back, letting them hang off the bed. Something broke then. That unseen, tentative connective membrane that wasn't strong enough to stand up to scrutiny.

Scott rolled off of her, his breathing still fast and shallow. She wanted to kiss him again, but something about that felt so intimate. Maybe more intimate than what they had just done.

Time stretched on, and Violet fought off sleep. She didn't want to sleep. Not yet.

"Where were you today?" asked Violet. Her voice cracked in the silence.

"I went to talk to my insurance agent and looked for a new car. I called a tow truck to take your car to the shop," he mumbled, sleep coming faster as he spoke.

"You didn't have to do that," said Violet.

"I don't mind."

Violet stared at the ceiling as her eyelids became heavy. He took care of her car for her? She wasn't sure what that meant. He was just being kind. Or so she wanted to believe.

"I miss the cat pajamas," mumbled Scott, quickly followed by a soft snore.

Violet closed her eyes, unsure of what to think. But sleep soon came before she could linger on it for long.

CHAPTER TWENTY-THREE

Scott held onto Violet's body as she slumped against his chest. She almost fell, holding on to him for support as she came. He could do nothing more than hold on to the kitchen counter as she tightened around his cock. He moaned a 'fuck' into her hair as he came too. Violet giggled against his chest, her hands wound around his neck, gripping it a little too tight, and it filled him with desire again.

Scott reminded himself to pace himself, not that it had helped all week. He had never been more thankful for a holiday break. He wouldn't have been able to concentrate for weeks if this had occurred at any other time. But he kept his promise to himself, fucking her in every square inch of her apartment. There didn't exist a surface anymore where they hadn't slept together. Kneeling in front of her while she sat on the couch, spreading her legs for him to lick. Standing in the shower and having her suck his cock in her closet as he dressed. Even on her balcony, as they watched the snow fall while he pleasured her with his fingers deep inside her.

He lifted his head to see Violet looking up at him, a wide smile on her lips. His own smile mimicked hers, unable to contain the happiness that had been growing all week.

Violet stretched in his arms. "God, I'm sore."

"Sorry," laughed Scott, but he wasn't sorry at all.

"Mm, I got my revenge," she said, pushing his face to the side to look at her handiwork on his neck.

"And then some. I have the scratches to prove it."

He couldn't explain the pull. The way his heart skipped a beat when she smiled in his direction. The urgent need to pull her pants down and make love to her standing when she touched any part of him with the lightest of touch. She had stopped wearing underwear around the house after the second day. It was a miracle they slept at all, but he had never slept more soundly in his life.

Scott realized one night, as he settled onto his side of the bed, that he was happy. Ridiculously so. When had he last been happy? He wasn't sure. Even his childhood didn't appeal to him anymore. Every memory of his mother corrupted it with regret and anger.

It didn't come without its complications. In about a week, they would go back to the office. He had no clue how they were going to hide the truth now. Before, he didn't care when he told people they weren't sleeping together, because well, they weren't, not in the sense his coworkers meant. But now? They were having sex multiple times a day. If he lied, he wasn't sure that he could sound convincing enough, or that the goofy smile plastered on his face wouldn't betray him.

Violet was another complication. Scott wanted to kiss her. Not to initiate sex, but because he wanted to. He wanted to kiss her before they fell asleep, while she studied, and as she did yoga in her living room. He noticed early on that she didn't like it. She would recoil upon realizing the kiss was spontaneous and not intended to start a hookup. So he stopped, only kissing her when he moved inside her, finding her then willing and begging for it.

She also wouldn't cuddle after sex. Scott found this worse than the kissing. His body moved towards her automatically, wanting to press himself against her and have her skin on his, but she moved away then too. The scowl on her face hurt Scott deeper than he realized it could. He couldn't help the morning cuddles. Her body betrayed her then, entangling herself in his limbs. But she shunned all forms of touch that weren't sexual. Scott told himself it was okay. Sex was all he wanted, anyway. He didn't need the rest, or so he liked to tell himself.

Scott awoke, spooning her in the chilly morning. He indulged in the warmth of her body next to his beneath the covers. Violet didn't stir, but seemed to melt into him as he held her closer. He breathed in her scent, letting it engulf his senses, knowing full well in a few moments, she would wake up and push him aside. He would enjoy this, whatever this was.

Love.

The voice in his head sounded soft. Testing the word, letting it fall as if by accident.

No, he thought. *This is something else, not love. I like her. It's hard not to. But this isn't love.*

Violet stirred in his arms, her ass pressing against his erection. He wanted to wake up like this forever. He stopped the thought, unsure of where it would go if he allowed it to continue. Panic made him list everything he needed to do that day to distract himself from where his mind wanted to go. He couldn't love Violet. It was out of the question.

Violet yawned, her body arching, stretching like a cat. She turned in his arms, her face inches from his. A sleepy smile followed, and Scott stopped himself from pulling her in for a kiss. In this state, in the in-between of sleep and consciousness, he thought he saw her true feelings.

But she was waking, and the smile soon left, leaving Scott's own heart empty. If he could keep her there, keep her close, maybe then she would see it too.

Violet's eyes narrowed, as if sensing what Scott was thinking. "Shit," she mumbled, bolting awake and fleeing the bed. Scott panicked and followed her in a sleepy daze, stubbing his toe on the door frame.

"Violet," he called. Violet ran into the bathroom. He tried to open the bathroom door but found it locked. "Violet?" he called again, worry gripping his chest. "Are you okay?" He pressed his ear to the door but couldn't hear anything. The silence was followed by a flush and then running water.

When Violet opened the door, she looked at him nonchalantly. "I'm fine," she said and walked towards her kitchen.

"You're okay?" he asked incredulously. "What was that?" he asked.

"I got my period," she shrugged. "Stop freaking out."

"Right," he said. His heart rate slowed. "Why did you run like that?"

"I had to run before there was a bloodbath underneath us. Anyway, I thought you'd be happy," she teased. "You don't seem like a daddy."

"I guess we've never talked about this, but we are safe, right?"

"Yeah, I know we haven't talked about it," her voice came in between chortles. "And you're not always quick enough to put on a condom."

Scott's grew warm with embarrassment. Sometimes, if the condoms were close enough, he could remember to put one on. He was normally very careful. The last thing he needed was to throw a crying, screaming wrench into his otherwise perfect ten-year plan. But with Violet, sometimes the need was so overpowering, it was as if his brain shut off and every responsible thought slipped away.

"But you're on birth control?" he asked.

"Now you ask," she teased, rolling her eyes.

"This is serious, Violet. If I had known, I wouldn't have been so careless!"

"Don't get so worked up. I have a friend who makes me a special tea."

"A tea?" he asked.

"Yes, trust me; nothing could get me pregnant."

"But why a tea? Why not normal birth control?"

"The tea works a hundred percent. Birth control has a shit ton of side effects and is only ninety-nine percent effective, if I remember to take it correctly. So tell me, how do you like those odds, Daddy?" she smiled, and Scott laughed uneasily.

"Okay, tea it is. Sounds a little witchy," he joked.

"It's just herbal medicine," Violet no longer laughed. "But people get so worked up about it like everything else now."

"I'm sorry. I trust you, but I'll be better about the condoms." Scott wanted to lighten the mood again, so he changed the subject. "Do you need anything?"

"What do you mean?"

"Well, I don't know? Chocolate or a heating pad? Do you need me to buy tampons? What do you need when you're on your period?"

Violet looked at him, her gaze strange, dreamy, almost. "You've really never lived with a woman before, have you, Scott?" He didn't know how to answer that. "I can feel my cramps about to start. I'm okay, but I have a heating pad in my closet that I need to microwave to heat up. I love salted caramel chocolate, and in two days, I'm going to crave pad see ew. And I have enough tampons. Also, sex is out of the question. I feel horrible."

Scott smiled, resisting the urge to lean in and kiss her forehead. She wouldn't like it, he had to remind himself. He went into her closet and found her heating pad and warmed it up for her.

Scott walked into a bar he thought would be empty but found a few sad-looking men nursing draft beer. Very few places were open during the day on New Year's Eve, but he had a long to-do list. He had been neglecting everything over the past week in favor of spending every moment with Violet, but he couldn't prolong it any longer. With Violet bedridden with her period, he finally had the time and space to work. While he argued with a car salesman for a better rate, he felt his phone vibrate in his pocket.

Hackman: Paradise. Noon.

Scott ordered a beer from the bartender. The man looked bored, placing a paperback on the counter to fill Scott's order. He didn't bother speaking with Scott, and he was glad about it. Scott wasn't sure his nerves would allow him to be the friendliest conversationalist. He was halfway done with his beer and contemplated another when the door chimed.

He turned to see the familiar gait of Arthur Hackman. He shook the snow from his coat as he shrugged out of it, wearing a rather formal-looking suit underneath it. Scott got the sense he had pulled Arthur away from his New Year's Eve plans. Arthur smiled a toothy grin when he spotted Scott and pushed his grayed hair away from his windswept face.

"Hi Scott, how are you?" he mumbled. A private investigator shouldn't be too loud, and Scott knew from experience that Arthur was the best in the city.

"I'm doing better," answered Scott. He didn't need to lie; Arthur would see straight through him.

"Heard about the shooting in the car." He motioned to the bartender and ordered a beer for himself.

"That's kind of what I wanted to talk to you about." The bartender came back, and Scott waited for him to leave before continuing. "Maybe we should get a booth?" Arthur nodded and followed Scott towards the back of the bar. They settled in, and Scott tried to memorize the faces of the other men there. He couldn't help it. He'd been paranoid after the first shooting, but now he looked for suspects everywhere he went. Arthur remained unfazed, gulping down his beer and settling into the warmth of the bar.

"I need your help. These cops are just wanking off at the station and doing nothing about these threats."

"Have you tried asking nicely?" joked Arthur.

"They're being difficult on purpose. I'm defending someone accused of witchcraft. I doubt they're happy about that."

"A witch getting a fair trial, yeah they would hate that." Arthur had a wheezy laugh, and Scott wondered if he took anything he said seriously.

"They wouldn't let me watch any of the camera footage from the library or the street outside in the square. I received a threatening letter at my workplace, and things are escalating. They won't do shit. They keep talking about due process suddenly."

"What can I do for you?"

"I need you to look into what the police won't. I need you to find out who this assailant is before he strikes again." Arthur looked surprised, but nodded his head. No doubt Arthur had expected him to ask him to track down another long-lost parent.

"I see. Do you have anything the cops don't have?"

"They won't let me see the evidence, but I know you can find something."

"I know I can do it, but it's gonna cost you."

"They almost killed someone I care about. I don't care what happens to me, Arthur, I really don't. But they crossed the line when they put her life at risk."

"Should have known this would be about a woman. It's always about a woman with you." Scott ignored him. He didn't want to think about his mother now.

He'd hired Arthur to track her down a year ago. Less than a month after, Arthur had deposited a thick yellow envelope in his mailbox. He tried not to think about the night he had opened it. After pacing for about three hours, and drinking an entire bottle of wine, his fingers wouldn't stop shaking as he pulled out the information. He didn't remember exactly what he'd read. His eyes became blurry after seeing a picture of his mother. What he remembered was his anger. His anger at seeing her with her new family, her new-step children, her new life.

"Do we have a deal?"

"Yes." Arthur downed the rest of his drink. "I'll message you later about payment."

"Has your account changed?"

"No."

"Then the money will be in your account tonight."

Arthur said his goodbyes, assignment in hand, and left. Scott shifted in the booth and looked around to see which of the patrons appeared fishy. His paranoia had too much power over him. No one looked curious or nosy. The other two patrons looked too depressed to pay any attention to him. The bartender ignored everyone there, his book covering his face.

Scott's paranoia had finally convinced him to call Arthur. He was almost embarrassed to see him again. He thought he would be better by now. That the memories of his mom wouldn't have affected him as strongly as they had the night he read over her file. Contacting Arthur resurfaced those memories anyway, bobbing up to toy with him once again.

She'd been so young when she died. Maybe she would have reached out when he was old enough to understand. Everyone had a story. He wasn't sure how he would have responded or if it would have been enough. But he never got the chance to try. She was gone, and now everything remained unsaid.

His mother remained forever young in his head. He was almost the same age as she was when he last saw her. He had no family to abandon. No relationship he'd built over ten years to ruin. Sitting alone at the bar, he wondered if he did that on purpose. If nothing tied him down, there was nothing to disappoint.

Scott left the bar, afraid of stewing in his feelings and memories for much longer. Violet soon replaced his previous thoughts. He pushed the memories away and drove to the supermarket. As he paid for chocolate, an electrical heating pad, and her favorite kefir drink, he calmed down. His turbulent feelings, which swirled in his body like an unrelenting wave, dissipated at his excitement at seeing Violet's reaction when he arrived home with sustenance.

Chapter Twenty-Four

Violet found herself a few days later at Lola's home again. She'd meant to visit the day after New Year's Day, but spent it with Scott instead. She had a surprisingly great New Year's Eve. There was no midnight kiss, not that she wanted one, but having Scott next to her to watch the ball drop had felt nice. Intimate almost. It made her skin crawl and her heart ache. The sharp ache made her finally reach out for help.

Lola's house was more modern than Molly's, but her penchant for color appeared all over the house. Lola had painted each room a different color, from the butter yellow of her kitchen, to the blues of her hallways, and the purple of her bedroom. She left no corner untouched. Her decor leaned kitschy, flea market and thrifted finds that sometimes came with an attached spirit or two. Violet didn't like these items, but Lola loved them. She particularly loved a haunted tea set that she didn't use because the previous owners had poisoned their dinner party with it. At night, Lola explained, the set would move, tinkling and shaking, adding to the sounds of the little footsteps from the haunted dolls she loved.

Violet had come over to peruse Lola's book of shadows, but she thought it polite to look at her newest acquisition.

"It's a casserole dish?" asked Violet, as Lola held a yellow porcelain dish with painted bees on it.

"Not just any casserole dish," Lola flipped it around, "it's a Pyrex from the fifties."

"Is it haunted by the spirit of an unhappy housewife?"

"No, it's just a wonderful find."

Lola flipped her blue hair out of her face and took the casserole dish back to her kitchen. She had dyed her hair a different color and cut it about three inches shorter since the shooting. Violet didn't think she had chosen a subtle color, but if the cops were still looking for a pink-haired woman, maybe this was enough to stump them for a while. Violet settled onto the couch, letting the coffee's warmth settle her nerves.

"So," said Lola, "I'm guessing you're not here to ask about my casserole dishes. What gives?"

"I've been thinking about the last time we all talked. About the accidental binding?"

"Ah," said Lola, "but why would you need to talk to me about it?"

"I know your book has a lot of love spells."

"Love spells, lust spells, spells to steal husbands. My ancestors clearly had one thing on their minds," laughed Lola.

"Does it have bindings too?"

"Some, but not what you're looking for. All the bindings in my book are very much intentional. I've already looked, and I didn't find anything about an accidental binding."

"Shit," Violet sat back, staring at the ceiling.

The past few weeks had been almost perfect. The days spent in each other's arms, making love and kissing the hours away. She had to be careful not to get carried away. If she focused on the physical, focused on the way her body reacted as his mouth sucked on her clit, focused on his abs beneath her fingertips, or the way he made her feel so full, she could easily forget the rest. She could forget the warmth in her chest and the way her heart skipped a beat when he looked at her. When her feelings popped up like spring bulbs, when the voice in her head questioned her actions, she buried it all away in a flurry of sex. And luckily for her, Scott was all too willing to let her get distracted.

But when he brought her chocolate, and remembered to buy pad see ew on day three of her period, she couldn't stop her heart from throbbing around him. She pushed him away, finding that sex no longer offered her the distraction she needed from her feelings. Sex made it much worse now.

"Bindings are a deliberate act, aren't they?" asked Violet.

"They are," said Lola.

"How did I accidentally bind myself to Scott? I didn't cast!"

"Molly can cast without saying a spell at all, you know that."

"But Molly is different. She's had decades of practice, she was born into it, and even then she's freakishly powerful."

"Molly is powerful, sure, but so are you."

Violet wasn't as convinced. Every time she tried to cast without speaking, she ended up giving herself a headache from squinting too hard. "But Ellie didn't know she had bound herself to Derek?"

"She might not have understood that the spell she cast was a deliberate binding, but that's what it was."

"Okay, but what about Ellie and River? Were they not being pushed by something magical to be together? I mean, what if Ellie didn't want to be with River? Would the magic stop?"

"Magic is not an exact science," said Lola.

"Yeah, okay, Molly," sighed Violet, rolling her eyes.

"We do still have free will, Violet. If Ellie didn't want to be with River or vice versa, I'm not sure if the magic would have stopped, but they didn't have to be together. They chose to be together."

"I'm not choosing to be with Scott."

"I never said you were. But do you think you're bound to Scott?"

"I think the sleep deprivation was because of the binding."

"Are you sure it was you?"

"What? Who else could it have been?"

"You said so yourself, Molly's had practice. She was born into a magical family, and she's had years to develop her skills. But you've only been a witch for what? Less than ten years? Everyone can develop their magic. Maybe Scott bound himself to you."

"There's no way."

"Stranger things have happened."

"Yes, magical things, but Scott is as mortal as they come. He didn't even like me before the shooting. He had no reason to bind himself to me."

"One of you did it. And I know you think it had to be you. I'm just suggesting that he found an anchor for this world, and he chose you."

Violet didn't know what to say.

"Are you developing feelings for him?"

"I'm afraid that Scott might develop feelings for me, and it wouldn't be right if it was because of a spell."

"I see." Her eyebrow raised as if she wasn't quite buying what Violet said. "We can check to set your mind at ease." She stood up and left the room. When Lola came back, she carried two large tomes and set one on the coffee table. She flipped through the pages, knowing exactly where she was going.

"Here we are." She turned the book over to Violet.

"You forget I don't know Spanish," said Violet.

"Right, sorry. It's a basic cleansing spell, but we can adapt it to see if there is anything in your aura that is clinging on."

"Okay, what do I need?"

"Something personal of his. Hair or toenail clippings would do, but if you're squeamish, you can bring clothes. You also need to take a cleansing bath for the next five days with," Lola squinted down at her book, "albaca, hierba buena, ruda, poleo, and romero. I'll get the translations for you."

"Okay, let's say we do this, and I am bound to him. What then?"

"We unbind you."

"Could there be any unforeseen consequences? Like, is he going to die?"

"I don't think so, but he might not be as interested in being with you anymore, especially when he learns he doesn't need you to sleep."

"That's what I want," laughed Violet, but even to her, her laugh sounded forced.

"Okay," said Lola, "bring me something personal and I can get it done."

Violet arrived home the same afternoon, and she walked straight into the bathroom. Scott's comb was near the sink. His dark hair twisted around its teeth, and she didn't hesitate before shoving the entire comb into a plastic bag. She hid the bag in her purse until the next time she saw Lola. Even though her stomach twisted in knots, thinking of the result of Lola's spell, she convinced herself in the hours that followed she had made the right choice.

She didn't move for the rest of the day. Unable to muster the energy to leave her couch as she flipped through her streaming services. Her mind focused on her conversation with Lola. She found herself down, depressed almost. She should be happy, shouldn't she? This nightmare would be over soon if she found out the truth. But she felt even worse.

The lock on her apartment clicked, and Scott let himself in. He greeted her with a huge smile on his face.

"What's up with you?" she asked.

"I finally got a new car." He sat down next to her, and she sat up.

"Glad to hear it," she said.

"And I talked to the mechanic, and your car should be ready in a few days."

"Any clues as to why it wasn't working?"

"Something about your battery? I honestly didn't understand what the mechanic told me. I should have written it down."

Violet had learned that while Scott could recite the history of case law and its impact on American history, and he beat her every time while they watched Jeopardy, he didn't understand cars. Violet found it rather refreshing. Many a first date had been ruined sitting across from a car guy that needed to spend the next three hours explaining why his car was better than others.

"Anyway, what are you doing tonight?" he asked.

"What I normally do. Watch TV and pretend school isn't starting in a week."

"Well, I have a better plan."

"Better than Henry Cavill? I doubt it."

"There is a rare astrological event tonight, a meteor shower."

"That's not rare, and the skies won't be clear."

"Wrong, there's not a cloud in the sky."

"Light pollution?"

"Won't affect it."

"We don't have a place to watch."

"My apartment has a rooftop, and we'll have the whole place to ourselves."

Violet was out of excuses. Her heart hammered in her chest, and her stomach churned. An empty rooftop to watch shooting stars, alone? How romantic.

She couldn't do it. He was compelled, pushed by an accidental binding. This wasn't real. None of it was. She didn't want to play along anymore. And yet, Scott looked happier than she had ever seen him. He was more talkative than she remembered. He seemed lighter, as if he had let go of whatever heavy burden he carried. His excitement was so palpable it made Violet's chest hurt.

He looked at her expectantly. How much longer could this go on?

"Fine," she agreed. "Let's go."

CHAPTER TWENTY-FIVE

When Violet stepped into Scott's apartment, she pretended not to be impressed by it. She wondered whether she had made the right decision to stay at her place. His apartment had tall gray walls, stainless steel appliances and a large kitchen island. The bathroom alone was almost the size of her entire apartment. The couches looked brand new and unused, a far cry from the old used couches Molly had let her take from her attic.

"I told you we should have stayed in my apartment." Violet turned to find Scott's smug smile glued to his face.

"Mine's cozier," she argued.

"I agree."

Violet looked away and pretended to inspect the backsplash in his kitchen. She couldn't trust herself not to break under his gaze. Her eyes roved over the countertop, and she gasped, surprised by what she found.

"The cactus," she exclaimed. The prickly green cactus sat in the same purple pot she had bought it in. It was the only color in his apartment.

"You were smart to think of getting me a cactus. I'm barely here enough to water it."

"I'm just surprised it didn't die at the sight of you. So where's this rooftop?"

"Follow me," said Scott, reaching out his hand for Violet to take. When his fingers grasped hers, her fast-beating heart betrayed her indifference. He led her out into the hallway and into a stairwell. The cold made Violet shiver as they climbed out onto the roof.

Someone had been growing a garden, but they left it abandoned in the winter. Lawn furniture pointed outwards towards the city's skyline. Violet's eyes fell on a padded mattress on the floor surrounded by blankets and pillows. Scott left her to turn on the heater by the mattress. He pulled out a bottle of wine and two wine glasses next to the blankets, motioning with his head for her to join.

Violet hesitated. Scott had put in a lot of effort for this night, and her guilt gurgled in her stomach. He wouldn't have done anything if not for the binding, but a small voice in her head protested. *It's not a sure thing that you guys are bound. This could just be him.*

She sat down next to him, pulling a blanket over her shaky legs.

"Are you cold?" he asked.

"Yes," she lied.

He wrapped another blanket around her shoulders and handed her a wineglass. Violet downed it. Scott appeared apprehensive, but didn't say a word. She handed him the glass, and he refilled it. After downing her second glass of wine, she grew warm under all the blankets and her coat. She pulled off her coat and lay down on the mattress.

Scott was right; not a single cloud covered the open sky. Some of the high rises around them had turned off their lights as well. The sounds of kids with their families getting ready to see the show floated to their lonely roof. Scott laid down next to her, and she tried to inch away from him, but the padded mattress was much smaller than Violet's bed. His heat warmed her body even through the heavy blankets.

"You seem upset today," said Scott.

"I'm just a little sad, that's all."

"Anything I can do to fix it?" he asked.

Violet wanted to cry. "I'll be okay."

Suddenly, a bright burst of light fell across the sky. Wondered oohs came from the surrounding buildings, along with happy squeals of excitement from children. The meteors fell in quick succession, creating brilliantly illuminated streaks through the sky. Violet watched in awe. She had never witnessed a meteor shower, and for a moment, her problems fell with the stars.

"There's that smile," said Scott.

Violet turned her head and met Scott's eyes. Their normal hardened edge was gone, replaced by a tenderness that threatened everything Violet fought against. "I thought you wanted to watch the shower?" She asked, looking back up. The stars put her back at ease, but she sensed his eyes still on her.

"I've seen a lot of meteor showers."

"You have? Why come see this one, then?"

"I thought you might enjoy it. And I don't know, I was thinking about my mom. She used to like this sort of thing."

"She did?"

"Yeah. She used to tell me that God plucked stars from the sky to put them into the eyes of lovers."

"That's actually very sweet."

"She was a huge romantic. She said we would recognize our soulmates immediately after meeting them, because we would see the stars reflected in their eyes. The same stars that were plucked from the heavens just for us to find." He grew silent, and Violet sensed his unease, causing her not to break it.

The stars fell until the number slowed, a star, maybe two, coming down every couple of minutes. But Violet stared at the sky as her tears fell from the corners of her eyes, pooling around her neck.

What would her mom be doing right now? With the time difference, she would be in the middle of cooking dinner. Asking her sisters to pitch in as they joked about an incident that happened years ago, but still brought tears to their eyes when they retold the stories. Her mom would tell them to hush up, but she would laugh too. A mischievous twinkle in her eye, not unlike Violet's. It wasn't all bad all the time. That's what hurt the most.

"It's looking like it's almost over," said Scott, as another star appeared after five minutes.

"Can we stay here for a bit longer?" asked Violet.

"We can stay as long as you want."

It took a while for Violet to get a hold of herself, but when she felt steadied enough, she asked, "Do you miss her?"

"Who?"

"Your mom?"

Scott waited a moment, and the silence made Violet uncomfortable. "Sometimes, but even my memories of her seem off. I can see the problems now. My parents used to fight almost every day. I hated hearing it. They would scream so loud that I couldn't drown out the noise. You know when you're a kid, sometimes you dream about having different parents. I used to pretend my best friend's parents were mine. They probably had problems too, but when I was over at their house, they seemed so perfect. I used to wonder how much happier I would be if my parents were different."

"I used to do that too. I used to fantasize Maggie's parents were mine, and that we were sisters."

"It was one of the few ways I could survive that time. Whatever problems she had with my dad, she didn't have to leave us. But even after all that. After all this time. I miss her. I always have."

Violet reached her hand under the blankets and searched until her fingers bumped into his freezing hands. She fought the urge to put them against her neck to heat them up.

She wondered how much Scott would've told her of his past if the shooting hadn't happened. If the binding had never forced them to spend time together. If they didn't need each other to sleep. It was all a forced illusion until Lola told her for certain that they weren't bound.

"Have you talked to your dad recently?" she asked.

"No, I can't bring myself to. He calls my phone every day, and sometimes he calls the office. Maybe in the future, I'll open that door again, but not now. What about you? Have you spoken to your parents?"

"That's different," said Violet. "Your dad wants to talk to you. He wants a relationship with you. My parents don't. The only way they would let me back into their lives would be if I did everything they asked. They would forgive me; I know that much. But I haven't been able to forgive them for what they did to me." Scott squeezed her hand, but she found little peace in it.

"What happened?" he asked after a moment.

"My youth pastor almost assaulted me." She waited for Scott to say something, but he seemed to hold his breath. "He asked me to come early to help set up for choir practice. I thought he had asked the others to come too, but he didn't. I was so young, so naive. I had no clue he was coming on to me. But I had a crush on him, and I used to be so jealous of all the attention he gave this girl named Savannah. And I was eager because he had asked me to come early, not Savannah. He was giving me attention and not Savannah."

"But I was so confused when he started touching me. First my face, and then my breasts. I couldn't understand what was happening, but I felt gross, and knew I had to leave. So I started pleading and trying to get away. I told him my mom was coming to pick me up early. He knew that was a lie. He didn't care how much I begged. The bastard probably enjoyed it."

Scott froze like a statue. She wasn't even sure he breathed.

"He got aggressive, and he pushed me onto the floor. But I fought. Oh, and he was so mad about it too! He couldn't believe I was fighting him. And then a few students walked in, and the bastard got up and had practice like normal."

"I thought I was safe. Now everyone was going to see this man for the creep that he was. And I wouldn't ever have to see him again," Violet stopped. Her whole body shook, and Scott's grip tightened on her hand, urging her to continue. It never got easier, no matter how many times she told it.

"My parents were furious at him, but also at me. They asked me what I did! How I acted! What did I do that caused him to stumble? My parents used to dress me up in modest clothing, so they knew my frumpy knee-length jean skirts couldn't have done it. So it must've been the way I acted. It must have been something I did. The worst part of it all was the following Sunday. He had confessed. But we were both brought up to be made an example of."

"What?" asked Scott. Finally, something broke through his stupor. His anger radiated from him, making his muscles taut. Her fingers grew numb in his hand.

"Yeah, I confessed. I said I made Grant stumble. It was my fault. They wouldn't believe me if I told them the truth. My own parents didn't believe me. I think at that point, I just wanted it to be over."

Her tears flowed down her cheeks. Her biggest regret — confessing in front of everyone — now lay open for Scott to judge, and she waited for the results. When she glanced at him, however, his face lacked any trace of pity. His eyes were dark; his anger was barely contained. He reached over, brushing away her tears.

She realized Scott understood. He saw the broken parts of her. He didn't think of her as ruined, the way her parents had convinced her. She was fallible. Human. She was saved until she wasn't. Until her parents told her she caused the other boys and grown men in the congregation to sin. That her modest skirt and blouse weren't enough. The night she had punched her attacker in the face when he tried to feel her up had been no one else's fault but hers.

She had been so scared that night. Her adrenaline pumped through her body as she pushed Grant off of her. He had been so determined, but she was fierce. She always had been, but they kept it locked away. Kept beneath bulky clothing, fear, and her faith. Her church and her parents would keep her safe, because she believed. But it didn't keep her safe. They were quick to sweep it under the rug. The idea of reporting it to the authorities was out of the question.

Even remembering it now, she became angry. How could the people in her life who proclaimed they loved her the most abandon her? She often wondered later if she had just kept his secret and if she had just kept quiet, would things be easier? Could she have gone on keeping his secret? Her parents would still be in her life. They wouldn't have made her stand alongside Grant in front of the congregation to confess their 'mutual' sin. She would never be a witch.

Violet smiled weakly, letting her fingers brush over Scott's furrowed brow. "It's over now," she said. She said it to herself, too. A reminder that she had grown, made her own family. Created a whole life that seventeen-year-old Violet would've loved. The life and community her younger self deserved.

"Violet," he said, his hands drifted to her face, cupping her head in them. "I could kill him. If you tell me where he lives, I know ways to make him disappear."

"You're a mercenary now?" A small laugh escaped, almost like a hiccup.

"I defended a hit man. He owes me a favor," he said, as if it was the most normal thing to say.

"As much as I would love that, you would deprive kids of their dad?"

"What?"

"He married Savannah the month she turned eighteen."

"Fuck, Violet," he said. He looked devastated.

"It's more normal than you think, where I'm from."

The photos hadn't even shocked her when she first saw them. They stood in a field of long grass. Savannah's hair lay in perfect blown-out waves around her shoulders; her engagement ring flashed prominently to the camera. Savannah looked up at him in the photo. A look of admiration and love plain enough to see in her smile, but Grant looked at the camera. Why they chose that photo to announce their engagement, she didn't know. But the caption beneath the photo made her want to throw her phone at the wall. Savannah's descriptions of the perfect godly man made her sick.

"None of that is normal, Violet. What happened to you wasn't right. They should never have put you in that position."

"I don't disagree. It's just difficult to hold hatred for so long. At some point, it burns you from the inside and makes you think that nobody out there in the world is good or kind. It makes you think everyone at one point will hurt you. When you were telling me you missed your mom, I realized that sometimes, as fucked up as it might sound, I miss my family."

"It's not fucked up. It's hard to balance the wonderful memories you have of someone with how they hurt you. Even after everything my dad did, I miss him, too."

Violet's eyes had never seemed heavier. Even though she wanted to keep talking, feeling lighter than she had in weeks, she struggled to keep her eyes open. She pulled the blanket in between her and Scott, and put it aside.

Scott didn't budge but watched her every move, almost as if she would spook with any sudden movement. As if her confession had made her more fragile, and in a way it had. She didn't feel grounded until she settled onto his chest and his arms wrapped around her. Nothing felt as secure as this. He kissed her forehead, and she melted. His heartbeat drummed beneath her ear, angry and frantic. She rubbed his chest with her hand, shushing it.

As sleep came to drift her off to the dream realm, she heard a whispered, "I love you." She smiled even though it hurt, finding consciousness slipping faster away the longer she held on to him.

CHAPTER TWENTY-SIX

Scott wondered for the next week whether Violet had heard him that night. The 'I love you' had slipped out, but as soon as it left his tongue, Scott didn't have an ounce of regret in the moment.

He loved her. He loved her incessant quips. The ones that used to irritate the hell out of him, but now made him laugh. He couldn't remember the last time anyone had made him laugh. Life had always been so serious for him. He loved the way she disarmed him with one look, melting every fortress he set up to protect him from hurt. He admired how hard she worked, and how much she cared about that work. Her laugh was his favorite sound in the world, followed by her groggy voice in the morning. Everything about her culminated in his love. After she shared her story, his raging anger made him realize he would do anything to make sure she would never experience pain again.

Now that the words had left his head and walked in the world, he had no clue what to do about it. Love changed everything for him. More than he realized it would.

Regret came later, and so did his anxiety, when she didn't address it. He tried in vain to remember the details of that night. He was a few drinks in, and her story made him so angry that the night blurred in his memory. The surrounding roofs had quieted down as people returned home after the meteor shower. He wasn't sure whether she had heard him.

He worried about Violet. He often caught her staring out into space, distracted from the world around her. Even though they were together, her thoughts were somewhere he couldn't follow. He worried she had left her mind and spirit behind on the roof. The Violet he saw now was a hollow version of the woman he loved. Devoid of everything he understood about her. Everything he loved about her. He searched for her, watching her every move to find the person he once knew. But after a long week of her absent stare, he tried his best to amuse her. She was open enough to it, often pulling him into her arms and away from whatever he worked on. He didn't fight it.

Love changed sex for Scott. He wasn't sure Violet sensed the difference. Did she sense the desperation in his every touch and kiss? He longed for her. An ache gnawed in his chest. It's only balm that could be found as he made love to her. As her eyes rolled into the back of her head as he moved in her. As he kissed every inch of her body, he felt the difference, wanting her eyes on him. She would refuse shutting them when asked. He had to edge her until she would. But he always had to ask.

Although it wasn't the change he wanted, something shifted in Violet. Her kisses had a bite to them. She enjoyed pushing him. Push him against the wall, against the bed, onto the couch. She had initiated sex plenty of times before, but there was an aggressiveness to her. Hungry. As if he would disappear tomorrow.

But there was a disconnect between Violet in bed and the Violet of every day. Nothing made sense to him anymore. Did she love him back, or was he trying to comfort himself?

However, other things kept Scott occupied. Arthur kept Scott informed of the suspects he followed, but nothing substantial had materialized yet. Scott became more paranoid, and while he had no new nightmares of Violet's death, the thought liked to pop up randomly. Their next moment wasn't guaranteed, not while the shooter walked free. If this was it, Scott wouldn't waste it. Perhaps those were Violet's exact thoughts as well.

With work and school starting again soon, he had little time to devote to his obsessive thoughts, but that didn't stop him from doing so. Any time he had a second alone with his thoughts, the spiral would start. But luckily for him, if Violet was near, she had a way of pushing all his thoughts away.

Scott lay in bed with her as she read through the syllabus for one of her classes. He was supposed to be writing an email, but he watched her instead as she became more and more anxious.

He could catch that now. The way her chest would move faster, and her foot would shake uncontrollably.

"How many books?" he asked.

"Five for one class alone. What a pain."

"You'll get through it."

"I have no clue how anybody survives law school."

"You're almost done. What, one more year, right?"

"Yeah, one more year," she sighed and turned to him. "What are you doing?" she asked.

"Just emailing Carl and the other associates. This is the last of the motions the prosecution sent. They set trial for two weeks from now."

"Are you nervous?"

"No, we'll win."

"You're very sure."

"You have to be. And Ms. Miller will be free from this bullshit." He'd met with Eve Miller earlier that afternoon. She'd been nervous, rolling the rings on her fingers over and over until she yelped as one loose prong in the setting pinched her skin. He had tried his best to assure her, but he doubted it did any good.

"You're a good person, Scott," said Violet.

"Where did that come from?" he asked.

"From me."

"Are you sick?"

Violet nudged him hard in his ribs. "Listen, I only give out a compliment a year. Take it."

"One compliment? What was that you said the other night? Oh yeah, something about me being the best sex you've ever had? A sex god, I think you said." Violet grabbed the pillow beneath his head, and Scott laughed as he fought her trying to smother him. "It's too late to take it back," he laughed.

"I'm never going to compliment you again, asshole. Also, I didn't call you that." She couldn't do much damage, but Scott held her wrists to her sides.

"I'm sorry. What were you actually going to compliment me on?"

"Forget it," huffed Violet.

"Violet," he said as sweetly as he could muster without bursting into laughter.

"All I was going to say was that you could have jumped ship like the rest of the firm and dropped Ms. Miller. But you didn't."

"I'm not as honorable as you think. I thought it would impress the partners if I stayed on," he admitted.

"Oh please, after the shooting at the square, it would be completely understandable if you referred her out, and you know it. Martyrdom doesn't impress the senior partners. You wanted to help. Even if she was a witch."

"I'll take the compliment, I guess. But I don't believe in witchcraft."

Violet paused, her mouth hanging open. "What do you mean you don't believe in witchcraft?"

"I've never met an actual witch. All these trials are political theater playing with the lives of women and marginalized people."

"I don't disagree with the last point, but witches are real."

"Please," scoffed Scott.

Violet burst out laughing, rocking the bed with the force of it. It had been so long since he had heard her laugh; it took him by surprise.

"What's so funny?"

Violet waved her hands, telling him to stop. Her laughter continued until she could barely breathe.

"What? I don't get it," he smiled, finding her laughter infectious. He raised himself on his elbows, which made her laugh more. "Tell me, Violet," he laughed now, too.

Violet shook her head no.

"Violet," he straddled her, pinning her arms above her head. "Tell me," he demanded.

She still laughed, and he pressed her wrists further into the bed. He leaned down, kissing her. Her laughter stopped, but a small giggle escaped her mouth into his as he ground his hips down onto hers. She bit his lip, but if she wanted to push him away, that was the wrong way to do it.

"Make yourself feel good," he instructed, pressing his hips down on hers. She pushed her hips up, meeting him. He wanted nothing more than to tear her tights off of her, but he relished the sweet pressure on his cock. She pressed herself against his growing erection, and he nipped her bottom lip. She liked that, a heavy sigh leaving her lips.

He grew impatient. He could never draw it out as long as he wanted. No matter how hard he tried, he needed her as soon as possible. It was a strange feeling, almost magic. No one had ever made him feel as desperate or hungry as Violet did.

His hands caressed down her arms and over her chest. She arched her back to help him take off her blue sweater. The same impatience made him skip unhooking her bra, and he pushed it to the side to kiss her waiting breasts. Violet moaned as he sucked them gingerly, and she arched her back again to unhook her bra for him. She threw it on the floor, but Scott had already moved on, kissing down her chest. Her hands went to his head, her fingers digging into his scalp as his fingers traveled down. He pulled down her skirt, tights, and underwear in one swift movement.

The dance was now so familiar to them both as Violet reached her hands under his sweater. Her hands ran over his chest, and he shivered at her icy touch. He pulled his sweater off, and her hands went back to his face to smooth the hair away. She traced his jaw, gliding her fingertips to his lips. It sent shivers through him, making his cock twitch.

Her hands traveled to his pants, and he helped her push them off. He settled in between her legs, kissing her neck, letting his tongue trace her jawline. Violet whined, bucking her hips up, rubbing herself against his abdomen.

"Not yet," he whispered.

"Now," she protested. Her own patience was as short as his.

He laughed, and she started laughing too, making his heart swell. His hands wandered down to her folds, separating them and letting his finger find her lovely clit. He hitched her thigh up to palm it. She moaned into his shoulder.

He kissed her then, slowly, deeply, his fingers running over her clit in slow circles, while her nails dug into his shoulders. Her eyes fluttered closed, and he kissed the thin skin of her eyelids. He liked her like this, soft and yielding beneath his hands. As if she pulled back the shell she hid behind, if only for a moment. For him.

"Inside," she gasped. "I want. You. Inside." Her hand moved onto his cock, and his breath caught as she squeezed his shaft. It wasn't fair. Watching her squirm with his touch had made him so hard. She pumped his cock, lingering on his head. He closed his eyes. His own movements on her clit lost their rhythm as the pressure built in his body.

"Not fair," he said.

Violet laughed. "I don't... play fair." She pumped harder, and Scott had to stop what he was doing, letting himself feel each touch. She dragged her hands, letting the slow ministrations both frustrate and excite him. He stopped Violet when he thought he would cum. Her eyes shone, proud of getting him so close. He couldn't hold back any longer. She had won.

Scott positioned himself between her legs and pushed in. He loved the first gasp, the startled breath at the first inch of his cock in her core. He pushed himself in, and each inch was an agonized test of self-control. Violet closed her eyes, and Scott craned his neck down to kiss her. He was in no rush, letting his movements be languorous and slow, even if it meant he would have to wait for his release. Violet moaned beneath him. The unhurried pace was getting to her. Her legs wrapped them-selves tighter around him. Her nails scratched his arms.

He started pushing faster, letting his hips grind against hers. Her fingers dug into his shoulders; her moans became guttural. He fisted her hair at the nape, pushing her eyes to meet his. He forced her to kiss him as he pumped harder, her mouth opening wide mid-moan. His hips relentlessly moved, and he couldn't take the way she felt on his cock.

"Scott," she pleaded.

"I love you," he said. Her eyes grew wide, and her lips stopped responding to his kiss. He moved harder. Her body responded, tightening around his cock.

He moaned as he dug his hips harder. Violet moaned in his ear as she came around him. His own release was swift and overpowering, stealing his breath. He tried not to collapse on top of her, but he didn't want to pull away yet. He needed to stay as close to her as possible.

"You love me?" she asked breathy.

"I—" Had he told her? It must have stumbled out.

"Do you love me?" she asked again as he raised himself. He couldn't read her face. She didn't look happy about it.

"I do," he said, cradling her face in his hands. "I love you."

"You don't know what you're saying," she whispered. Saying it more to herself than to him.

"What do you mean? I love you, Violet. That's how I feel."

"How do you know?"

"I just... do." Violet stood up, pushing him aside. She looked for her underwear and hurriedly untangled them from her tights. "Violet, what's wrong?"

"You don't know what you're talking about," she sounded frantic, and she struggled to put on her tights.

"Wait, stop." He reached out, pulling her back into bed. His grip only made her wind into herself tighter. "What is this, Violet?"

"What is what?" she asked, annoyed.

"What is this between us?"

"We're sleeping together," she said.

"Yeah, in more ways than one," said Scott humorlessly. "I love you, Violet. I've never felt that way about anyone else."

"There's a reason for that," she whispered.

"What's that supposed to mean?" he asked. Violet's eyes searched his. What she looked for, Scott couldn't figure out.

"I need to go," she said, standing up again.

He didn't bother stopping her. He watched helplessly as she grabbed her coat and her bag and left the room. The apartment door shut with a bang, and he jumped at the noise.

He had ruined everything.

Chapter Twenty-Seven

Violet sat in her car for five minutes. She felt cold, her hands numb in the January freeze. Scott loved her. *No, she reminded herself, it might not be real.* She compulsively checked her messages with Lola. She had given her Scott's hair five days earlier, and Violet had been taking the cleansing baths every day. Surely by now there should be an answer, but Lola still hadn't responded.

She couldn't go back to her apartment. Her imagination ran wild with what Scott was doing now. She pictured him angry, hurt, pacing her apartment and picking up his things to leave. She needed to call Margaret, see if she could stay over at her place. Even if it meant no sleep. Her thumb scrolled to her favorites when her phone started ringing.

Molly's name popped up on her phone's screen. She stared at the number, confused. A picture of Molly drinking coffee on her screen stared back. Last she checked, they were still on shaky terms. She didn't want to answer, but reasoned there could be an emergency. Molly probably wouldn't call her unless she had no other choice. Against her better judgment, she answered.

"Hi, Violet?"

"Yeah, hi Molly. What is it?"

"Are you busy? There's something I need to show you."

Violet wanted to make an excuse. The last thing she wanted was to hang out with Molly. There weren't enough sleep potions in the world to make her suffer through yet another lecture.

"Come on, Violet, I know you're running through your Rolodex of excuses."

"What's a Rolodex?" she asked, annoyed.

"Just come over to my house. It's important."

"Fine," she said. "Be there in ten."

Violet sat in Molly's kitchen, a simmer pot boiling on the stove. Its fragrance wafted through Molly's entire home. Cloves, cinnamon, oranges, and a few peppercorns. *Deceptively welcoming*, thought Violet. Her pocket vibrated. She pulled out her phone and saw Scott calling. She muted the call.

Molly joined her, offering her something to drink, but Violet declined. She wanted to be in and out. No time for pleasantries.

"So, what did you want to show me?" asked Violet.

Molly reached into a small bowl on her kitchen counter. "Catch," she said, throwing a small object at Violet.

Violet's fingers closed around something cold and round. She opened her palm to find a squished bullet in her hand.

"What the fuck, Molly!" she yelled, dropping the bullet from her hand. It bounced off the counter and rolled onto the wooden floor. Molly sighed, picking it up from the floor.

"Is that the bullet that burned Rosie?" asked Violet.

"Yes, but it won't hurt you." Molly held the bullet between her fingers and handed it back to Violet. Violet let the bullet roll around in her palm. Her phone vibrated again, and she pulled her phone out to see three texts from Scott. She set her phone to silent.

"I don't understand?" Violet said, focusing on the bullet. "When Rosie had this, it almost burned a hole in her palm."

"Smell it," said Molly.

Violet hesitated, not wanting to bring it up to her face. "It smells like... sulfur." She wondered why they hadn't caught the potent scent before. "There's something more though," she said. A hint of something herbal, grassy.

"Henbane," said Molly. "Also known as Black Nightshade, it's a poison. The Assyrians used to make a mixture of sulfur and henbane to protect against magic. They'd dip amulets into the potion so no one could cast a spell on them."

"Protect against magic?"

"It burned Rosie because she used magic directly on it when she tried to trace who the killer was. But us just holding it, nothing happens."

"I don't understand. So they're magic-proof bullets? But how did Scott and I survive the shooting then? Weren't you guys casting to make them not hit us?"

"We were. And I thought that might have been what stopped you guys from getting shot, but the more I think about it, the more I realize that's not what happened. The only thing I can think of that protected you and Scott that night was Lenore's amulet. Since it wasn't a direct spell on the bullets, it protected you. But any direct spell around these things and you're as good as dead."

"Magic proof bullets. Who knew such a thing existed?"

"Violet, the person who tried to kill Scott, had the foresight to dip their bullets in a potion of henbane and sulfur. We're not dealing with a random person who hates witches enough to kill their defense attorneys. This is a witch hunter."

Violet realized she'd never seen Molly scared before. She was always such a steadying force for the entire coven. Her beautiful face, still and poised. Never letting on what was going on in her mind. Even when Ellie's ex-boyfriend rampaged and threatened to expose the coven, she had appeared strong and unfazed by it. But now, she looked graver than Violet had ever seen her. Violet had known Molly for four years, and she felt ashamed, knowing she had never asked Molly what had happened to her. Something must have. Everyone had a story. Why had she never asked Molly what made her so intense and so cautious? Guilt slinked over her conscience, remembering all the times she thought Molly's caution was overkill.

"So what do we do now?" asked Violet.

"We lie low, we stay vigilant. Nothing changes for the coven. But Violet, we need to unbind you from Scott."

"What?"

"Lola told me about the spell to figure out if you're bound to Scott. You are. Violet, the longer you're with him, the more danger he's going to put you in. This is a witch hunter, and we can do our best to protect Scott for you if you wish, but you need to be physically away from him as much as possible."

"I..." Violet didn't know how to respond. They were bound. None of it was real. A spell made him love her.

"I know this is a shock, but we can reverse it. It's not the same spell that binds Ellie and River."

"I can't leave him. We can't sleep if we're not together. Molly, they'll kill him! Binding or no binding, I care about him. He's safer with me."

"But you're not safe."

"We survived the shooting thanks to Lenore's amulet. We're protected."

"How long do you think it will take the witch hunter to realize that his anti-magic bullets didn't work? He'll figure out another way."

"I'm not doing it," Violet shook her head.

"Violet—"

"I'm not! I won't do it. I won't abandon him when there is a witch hunter after him."

"Violet, be serious! Is he worth it?"

"What?"

"Well, it wasn't like you liked the guy before the binding. This could all be a spell! The longer you're with him, the longer you're in danger."

"You mean the coven is in danger?"

"No, you're in danger, Violet! Why can't you see that?"

"Why can't you see I care about him? And it isn't because of a spell. Lola said we have free will, spell or no spell. I chose to fall in love with him. And he chose me." Before Molly could respond, Violet stood up. "I have to get out of here."

Violet began gathering her things. She grabbed her phone off the counter, flipping it over. She noticed five missed calls from Scott and five missed messages.

Violet opened the messages and read through them quickly, trying to shove her hands through her coat sleeves.

SCOTT: Violet, please answer.

SCOTT: I'm sorry.

SCOTT: I didn't mean to spring it on you like that. It just happened.

SCOTT: Violet, I got a call from work. Answer, it's an emergency.

SCOTT: The client is dead.

Violet read the last message several times, not believing or registering it. Her coat hung midway on.

"Violet?" said Molly. "What's wrong?"

"Scott's client. She's dead."

"Is this the woman they accused of witchcraft?"

"Yes," said Violet. She flopped down on the couch, her head spinning. Molly sat next to her. "What if it was the witch hunter?" asked Violet.

"We would need details, but it's a possibility." Molly smoothed down the flyaways on Violet's head. Violet wanted to lean into her touch, take in some of the comfort being offered, but she didn't feel like she had earned it. Not after yelling at Molly.

"What do I do?" she asked.

"We unbind you."

"I can't do that."

"Violet, if you're afraid his feelings for you will change, it's not right to keep him bound for that reason."

"I know. But it doesn't change the fact that he's safer with me. And if being bound means he's safe, then I can't break it. Not yet."

"Are you sure you can be with him? Even if his feelings are being influenced?"

"I don't know," said Violet. She tried her best to push the tears away, wanting to hide it from Molly, but the choice lay heavy on her chest.

Violet walked into her dark apartment. If it hadn't been for Scott's car in the parking lot, she would never have known Scott was home. She found him curled up in her bed, staring out the window. Violet crawled under the covers, not bothering to change her clothes. She wrapped her arms around him, pulling him back onto her chest. He resisted, his muscles tense and taut, but the longer she held on, the resistance melted away. He leaned back into her, bringing her hand up to his mouth to kiss her open palm.

"I'm glad you're back," said Scott after a moment.

"Me too."

She would stay, but she wasn't sure how much longer she could justify this. How much longer could she watch his sad eyes stare at her without guilt eating away at her conscience? But for now, this moment, and until the threat passed, she would bask in whatever love he had for her.

As sleep came, she wondered bitterly why, without a spell's influence, Scott would never have loved her. She was unlovable, as she always had been. Too brash, too intense, too intimidating. Nothing like the demure girls she grew up with. Not the model wife she was told to be. Or the girls she observed in college, who seemed to figure out exactly how to get a man to love them.

Even after she'd left the community she grew up in, no one had ever taken a genuine interest in dating her or asking her out on dates. She took what she wanted and boasted of her conquests to the coven. Now she felt something different. Now that she knew what being loved was like, she thought it cruel that no one would love her the way Scott did now. Love was never supposed to happen to her.

The most terrifying part of it all, the part she pushed, denied and pretended didn't exist, slithered away from her tight grasp.

She loved him too.

Chapter Twenty-Eight

The sun set early, and its weak rays highlighted the veins on Scott's hands. He flexed his hand, remembering how Violet had traced those raised lines over and over as she consoled him. He thought it strange looking at them now. She had found a part of his body he rarely gave any attention to and made it his sole focus. He would have never guessed out of all the parts of his body that Violet had access to, she would choose his hands to find the most attractive. He hoped it would be a part of him he worked hard to build, but her mind was a strange place.

It reminded him how much of Violet's inner world remained a mystery to him. All her reasons were unusual and unexplained, but he no longer had the energy or the want to question them.

He no longer knew where he stood with her. Violet had been kinder to him since the death of his client. They left their argument untouched, too afraid of what might arise if they tried again. And while Scott wanted to bring it up again, the death of his client took precedence.

It bothered him to have expressed his feelings and not had them reciprocated. It was a vacuous hole left in the middle of the room for them to cross. Yet, Scott traversed it every day, kissing, holding, clinging to her, feeling the fear creep in the dark as she slept next to him.

She could be next. He could be next. The killer was getting closer, and as much as Scott wanted to bring up the subject, he feared Violet running off again. Afraid to be where she was not, unable to keep her safe, he tried his best not to scare her away.

Scott hated going to work now. The hours drifted by, working on other cases and interacting with the other associates, but his client's death attached itself to his mind. He wondered what he had done wrong. Where he should have helped more, or what he could've done to prevent her death.

"This isn't your fault," said Carl the day after in this office. "I know what you must be feeling right now. I've had a similar experience, but I have to tell you, Scott, as your mentor and friend, you can't let this experience stop you from your work. That's how the bastard will win."

"Thanks, Carl. Can I go now?"

Carl nodded, with a resigned furrow on his brow. Nothing reached Scott. No matter how many times Scott repeated it to himself, it never made it any truer. It was his fault.

If he had only contacted Arthur sooner. If he hadn't waited for the police to do something, they would have caught the killer long before he had the chance to strike again.

He went home early every day, causing Beatrice to stare open-mouthed each time. Her tight smile and worry etched into every line of her warm face. The other associates salivated at his departure. No doubt planning their next move to oust him. Scott didn't care.

He lay on Violet's couch in the middle of the afternoon. His eyes unfocused and his brain elsewhere as the TV blared. He wanted Violet at home. She would be the perfect distraction, but checking his phone for the time, he realized her class wouldn't end for another hour.

He fell into a restless sleep somewhere between episodes, and the jangle of Violet's keys at the door startled him awake. He wasn't sure if he was still jumpy or just attuned to her like a dog.

Her sigh broke the silence as she stood in front of the TV. He dared not peer up to see her disappointment, deciding to focus instead on the specks of snow melting into her maroon coat.

"Scott, it's three o'clock."

"Is it? Weird, I thought it was eight."

"Scott, why are you home?" she asked.

She sat next to him, forcing his head onto her lap. Scott closed his eyes as her hands moved to his scalp. She ran her fingers through his hair, and the tension that Scott had held in all day melted. Her salty vanilla perfume engulfed him, warmed by the heat of her neck. God, he wanted to kiss it. Lie in the crook between her head and her neck and forget everything that had transpired over the past couple of weeks. Violet would make him forget. Licking her sweet pussy as her thighs clenched around his head would make every horrible fear disappear.

"I wasn't feeling well."

"Are you getting the flu? Because I have a test next week, and if I get sick—"

"It's not the flu. I promise, you and your precious grades are safe."

"Scott, what's wrong?"

I love you, and you'll never love me back. That's my fault too. Like everything else.

"Everything is fine, honestly," he said. "I'm just tired, that's all."

"You're sleeping fine every night."

"That's because of you."

"Is it because of your client?"

"I—" Eve's death was part of it, but he wondered whether it was worth telling her the truth. He didn't want to risk losing her now. "I'm in a rut, that's all, Violet." She traced the veins on his hands again. Her cold fingers made him shiver, but her touch hurt. His chest grew tight with each soft pass. It was all so intimate, and it hurt.

"Scott," said Violet. "Beatrice told me your birthday's next week."

"Is it? I forgot." It wasn't a lie. He didn't have the faintest idea what day of the week it was.

"You're an Aquarius. I should have known." He chuckled and opened his eyes to see Violet's soft gray eyes staring down at him.

"Are we compatible?" he asked.

"Only if you like putting out fires. April 5th."

"What does that make you?"

"Aries."

"Explains a lot."

"Does it?"

"No, you'll have to tell me later why my being an Aquarius makes so much sense to you." His head bobbed up and down as she laughed.

"Can I throw you a birthday party?" she asked. Scott stared at her, dumbfounded.

"Why?"

"It's your birthday. It's not everyday you turn forty-five," she said as her mischievous smile spread across her face.

"I'm not forty, Violet, and I don't know if a party is a good idea."

"Scott, I know you don't like most people, but you're home at three in the afternoon. You haven't left my apartment in days. You're depressed, and before you ignored your feelings with work, but now you're not even working."

"So a party will fix it?"

"I think a party celebrating the fact that you're still alive is a good thing. And I know you won't go to therapy."

He groaned. "You're wearing me down on that front."

"Good! Margaret has a number for a great one. She can give you the details at your birthday party."

"You would invite your friend?"

"Well, you're not the friendliest guy, and I need to pad the guest list."

"You want to introduce me to all your friends?"

"The ones who show up at least," she shrugged.

"Seriously?" Violet's fingers stopped running through his hair. What did this mean? Was she was finally crossing the abyss of his slipped out 'I love you?' "I guess a party wouldn't be the worst thing in the world right now."

"Just say yes," she said, rolling her eyes.

"Fine, yes. Okay, throw me a birthday party."

CHAPTER TWENTY-NINE

"Can you hand me those numbers?" asked Violet.

Margaret fumbled through brochures and menus on her coffee table until she found the right stack for her. Her house had turned into party-planning headquarters. What started as a small get-together had quickly grown the more Violet worked on it. She wanted to hide most of it from Scott. The guy needed a good surprise. Luckily, Margaret was kind enough to volunteer her house.

"I still don't get why you're doing this," said Margaret as she handed over the sheaf of papers.

Violet didn't respond. She peered at the papers in front of her, hoping they gave her an excuse to seem distracted enough for Margaret to move on. It was the first time she had ever planned a party, let alone a birthday party. Most parties in the past involved trying to buy a keg and hiding any valuables from drunk college students. This party had to be different, but planning everything last minute left her with few options for venues, cakes, or guests.

When she finally looked up, she found Margaret's interrogating gaze still on her.

"Scott's having a hard time right now. I thought I would be nice," she shrugged.

Nice was one way to put it. Another would be trying to rid herself of the guilt that kept chewing on her insides. Since Molly's revelation and Eve Miller's death, Violet did nothing but try to convince herself she was right not to unbind them. Eve's death was a warning. The killer wouldn't be satisfied with stopping there. Scott needed her to keep him safe.

But there was something else. A little grating voice that questioned everything. She couldn't do anything without that voice popping into her head like a jack-in-the-box from hell, pulling her from every moment with him.

Was she selfish in tying him to her while she knew the truth of their binding? If answers were what she needed, she was nowhere close to getting them. Although planning the party was a welcome distraction that kept her mind from eating itself.

"This is a lot of work for someone you hardly care about," continued Margaret. She tucked a large red curl behind her ear as she peered over Violet's to-do list.

Violet had made Margaret more of a priority since their last fight, but it meant she could no longer hide the thorny problems she wished to ignore. Margaret had a sixth sense with Violet, and if her expression was any sign, she didn't buy a single word out of her mouth.

"Yeah, well, I have a lull in my schedule."

"Vi, come on."

Margaret had a knowing look on her face, and Violet realized that if she continued to make excuses, it would only be harder to dig herself out of them. Sure, she had told Molly she loved Scott, but telling Margaret was something else. Telling Margaret made it real, and it made her keeping him bound even worse. She had told Margaret about the binding a few days after she learned of it, but she didn't have the strength to tell her the rest.

"I'm just being nice," she assured her.

"Violet, you love him, don't you?"

The words made her heart skip a beat. "And...what if I do?"

"I would say it was great, but you honestly look like you're about to puke."

Violet groaned and collapsed her head into her hands. Margaret's house had always been a comfortable hangout, but all she wanted was to go home and make sure Scott was okay. Being away from him filled her with a sense of longing she couldn't comprehend. No guy before ever made her want to be with them past the one night. Some guys made her run the other way as soon as she spoke to them. Others needed more of a repellent to push them away. Not Scott. At least, not lately.

She wasn't sure if that was the binding or her. She would never know unless she did the one thing she wanted to avoid.

"Okay, let's say I love him. What does that even mean?"

"You lost me."

"I mean, let's say I unbind him, like Molly wants. What if my feelings disappear? Or his? But if I keep him bound, what if we get married and one day it just breaks? Like the spell has a time limit or something, or the guilt gets to me one day and I tell him. What then?"

"Wait, you would keep him bound for that long?"

"No, I wouldn't. I'm talking hypothetically here."

"Vi, I've never seen you this strung out over a guy."

"Exactly! This isn't normal. My feelings aren't mine. It's all the spell."

Margaret, perhaps sensing the oncoming panic attack, quickly drew Violet's hand to hers. "Do you love him?"

Violet hesitated, although she had no reason to. She felt it deep within the heart she thought had long frozen over. The mere thought of him leaving her made her chest hurt.

"Yes."

"And he loves you?"

That hurt more to admit than her own feelings. "Yes."

"Spell or no spell. Those feelings don't come from nowhere."

"What do you mean?"

"I've looked through some of Lola's spells. I've translated them when I get home because I'm too embarrassed to ask Lola to translate them for me. Most spells I saw will only work if there were feelings there before. The stronger the feeling, the stronger the spell."

"But there were no feelings before Maggie. That's the problem. I hated him. He hated me too. We couldn't stand being near each other."

"Those are still strong feelings."

"But they're not the right ones."

"Maybe it wasn't all hate all the time. Maybe there was always something there. You two just needed something to force the two of you to see it."

Violet shook her head. No matter how Margaret tried to explain it, the uncomfortable truth remained that one day she would need to unbind them. The killer was an excuse. She couldn't live with herself if she made more excuses.

"I can't unbind him yet, but I will. I have to. It's just I'm not sure what will happen when I do."

"Whatever happens, I'll be here. You know that, right?"

Margaret draped her arms around her, bringing in for a hug. It helped. The tension in her shoulders eased, but not much else did. Yes, she knew no matter what happened, no matter who was in her life, or out of it, Margaret would be the one person left standing.

She hoped it wouldn't be just her.

CHAPTER THIRTY

Scott regretted telling Violet to throw him a birthday party. He stood awkwardly in the middle of a bar he had already forgotten the name of. His coworkers, his two friends, and a group of women he didn't recognize were there. Along with what Scott assumed were the bar's usual questionable patrons. He wanted to back out of the party twenty minutes after agreeing to it, but Violet's excitement stopped him. She wanted his opinion on everything: cake, venue, and guest list. Once she started, he realized he couldn't stop her.

His two friend's numbers had to be blackmailed out of him. Violet threatened to send their wives the sexts he had sent her over the course of their relationship. A cruel joke indeed, but Scott didn't believe that she would have actually done it. Violet chastised him for having only two friends and complained the party would be boring if they didn't invite more people. So Scott invited some coworkers to fill in the gaps. He didn't mind Beatrice or some of the other junior associates coming, but he wasn't looking forward to seeing Carl or some of the more cutthroat, social-climbing partners at his party.

"Are you sure inviting the firm is a good idea?" he asked.

Violet didn't glance up from her textbook. "Why not?"

"We were trying to keep this a secret."

"Beth is onto us."

"What? Beth can't even tell the difference between opening and closing remarks, and you think she knows?"

"She asked me yesterday how long we had been seeing each other. She guessed we've been together since the start of my internship."

"Like I said, not the brightest."

"Yeah, except then Judy, Roland, and Adi all asked me the same thing. I'm guessing our being together in the square during the last shooting was a tipoff."

Scott stared at her, but she didn't seem as shocked or upset by it as he thought she would be. "So what now?"

"Why hide it?"

"Hide what exactly?"

"Hide from the fact that I'm throwing you a birthday party." Not the answer he wanted to hear, but he would take it. "Honestly, I'm just surprised that anyone would want to come," continued Violet. "But it seems like someone's new attitude might be winning him some friends."

"I should go back to being mean." He didn't feel like he had changed much at all, but a couple of fewer scowls thrown at random interns had them flocking to him. He had never had more conversations in his life at work.

Scott became more anxious as the party loomed closer, but he couldn't stop Violet's enthusiasm for the party. He didn't want to stop her fun. She called venues and restaurants, but accommodating at least fifteen people last minute was difficult. She settled on a bar when Scott told her venues were overkill for a birthday.

He watched her over the week, both awed and confused. Perhaps Violet couldn't tell him she loved him. The words got stuck between her head and her throat. Maybe her effort, the way she looked at him, the deep satisfied sighs when he moved in her, would be enough. Love needed to be more than a platitude given absently. Love was this. In the actions. He would do the same for her. He didn't want a party, but Violet wanted a party for him. And that was enough for him.

With a beer in hand, Scott stood and greeted his coworkers with a forced smile at his birthday party. He couldn't help but feel like a six-year-old with friends his mom had invited to his party. The junior associates didn't appear as awkward, joking and drinking with him as if they liked him and weren't trying to find a weakness they could exploit later. Carl slapped him hard on the back, making Scott almost drop his beer.

"So, thirty-one, eh? I remember being thirty-one. I had more hair back then," he joked. Scott choked out a laugh.

"Yeah, well, hopefully it won't start falling out," said Scott, running a hand through his dark hair.

Carl wound an arm around Scott's neck and pulled him down a few inches to his face. "You and Violet, huh?" he asked. His beer breath made Scott nauseas.

"What about me and Violet?" said Scott, clearing his throat.

"Are you two together?"

"No," said Scott quickly. Carl burped, already drunk.

"I'm just asking. But listen, technically it's okay cause I'm her boss, you're just a guy who works there, but I'd be careful."

"Why?" asked Scott. He hated this conversation. Carl motioned to the bartender for another beer. Violet shouldn't have insisted on Scott inviting him.

"I'm just saying it doesn't look very professional, that's all." Carl took another swig of the scotch he held in his hand. "If I were only younger," he sighed.

Scott excused himself from the conversation, resisting the growing urge to punch his mentor. He raced towards Violet, noting that it wasn't a great idea with everyone watching, but he only wanted to be around her, anyway. Forget the others, and their misconceptions about them. Their opinions never mattered to him, anyway.

Violet wore a black velvet dress; it had see-through mesh sleeves, and his eyes lingered on her bare legs. He wished they could go home. He wanted to leave the crowded, dirty, and loud bar and spend his birthday in the warmth of her bed.

"Hey," yelled Violet as he approached. She stood next to a woman with red hair and giant green eyes. "This is Margaret." Scott said hello reaching out to shake her hand. After all of

Violet's stories about her, he had expected someone younger, like a kid sister. Ellie said hi after an awkward chuckle. Not that he blamed her. Although he no longer belittled them, some interns were still skittish around him.

Violet pointed to the rest of the group. Rosie and Lenore were taking tequila shots at the bar. Wincing as they sucked a lime after each one. Rosie's black hair was blunt around her shoulders, wearing all black and combat boots, as if she was going to battle later. Lenore threw her head back, laughing as Rosie whispered in her ear. Her flowery dress and demeanor seemed much less intense than Rosie's.

Lola and Molly shook his hand as Violet introduced them. Lola made him feel at ease. He was unsure why, but he chalked it up to her warm smile. Molly's smile didn't reach her eyes, and he felt as if she were attempting to read his mind.

"Is this everyone?" he asked into Violet's ear.

"Yes, well, there's River. That's Ellie's boyfriend, but he couldn't make it out today. Emergency at the morgue, I guess. By the way," said Violet, hugging him. "Happy Birthday. Fifty-two, who would have thought?"

Scott laughed, the sound turning a few of his coworkers and her friends' heads. Violet's smile was awkward and apprehensive, glancing at the others. He resisted the urge to scoop her up and kiss her.

Violet talked with her friends, trying her best to include Scott. He found them nice enough, although Rosie and Molly were shooting daggers at him. But Violet was happy, and if this birthday party brought her joy, Scott figured it was worth a couple of awkward introductions and conversations.

"Your cake is in my car," she said. "I'll be right back."

"Don't go alone," he said, grabbing her hand. He didn't care anymore. He didn't care who looked. Violet had thrown him a birthday party. She introduced him to her friends; she crossed the other side to meet him now. Why hide anymore? Carl already suspected it, Beatrice probably knew, and the other associates and interns threw furtive glances their way. He wanted to kiss her in front of everyone. Letting everyone see he loved Violet.

"I won't go by myself," she pointed out to Rosie, standing by the door, her arms crossed over her chest.

Scott nodded and watched her leave. Beatrice approached him soon after, her smile crinkling her soft eyes.

"You look happy," she said.

"Don't say that, Beatrice."

"Why?"

"Something bad always happens when I'm happy. Let's just say that I'm content."

"Content, happy, same thing. Don't be afraid. I always knew you two would be together."

Scott wanted to question her further. At what point had she figured it out? But he kept his eyes on the door, waiting for her to come back. He should have gone out with her. Anxiety made the beer in his stomach burn like acid. What was taking her so long?

Then he saw him walking through the door with Violet. A man with graying black hair, standing six feet tall, and with a more weather-worn and tired look than Scott's own face.

His father.

Scott's heart raced. What was he doing here? Why was he talking to Violet? Had she invited him? Violet's eyes searched the crowd until they landed on Scott. He didn't know what his face looked like, but Violet's own looked terrified. He excused himself to Beatrice and walked towards his father. Without looking at him, he walked past him out the door.

"Scott," he heard his father's voice behind him. The blood rushed through his body, making his head swim and his heart beat loudly in his ears. "Scott," he heard again behind him. He finally turned around.

"It's nice to see you again," said his father. His eyes scanned Scott, taking him all in.

"I can't say the same about you." His father gave a half-smile. His tired and weary face hadn't changed in the year since he had seen him last. Scott ignored the part of his conscience that told him to be kind and respectful. Childhood habits long instilled in him. His father didn't deserve any of it.

"Really? Scott, after all this time, you still haven't gotten over it?" he sighed.

"Gotten over it?"

"Wrong choice of words."

"No, Dad, it's exactly what you wanted to say. No, I haven't, so if you'll excuse me, I'm leaving." His father stood still.

Dumbfounded that his planned birthday party ambush hadn't worked.

"You would be so cruel as to not let me see you? After the shooting? Your girlfriend was hysterical over the phone. Can't you for a second see it from my point of view? I didn't hear from you for three years, and the only piece of news I have is that someone shot you. The only reason I knew you were alive was because of your girlfriend. But you couldn't have done the decency of calling me just to let me know you were okay?"

"The same decency you had to lie to me about Mom my entire life."

"Scott, this isn't about your mother!"

"It is! It's about what you did to drive her away!" His father stood still, silent. Scott hadn't meant to say it, but now that it was out, he was glad he had. His father drove his mother away. There could have been no other reason. After all this time, the least his father could do was admit it.

"I didn't do anything, Scott," his father's voice sounded deflated. As if replaying the past was the last thing he had wanted to do tonight. There was no fight left in him, and instead of giving Scott pleasure, it infuriated him.

"Yes, you did."

"No, I didn't. Could I have been a better husband? Of course. I don't deny that there were things I wish I had done differently, but I didn't drive away your mother. She left us for her own reasons, and she never clued me in on what they were. But Scott,

I'm the only family you have left. And I didn't leave you! Your brother didn't leave you! You left us."

"Don't you dare try to put this on me! I told you that three years ago. We're through. I meant it then. I mean it now." His fists balled up. His dad nodded, as if realizing the finality of it all. He turned, walking back towards his car.

Scott took a deep breath, holding on to whatever small bit of control he had. His hands shook, and his eyes watered. His breath fogged in front of his face. He felt small again. Small and scared, looking into his mother's closet, confused why it was empty. He closed his eyes. The icy wind cut through his body, making him shiver. He could hear his dad pulling out of the parking lot, but he didn't want to bother looking.

"Scott," he turned, seeing Violet behind him. She wrapped her arms around her chest. There wasn't a trace of guilt on her face.

"How could you?" he asked.

"What?"

"Why did you invite my dad?"

"I didn't." Scott turned away from her. He needed to leave. He needed to go back to his place. "Scott," she ran ahead of him, putting her hand against his chest. She had run out in the cold without her coat, but it didn't seem to affect her. "Scott, I didn't invite your dad."

"How did he know about the party?"

"I don't know, but it wasn't me! Believe me, Scott, I would never do this!"

"Just leave me alone, Violet. I need to be alone."

"Wait. You believe me, Scott, right? I didn't do this!"

"I need to be alone," he repeated. He stared away towards his car. One look from her and he would fold.

"What are you doing?" she asked. Her voice soft, the cadence skipped through a half-swallowed hiccup.

"I'm leaving. I told you."

"You don't believe me," she whispered.

He looked at her then, her gray eyes filled with tears. What was he doing? This was the person he loved. *That doesn't love you back*, he thought furiously. He was stupid to believe that she ever would.

"I don't believe you." The words sounded false to his ears, but they were irreversible.

"That's enough."

He turned to find Molly standing behind him. She had Violet's coat in her arms, and her eyes glowed with a controlled fury. He took a step back, away from Violet.

He turned back to Violet and found her eyes laced with the same anger as Molly's. With something else. Something that stung. Disdain.

She didn't love him. She never would.

He walked past Violet into his car and drove away as fast as he could.

CHAPTER THIRTY-ONE

A heavy coat fell onto Violet's shoulders as Scott pulled out of the parking lot fast enough for his tires to skid. Violet had stopped thinking about the cold somewhere in the fight, but the warm coat on her back made her realize her teeth were chattering.

"Violet," said Molly behind her, but she didn't dare look away from the parking lot exit. He would be back. He had to. He couldn't sleep without her. She needed the promised oblivion of sleep tonight. She couldn't bear feeling this way all night. But he didn't return, and her tears came out then, leaving warm trails down her frozen cheeks.

"Violet, let's go inside." Molly's hands wrapped around her arms.

"I can't go back there," she hiccuped.

"Then let me take you home," she turned to Molly. Snow poured down, and it clung to Molly's curls like a baby's breath wreath.

"I can't go home," cried Violet. She fell shakily into Molly's arms. Her tears pooled in Molly's coat, but she held her tight. Her steady hand caressed Violet's head, smoothing the flyaways.

"You're okay," Molly repeated, in the shushing tone of a mother. It made Violet feel worse. "Let me take you home. We don't have to go back to the party. The girls will clean up."

"Take... me... to your... house," said Violet, her words came out between choked gasps.

"Okay, I'll set up the guest room." Violet shook her head. Molly didn't understand what she had asked.

"I need you to unbind me," she said. Her breath fogged in front of her as she pulled away from Molly's shoulder.

"What?" asked Molly.

"I want you—no, I need you to unbind me from Scott."

"But you said—"

"I know what I said! Okay, I regret it! I was stupid, and I was wrong! Unbind me!"

Violet didn't want to look at Molly too closely, but her sadness was clear on her face. Molly reached out, smoothing Violet's hair away from her face.

"Are you sure?"

"Yes."

Violet's body still shook even though the fire roaring in the fireplace in Molly's kitchen made the room balmy. The house lay unusually quiet. Violet was used to the chatter of the coven when they were all together. Those warm moments felt far away.

On the counter, Violet stared at the materials for the spell. Candles, herbs, string, but she didn't have the heart to ask questions. She didn't want to know what the spell entailed. How Molly would cut Scott from her life.

Molly approached her with an athame in her right hand. She handed it to Violet. The cool metal delicate in her shaky hands. It didn't break through the numbness. Nor did it center her at the moment.

She kept her mind blank on purpose, keeping her thoughts of Scott away. Batting them away like flies. They weren't important anymore. He wasn't important anymore. She had deluded herself into staying in a relationship with someone compelled by a spell. What was wrong with her?

Molly had been right from the start. She should have listened.

"Are you sure this will work?" asked Violet. She needed to be done with it, but a part of her screamed to slow down. She wanted to call Scott, to explain, to beg, to cry, but she fought the urge.

"It should."

"It won't be like with Ellie, right? You won't have to attach my soul to someone else?"

"No, Lola and I discussed it. That was a different spell. She attached Derek to her soul and body with a sacrifice. You cast a spell to anchor him to you. What you did was a simple love spell. That's all."

"I didn't mean to fall in love with him," she whispered.

"I know," said Molly. She grabbed the red string on the counter, and without measuring, cut a large strand. Violet sat transfixed to it as Molly looped it between her two index fingers. "I'm going to ask you again. Are you sure you want to do this?"

"It's what you wanted me to do from the start. Why do you even bother asking?"

"I didn't want it to happen like this," said Molly. Violet looked up at her, confused and angry. The sight of Molly's sorrowful eyes intensified her anger.

"What are you talking about? This is what you wanted. This is what you've always wanted. Isn't it? Because you're right! You're always right! And I don't listen, and bad things happen to me because I don't do things the right way and—"

"Stop it," said Molly. She put away the string and hugged Violet close. Her muscles froze, stiff and awkward in Molly's arms, but the tension lessened, and she relaxed into the hug. "That's not what I meant. I worry about you, and I know that sometimes my worry doesn't come off the right way. And I know I can be overbearing sometimes. The only thing I've ever wanted was for you to be safe. Violet, you frustrate me to no end sometimes, but you're a part of this coven and a part of my family. And just as you killed Derek to save Maggie, I would do the same for you."

Violet hugged Molly hard, her arms wrapping around her slender frame.

"I'm sorry, Violet."

"No, I should apologize."

After all the disparaging things she had said about Molly and after all the trouble she had caused, Molly didn't care for her any less. Her decision to kill Derek without the coven's help put everyone in danger, but Violet thought she had protected her family. Her family was much bigger than just Margaret now. A part of her feared it. But this family would never hurt her the way her biological family did.

"Let's not apologize too much or we're going to be here all night," Molly pulled away, wiping her tears away from her eyes. Violet sniffled, her heart feeling a little lighter.

"Do you still want to unbind yourself from Scott?" asked Molly.

Violet thought of his body in her bed. The steadiness of being in his arms. She thought of how beautiful she felt when he looked at her and the joy that swelled in her when she made him laugh. *All built on lies*, she reminded herself.

"I have to, Molly. You were right. It's not fair for him to stay bound. I can still protect him, but I can't hold him against his will."

"We'll protect him. The entire coven. I promise," said Molly. She grabbed the string again. Violet saw her ring securely tied to one end of the string, and on the other, some of Scott's hair. Molly gripped the string with her eyes closed. Violet watched as it began to glow. The light cast golden shadows across the room. The light was warm and inviting, and she wanted to sink into it.

"When you're ready." Molly's voice broke her away from her trance.

She wanted to touch the string to see if the heat was real. If the connection between her ring and his hair had the energy of them together. Was it embedded in the spell? The way he looked at her when she first woke up? Did his laughter, the one that shook his whole body, vibrate on the string itself? If it had all been a spell, why could she feel her heart breaking?

Violet hooked the string in between a ridge of the dagger, and closing her eyes, she pulled the blade upwards. When she opened her eyes again, the string hung limply in Molly's hands. Mundane and lifeless.

Violet woke up at ten in the morning, crying. Her hand reached behind her, half expecting to bump into Scott's body, but the other side of the bed lay cold and empty. She shivered and pulled his pillow close to her body. His scent clung to the pillow, and she inhaled it slowly.

She had slept the whole night without him. The unbinding had fixed the insomnia, but she still loved him. The feeling didn't go away. It stayed burrowed deep in her chest, and her whole body shook with her cries.

Chapter Thirty-Two

Scott startled awake. For a moment, he forgot where he was. He was in his own bed, in his own apartment. The bed felt cold, and he fumbled around his nightstand, looking for his phone. Through his blurry vision, he made out a nine and a thirty-something.

He had slept without Violet.

He'd been exhausted, but he didn't expect to sleep. Somewhere between his heartbreak and anger, he had drifted off. His first instinct was to call Violet, to ask her if she had experienced the same thing, but the memories of the night before rushed back.

The night's events filled him with shame, and scrolling down his phone, he had a missed call from his brother, a few from his dad, but none from Violet. He shouldn't have expected Violet to call, but he wished for it. He needed to call her, apologize, grovel if necessary. How did he fuck up so badly?

He scrolled to her number, his thumb poised to call, but he hesitated. A small voice deep in his mind asked if maybe this was for the best. They had moved too quickly. This relationship hadn't been like the rest. He had never fallen so hard, so fast. Never wanted to spend all his waking hours with one person. Violet didn't even annoy him enough to drive him away.

A break would be helpful. He could reconnect with himself. Set his priorities straight. She didn't love him; he reminded himself. Regret bubbled its way to the surface of his consciousness, but he pushed it away. He would give it time. But deep down, he created excuses again to not be vulnerable and to keep her at arm's length. He thought he'd gotten over that. Why was he too afraid to call her now?

He turned off his phone. He would decide over the weekend.

Scott didn't call her over the weekend. He figured they would talk in person at work. Come Monday, he walked by her desk expecting to find her there chatting away with some paralegals, but he just found Ellie by herself. He assumed she was late, so over the next few hours, he came up with excuses to keep walking by. He needed a copy of some letters, a paper clip, and coffee. Finally, after his fifth go-around, Ellie stopped him.

"She's not coming," she said, not bothering to look up from her computer.

"What?"

"She's sick. She's not coming in today."

"Oh," he hesitated. "Did she call you this weekend?"

"Yeah, she did."

"Is she okay?"

Ellie finally looked up, her anger palpable. "She doesn't want to talk to you."

"Ellie, I just need to know if she's okay."

"What do you think?" Ellie stood, closing her laptop a little too hard.

Scott dragged his feet back to his office and sagged in his chair. No matter what, he would try again the next day. Except Violet didn't show up the following day, or the day after. He wondered if he went to her apartment to take care of her, if she would forgive him. But he thought better of it, placing the key to her apartment in his briefcase.

Nothing he did over the following week helped his suffering. Every night, he resisted the compulsion to call. What could he even say? He had no clue what to think now. He second-guessed himself at every turn. Maybe she had been telling the truth. Maybe she hadn't called his dad. How would she get his number, anyway? But then he remembered her getting the numbers for his friends. She had access to his phone. Violet, of all people, understood why he didn't want to talk to his parents. So why would she do it?

He didn't work during the day, preferring to use his time to stare out the window. He could survive the day, but nights were the worst. At night, sleep would come faster than he expected.

He almost hated it, wishing to feel her next to him. Craving that weight on top of him as her eyelashes fluttered against his jaw.

He tried to convince himself that he had never loved her. He'd known her for only a short while. How could it be love? He cared about her and wanted the best for her. But did he love her? Or was he just grateful to have someone to talk to? Someone to hold, who could understand him, who he could trust enough to let her into his life. It sure sounded a lot like love to him, but he didn't want to admit it. Not after he lost her.

As much as he argued it in his head, his heart still hurt. He'd lost the little fun he had in his life. His career had been his focus. The end goal, a law partnership at a prestigious firm. Now, he wasn't sure if it mattered at all. Since the death of his client, he found working on the other cases tedious. He neglected the motions sent by opposing counsel. Carl took him off two cases, and it didn't even faze him.

His week passed in a daze, and on a lonely Thursday evening, while he debated between Indian or Chinese food for dinner, he received a call from Arthur.

His heart dropped reading Arthur's name on his phone. "What do you have?" he asked as soon as he answered, wanting to cut all pleasantries.

"I'll head over now," Arthur's gruff voice sounded out of breath.

"Where?"

"Your apartment. This can't wait."

"Can't you tell me over the phone?"

"Not this information. I'll be there in ten."

Before Scott could try to suggest they meet somewhere else, Arthur hung up. Scott wasn't used to house calls from Arthur, but he figured the meeting wouldn't last too long.

He tidied up a little, throwing his dirty dishes in the dishwasher, although he doubted Arthur would judge him for a messy apartment. Once he cleared the boxes of takeout and dumped them in the trash, he saw the cactus.

He remembered the night of the meteor shower. He had loved watching Violet react to his apartment, the square-footage and size far more impressive than her tiny student apartment. But his apartment felt sterile, cold. He had let one of his ex-girlfriends decorate it when he had first moved in two years prior. The clean minimalist style reflected her, but Scott felt out of place in it. Violet's apartment felt like home, with its mismatched furniture, colorful artwork, and haphazard organization.

He pushed the memories away, wary of living in them. He couldn't live with himself if he clung to a person who never loved him. His love wasn't enough. The fight had been what Scott needed to put an end to a situation he hadn't realized wasn't good for him. He needed to remember the fight. Not the way she held her stomach when she laughed, or the satisfied little sighs when she lay in his arms.

His phone rung and Scott buzzed Arthur in. He paced as he waited for him to arrive. Arthur appeared haggard at his door, as if he hadn't slept in days. Yet he gave a cheerful smile and plopped down on the couch. He looked calm despite his appearance. Good news perhaps?

"How are you, Scott?" he asked.

"Fine, what have you found out?" Scott wanted to cut the small talk.

"You're not going to like it." Arthur scanned the apartment. "What, no drink?"

"Sorry, where are my manners?" said Scott through gritted teeth.

"I'll have scotch if you have any."

"I don't have any."

"Beer?"

Scott sighed, walked to his fridge, and pulled out a beer for Arthur. He pulled another for himself. Arthur sipped his beer leisurely, and Scott wondered what was an acceptable amount of time to pass before he could cuss him out.

"So, what did you find out?" Scott asked again.

"What do you know about Violet Caldwell?" asked Arthur.

Scott's skin grew hot. "She's an intern I work with."

Arthur laughed. "Sure, okay. How much has she told you about herself?"

"Stop this, Arthur. Tell me what you know." He didn't like where this was going, and the smile on Arthur's face made him more nervous.

"Violet is a witch."

Scott scoffed, rolling his eyes. "Please."

"She's a witch," repeated Arthur, looking pleased with himself.

"Did I pay you to investigate Violet? I asked you to find out who was responsible for the shootings." Scott's heart raced. How did she hide this from him? Was he so unobservant? But around her, he found it hard to pay attention to anything else.

"You didn't let me finish. The shooter at the library wasn't after you. He was after Violet. He was also at the square for her."

"What?"

"She's a witch. This person is after her."

"Who?" asked Scott.

Arthur pulled out his phone and pushed it towards Scott. He saw the image of an older man leaning against a car. He had a paunch belly and a shiny bald head, with a few faint hairs left. Scott squinted his eyes, looking at the photo closer. The man looked familiar, and it came back through the fog of the memory. "I know that man. It was the police officer who spoke to me after the shooting in the square. It's him?"

"Yes, Jason Wharton. He's been on the force for over twenty years. I found the posts he made online about witches, and let me tell you, the man hates them."

"People write hateful things about witches all the time. It doesn't make them killers."

"No, but this does." He swiped through the photos on his phone until he found the one he wanted. He pushed his phone back to Scott.

Jason Wharton stood with another group of men, each covered in body armor, with enormous guns strapped to their chests.

"It's a group of witch hunters. A lot of the attacks you see happening to the accused witches have come from this militia. This one here," he pointed to a younger-looking man with dead eyes. "He killed three women in Arizona accused of devil worship. They never saw their court date. I don't think Jason was after you at first, but I'm sure killing the defense attorney of a witch would be a bonus."

"Are you sure it's him?"

"You paid me to find out, and I found him." He pulled a manila envelope from his briefcase. The thick envelope landed with a soft thud on the coffee table. "I got it all in here. Information, photos, his family, his properties — all of it. This won't surprise you one bit, but he killed your client."

"What?" asked Scott, his stomach sinking.

"If I had found her in time, I would have tried to save her, but I got there too late. I found the body," Arthur shuddered as if reliving the memory. "I called the paramedics, and I stayed long enough to tell them what I found, but it was too late to do anything."

"Are we done?" asked Scott. Arthur downed the rest of his beer and stood up to leave.

"Scott, I don't know how you're going to handle this, but a word of advice. If you're gonna go toe to toe with this man, you better be prepared. Other police officers might be involved, and they won't give up one of their own."

"Thank you, Arthur." He meant it too.

Scott locked the door behind Arthur, and he paced back and forth in his living room. Violet had kept the biggest secret he could imagine from him, and he felt furious. Who had he fallen in love with? And here he thought she had let down her walls to let him in. All of it had been a facade. He had deluded himself into assuming that she loved him in her own way. Love included honesty and trust, and she had never trusted him.

As angry as he was, a stronger emotion took over. He would deal with his anger later, but Violet was the target. She needed to know. He pulled out his phone and called her. The call went to voicemail. He tried again, guessing she ignored his call, but she didn't pick up again. He thought back, checking the time on his phone. It was almost six o'clock on Thursday. She should be home by now. He grabbed his coat and the key to her apartment and left.

CHAPTER THIRTY-THREE

"Violet?" he called as soon as he entered her apartment. He didn't bother knocking and let himself in. He would rather she yelled at him to get out. At least he would know she was safe.

"Violet?" he called again. He checked every room, but she wasn't home. The dishes were piled high in the sink. Her bed lay unmade. She should have been home by now, and nausea bubbled up in Scott's throat. Out of all the days for her to change her routine. He scrolled through his phone, but there was no one else to call. Violet had never given him her friends' numbers. But then he remembered Books & Beans, Molly owned the place. Violet might not be there, but he could bump into one of her friends.

He left Violet's apartment and sped through traffic. People struck their horns as he passed and cut them off, but he didn't care. He had barely shut off the engine before he rushed out the door and ran inside Books & Beans, searching for her. The customers in the cafe stared back, confused. He thought he must look strange to them. Molly and another employee watched him from behind the counter.

"Have you seen Violet?" he asked as he approached Molly.

"What? No, not since this weekend. Why?" she asked, narrowing her eyes. Scott looked behind him. The customers were too engrossed in their laptops or books to pay attention to them. The other employee talked with another customer, but Scott worried about informants. Who did the cop use?

"Is there somewhere we could talk in private?" he asked, lowering his voice. Molly nodded, and she instructed the other employee to take over, and led Scott into the back of the shop. Between boxes of coffee and syrups, Molly settled into a chair by a small desk with papers strewn on top.

"What is this about?" she asked, crossing her arms.

"I know Violet is a witch." Molly's eyes grew. "And by your reaction, I'm guessing you're one, too. You can trust me. I promise. I would never turn you or Violet in," he added before Molly could react. "Do you know where Violet is? The killer, he's not after me. He's after her. Can you get a hold of her? She's ignoring my calls, which I get why I deserve that. But I need to talk to her. I need to know she's safe."

He wasn't sure if it was the desperation in his voice, or what he'd just revealed, but Molly, without skipping a beat, pulled out her phone. She dialed Violet's number and set the phone on speaker. The phone rang and rang, each ring building the bile in Scott's throat. Violet's voice echoed through the small room, asking them to leave a message.

Molly said nothing, but scrolled through her phone and called another number.

"Hello," an unknown voice answered almost immediately.

"Margaret? Is Violet with you?"

"No, why?"

"Call the rest and see if anyone has seen her."

"What's going on, Molly?"

"I'm not sure yet. We just need to talk to her."

Scott's leg bounced uncontrollably. He had to find her. His thoughts raced through his head. His nausea getting worse, he wondered if Molly would hate him if he threw up in the yellow bucket that held the mop. He had already ruined her first impression of him. What was one more thing?

Molly didn't offer platitudes or small talk. Nothing to ease his worries. After about five minutes, her phone rang. Scott perked up, hoping to hear Violet, but he became dejected when Margaret's voice rang out.

"I called Ellie and Lola. Lola called the others. No one knows where she is. Rosie's trying to locate her." Margaret sounded as if she had been crying.

"Okay, I'll meet you at my house." She hung up the phone and started gathering her things.

"I'm coming with you," said Scott. He stood up and waited to see if Molly would argue with him. He got the sense that she wanted to. She had witnessed the fight between him and Violet, and she probably didn't have a great opinion of him. But she surprised him, nodding her head yes.

"I'll drive," he said as they ran out of the back of the shop.

Molly's house was sweltering, and Scott's arm pressed into Margaret's as he crammed into a kitchen with six witches. The witches sat silently as they watched Rosie. Her eyes moved beneath her closed eyelids. Scott wanted to yell at her to hurry.

"It's no use," said Rosie. "Everything's blocked. And sometimes I think I'm getting somewhere, but it's weird. It's like I get pushed."

"Did you see anything at all?" asked Lenore.

"I saw some trash — well, a lot of trash. It kind of looked like a junkyard of sorts, but I can't tell if that was true or another redirection!"

"I don't understand. What's happening?" asked Scott, frustrated. There had to be a faster way of doing this. He had a lot of questions about what everyone did, not to mention he'd just learned Ellie was a witch too, but thought better than to ask specifics. There was no time.

"This isn't a normal person, Scott. This is a witch hunter. And it's just as I feared. He has protection against our magic," said Molly.

"So you can't find her?" he asked, panicking.

He looked away, and his eyes met Margaret's. Her mascara streaked down her cheeks as she cried. They were trying; he reminded himself. They cared about her too. This was her family.

He watched as they shuffled around him, grabbing books and muttering to each other. He took a deep breath. It came then, in the small calm he created, a memory.

"Shit," he said, running to the kitchen and grabbing his coat. He pulled out the manila envelope that he had tried to squish into his inside jacket pocket and spilled its contents on the island.

"My P.I. has been tailing this guy. There might be some information here." They dug through the papers. A flurry of hands grabbed at whatever was closest to them. Scott got stuck with papers full of information about Jason Wharton's daily activities. His frantic hands tore a corner of the paper. His eyes skimmed across the words. There had to be something. But Jason's daily activities were boring and normal, except for the weekly meeting at his friend's place to practice shooting.

"Wait!" He looked up to see Ellie holding a photograph. "Is this what you saw, Rosie?" The low-resolution photo was hard to make out, but it looked like a shed made of concrete. He noted that there were no windows, and the place was littered with junk. Rusted and broken bicycles, old red gas cans, discarded metal and trash.

"Yes," said Rosie, her eyes growing wide. "This is it. She's here."

"Where is this?" asked Lola.

"Look for anything that has his properties," said Scott. Margaret held the paper up, her hands shaking. A quick search online and they found it. A satellite photo showed the shed standing next to a home about twenty minutes outside of town. Before Scott said anything, they moved, running to their cars.

He had no clue what the plan was. Or how they were going to get there fast enough without the cops stopping them for speeding. But he only prayed and wished to whatever would listen that it wasn't too late.

CHAPTER THIRTY-FOUR

Sound came first. Muffled like a scream in a pillow. Violet tried to move, but something was wrong. Her limbs wouldn't cooperate with her brain, refusing to move no matter how hard she tried. She opened her eyes, but her vision blurred. Her head hurt, and the blood pounded against her temples. Her eyes adjusted to the dim light coming from a solitary flashlight on the floor. Oily boxes were stacked along the walls of the room, and a rusted, broken gate lay mere inches from her feet. Windowless concrete walls surrounded her. She spotted a metal door on one wall, and she wondered if it was locked. As she became more conscious, she realized her arms and legs were bound tightly with duct tape.

She struggled against the tape and winced as it pulled her arm hair off. Her mind finally caught on to what was happening. Her breathing became shallow with panic. Where was she? The last thing she remembered was walking towards her car when class ended. Her mind was occupied with the humiliation she experienced when her professor cold-called her and she didn't know the answer. She was about to open the door, and she remembered hearing a shuffling noise...

She stopped struggling when the sound of keys jingled on the other side of the door. The metal door scraped against the concrete floor, making her cringe and wish that her hands were free to cover her ears. An enormous figure emerged through the door. The dark obscured his face, but as he closed the door behind him, Violet's heart raced. He walked into the light, and Violet recognized him right away. Jason Wharton, the police officer who questioned her and Scott after the second shooting.

"You're awake," he said. He didn't seem happy about it. Violet didn't want to say anything. Her mind raced as she tried to figure a way out. "Nothing to say?" He squatted down, his eyes level with her face. His eyes traveled farther down, and Violet panicked. His lecherous eyes scanned her body, stopping back up at her throat. Violet followed his gaze to her neck and realized something was missing.

"Looking for this?" he said, pulling out Lenore's amulet from his pocket with a gloved hand. "Tricky thing, this amulet, but once I tore it off your neck, I had no trouble getting you into my car." He tenderly pulled off the blue surgical glove. His hand glowed in the low light, raw and pink, as if it had been boiled.

He started laughing. "You really are something," he said. "You've been so hard to find, to kill." He savored the last word, the corners of his mouth lifting into a smile. "You're not like the other witches, are you?" He waited for Violet to do something, but a mix of anger and fear kept her quiet.

"Not going to talk?" The smile on his face faded. He lifted his hand, and before Violet could react, his fist slammed into her face. She fell on her side, unable to flip over. Her jaw burned, and his hands flipped her over onto her back. She stared at the ceiling, another concrete wall. He appeared on her left and pulled her back into a sitting position.

"I've been looking for you for months," he said. He lifted his hand, and Violet flinched away. His thumb traced her lips, smearing her blood like lipstick. His face contorted with disgust and anger, yet curiosity bubbled beneath. Violet realized this man would enjoy every minute he got to torture her. She prayed it wouldn't last long.

She closed her eyes, thinking of a spell, any spell to get her out. Lola's death spell popped into her head, but she didn't have the ingredients. When she killed Derek, she had Margaret there. She wasn't strong enough to cast it by herself, but she had to try.

"What are you doing?" asked Jason. "Your spells don't work here," he laughed. Violet remembered the bullets. Her eyes snapped open. He was protected, and she was screwed.

"What do you want?" she asked, her resolve falling away.

"I just want to talk."

"How did you know?"

"I saw you kill Derek Emerson." Violet's breath caught in her throat.

"How?" she asked. She had cast the death spell at Margaret's house. She remembered her anger and her frantic need both to comfort Margaret and to cast the spell. He had no way of witnessing it.

"I saw you in the woods that night. You were running out with the other witches. She's next, in case you were wondering. I was off the clock and I shouldn't have bothered, but I checked the woods anyway and saw Derek. He wasn't dead yet. He was passed out, but I woke him up and helped him get to his car. Nice guy, but he got mixed up with the wrong sort of trouble. Then, right before he was about to drive off, I watched a healthy thirty-year-old man drop dead in his car. Just like that," he snapped his fingers.

"I knew then it was a witch's death. Healthy young men don't just drop dead. I put him back in the forest and let the rest of the force take care of him, but I knew it was you. It took a while to find you, but I recognized you right away. Long black hair, a look on your face like you were above people. Like you were too good to face punishment for your perverse practice. After that, I followed you and waited for the right time to kill you. But damn, you're good at hiding. I'm sure this helped you," he said, swinging the amulet in front of her face.

Violet felt sick to her stomach. She had been too careless with Derek. This man didn't care about his murderer. He cared only that he had caught an actual witch. She didn't want him to know about the rest of the coven. She might not get out of this alive. Would the others even notice her gone in time? But she had to find a way. He knew about Margaret. He might find out about everyone else, too.

She needed to talk, to distract him long enough for her to figure out how to escape. "Why... why did you shoot Scott in the library?"

"I had already made a mess of things going into a public place. I was inpatient with you. You hid from me for months, and I finally had an opportunity, and I thought making it look like a random shooting would help me escape. It was the first time I had ever done something so public. I'm usually a little more careful, but I was there. I couldn't find you, and I saw the news conference the day before with that motherfucker talking about defending the witch. He's just as bad as you are."

"Why do you bother? Why do you want to kill me? Is it really because I am a witch?"

His hands went to the back of her head. She squirmed, trying to get away. He grabbed a bunch of her black hair at the root and yanked her head back. His putrid breath blew in her face. "I'm doing my part as a citizen to take care of the problem. Once I'm finished with you, I'll take care of your boyfriend, too."

Violet's anger flared at the mention of Scott. A scream erupted from the depths of her. Guttural and loud, vibrating the junk in the room. Before he could react, a force greater than Violet had ever witnessed pushed from her body. Officer Wharton's body hurled from her, smashing into the wall.

Her scalp stung from the hair he had yanked off as he went, but she stared at his slumped form in shock. Somehow, without casting a spell, she used her magic.

Violet couldn't admire her handiwork for long. She inch-wormed her way forward to get to the door, but found her achy body not cooperating. Before long, she heard stirring and groaning behind her.

She turned to see Officer Wharton clasping his head. Blood dripped onto the floor. He looked disoriented, but it was only for a brief moment. His gaze fell on her again. Rage and hatred moved him towards her.

He dragged her up by her hair, and Violet cried out in pain. He pushed her down again. The quick warm drip of blood down her face accompanied the pain in her head. He paused before digging his boot deep into her abdomen. Violet cried out, coughing and trying to catch her breath. His laugh echoed in the room, and she tried worming her way up. He struck her down with another blow of his foot. She struggled to breathe. Tears blurred her vision. His feet came close to her again, and she shut her eyes, waiting for the next blow.

It never came. A bang against the metal door made him pause mid-kick. Spots covered her sight. The banging continued, over and over, until it gave way. Violet tried to keep her eyes open, but they were fluttering closed.

"Violet?" Scott's voice pierced through the fog.

Footsteps echoed along the concrete floors, as did the sound of two men fighting. A warm hand tenderly touched her face, and she blinked up, seeing Molly and Ellie near. She could feel their hands on her body, and she felt the tapes ripped from her arms and legs. She tried to keep her eyes open, but they shut as the sound of a gunshot rang through the small room.

CHAPTER THIRTY-FIVE

The delicate sensation of someone caressing her cheek woke Violet up from her deep sleep. Her eyes fluttered open, and a wave of relief washed over her when she saw Scott. He smiled weakly, his eyes soft and happy. The familiarity of her own bed and pillows comforted her. But what comforted her more was Scott's arms wrapped around her.

"How are you feeling?" asked Scott. Violet raised her hand to smooth his brow. The tension in his face relaxed as her fingers brushed him.

"I feel like shit," she said, smiling. Even her little joke wasn't enough to ease the stress from his face. Her body ached, but she felt only a little pain. No doubt, Molly and Lola were responsible for dulling her pain.

"Who shot the gun?" she said as the memory flooded back. She panicked, and if she had had the energy, she would have shot up. Scott lay next to her, very much alive and unhurt, but she swore she heard a gunshot.

"We fought over his gun, and I got a hold of it as it went off. He's dead. You have nothing to worry about." He pulled her closer to his chest. Hearing his steady heartbeat beneath her ear grounded her. They were in her room, they were together, and they were safe, but something itched at the back of her brain.

"Aren't you supposed to be mad at me right now?" asked Violet. His heartbeat sped up.

"I'm sorry, Violet. You didn't deserve my anger that night. I should have known you wouldn't invite my dad. Everything clouded over when I saw him."

"He surprised you."

"It's not an excuse. I don't know what was wrong with me that night. I can't believe I would hurt you like that. I'm so sorry."

"I accept your apology," she said, sounding rather formal.

"Not partially?"

"No, fully."

Scott's arms wrapped tighter around her. "There's something else. My dad told me something that night. Something I've been too afraid to even think about."

"What?"

"My mother didn't leave because of my dad. I accused him of driving her away, but he still insists it wasn't his fault. Which means—"

"Stop, Scott, she didn't leave because of you." Violet wanted to raise herself up, but she couldn't. Her body was too exhausted and achy to move.

"I know," he said. "But I think it's one mystery I'll never be able to solve. And I have to live with that."

"Did you ever find out who invited your dad?" asked Violet.

"I got a call from Beatrice about an hour ago. She confessed to inviting him. She was very apologetic about it. My dad's been calling the office since the shooting. And Beatrice knows I don't take personal calls, so she's been politely telling my dad that I'm busy. She slipped up about the birthday party. She didn't mean to tell him about it, but she would never have guessed he would show up."

Violet stayed silent. She wasn't angry anymore. Anger drained too much energy, and she was already struggling to keep her eyes open.

"I'm sorry," he repeated. "I shouldn't have done that to you. Nothing excuses it."

"You need to stop apologizing," she said. Scott chuckled, pulling her even closer. She grimaced in pain, but she didn't care. "Maybe you don't want to hear it, but at least he showed up. That has to count for something, right?"

"I'm not sure if I'm there yet. One day, maybe."

His fingers ran through her hair, soothing her into sleep again. She didn't want to sleep. She wasn't sure how long she'd been unconscious, but she wanted to stay with Scott. Things were almost normal again. Well, if she ignored the fat lip and bruises. But she had missed him. Missed wrapping herself around him, and the soft caress of his hands. The heat from his body warmed her up in her drafty apartment.

"How did you know where to find me?" she asked.

"Rosie tracked you. To be honest, I still don't understand what she was doing, but with the information from my P.I., we found you."

"Wait, Rosie? P.I.?" she asked, lifting her head up. Scott's smile was gone, and instead she met hurt. "They told you," she said.

"My P.I. told me. I kind of just assumed your friends were witches, too."

"So, I'm a witch." She couldn't think of what more to say and settled on, "Any questions?"

"Just one. Why didn't you tell me?"

"I'm not sure. I was afraid, but not because I thought you would have a negative reaction, or you would turn me in. I mean, you didn't even think witches were real. My world is dangerous sometimes. I mean, you got shot because of me. Twice. There's so much good in it, but I was trying my best to keep you safe."

"You were trying to keep me safe?" said Scott, rubbing his face in his palms. He started laughing, shaking the bed with it. She waited for him to stop, but the laughter kept coming.

"If you're about to have a nervous breakdown, can you please get out of my room?" said Violet, annoyed. "Here I am trying to have an honest conversation with you, and you're losing it."

He sighed. "I was keeping you safe, Violet."

"Mm, wrong. I was keeping you safe. The cop didn't learn where I lived because of my protection spells. I put a protective sachet under the mat of your new car, and it was my amulet that protected us in the square."

"Well, I hired a P.I. who investigated and tailed the cop. That's how I found out he was after you! And that's also how I realized something bad had happened to you, because I kept calling you and you wouldn't answer. God forbid you tell me something as important as you being a witch!"

"Are we fighting, Scott? 'Cause I gotta tell you I can't handle it right now. I'll fight you tomorrow," she said, closing her eyes.

"I'm sorry," he said. Violet opened her eyes again. His exasperation was gone, but his curiosity made her nervous. "I don't care that you're a witch. It would never have mattered to me. Was the insomnia magic-related?" he asked.

Violet's stomach sank. She needed to be honest. She wouldn't hide anymore. "Yes, accidental magic, but magic."

"How?"

"When I saved you in the library, I cast a spell without meaning to. I don't a hundred percent understand how it happened. I think I was so desperate for you to live that I bound myself to you. I think the insomnia was a symptom of the spell, along with... other things."

"What other things?"

Violet wanted to puke, but she had to tell him. He had just saved her from a witch hunter. He deserved the truth. She raised herself off his chest with some difficulty. Her body wobbled as she tried to sit up straight. His hands shot up protectively, trying to steady her.

"Your feelings for me... they're not real. They're influenced by the spell. I didn't mean to cast it; I promise. But everything you felt was all an effect of the spell."

Scott stayed silent, his attention drawn to the view outside the window. Violet wanted to turn his face towards her, force him to speak to her, but she held herself back.

"So, everything was because of a spell."

"Yes," she wanted to cry.

"That's not possible."

"It's true. I unbound us. We're no longer connected."

"After my birthday? I could sleep after my birthday," he said, finally turning to look at her.

"Yeah, but I want to be honest with you. I found out before your birthday that we were bound. But I couldn't bring myself to let you leave me. I convinced myself that it was because I wanted to keep you safe. But I was selfish. I just wanted you. And I manipulated you into staying with me. I shouldn't have done it. And I'm sorry. But you're free now."

"Free?" he asked. "I'm not free, Violet. I still love you. If this love spell thing were true, wouldn't that go away?"

"I... I'm not sure."

"Were your feelings influenced, too? Did you like me only because of the spell?"

"I wish I had an answer for that. And I'm not sure how much of this will matter to you, but I tried to fight it. I tried to fight everything, but it didn't work."

"So, do you love me?" he asked.

"Yes." Her lips quivered, and his finger gently brushed over them.

"Violet, I still love you. My feelings didn't appear out of nowhere. I don't think it was because of your spell. They grew. They grew as I got to know you, as you let me in. As you let me hold you, kiss you." His hand moved to cup her cheek, careful not to hurt her achy face. "You say it's a spell you cast, but it wasn't you, Violet. I remember that day; I remember looking into your eyes. I attached myself there. It was the only thing I could cling to. I wanted to be with you, to be around you. You're fun, you care about people, you care about your future, about school. You pretend you don't; you pretend you're above it all. Like you're afraid if you show you care too much, someone will take it away from you. Nothing is going to take me away from you. Nothing."

"I still love you too," she said. Her heart raced, telling him the truth, but the words sounded right. No part of her wanted to take them back. A warm glow spread through her, filling her with a joy she couldn't explain.

Scott smiled, leaning down to press his lips to hers. His kiss was gentle, not wanting to hurt her more, but it only fueled her need for him. Spell or no spell, she loved Scott. Her feelings hadn't gone away either, and as she held on to him, she realized that perhaps her spell only amplified whatever existed between them. But now that it was gone, nothing could replace the love she felt for him.

He pulled away, and she could read on his face how badly he wanted her too. He smirked and kissed her again, this time with a quick peck.

"There will be time for that," he whispered, as if reading her mind. "You need rest."

He led her back down. She couldn't turn to the side without wincing from the pain, so she lay on her back, and Scott settled around her, his head on her chest.

"Now that you know I'm a witch, there's something else I need to tell you."

"What?"

"What do you know about an herb called slippery elm?"

"Don't people take that for stomach aches?"

"It has other purposes."

Scott laughed, raising himself up to kiss her again. "Tell me tomorrow. Now go to sleep."

Sleep embraced her as soon as she closed her eyes, wrapped in bliss and love.

EPILOGUE

"We're not keeping it," said Scott with a scowl.

"Are you kidding? Look at this face," Violet held the puppy up to his nose. Scott pulled back as the little golden lab's tongue popped out to lick his mouth.

"Violet, we're not taking it home."

Violet lowered the dog back down into its little enclosure. The puppy ran in circles with the others nipping at its head. Violet took off her sweater and wrapped it around her waist, finding the day growing too hot for her planned outfit. Scott hoped she would want to leave the park, but she remained fixated on the dogs. He snaked his arm around her waist to pull her away, but she oohed and awed at the small family of labs yipping at her to pick them up.

"A dog would be good for you. It will keep you young," she said. Scott wrapped his arm around her shoulders and tried harder to drag her away. Violet dug in her heels, trying to stop him.

"Can you at least think about it?" she asked.

"Fine, I'll think about it," he said.

"Seriously, think about it."

"I will, Violet."

"We can go on walks together."

"I know."

"We can take a family Christmas photo with our dog. Your dad and brother would love that."

"I think they would make fun of me."

"Please, Scott!"

"I promise, I promise. We need to go. Molly and the rest are waiting."

He would give in; he always did. Violet would get her way, and he would glower for a few weeks, but watching her glee would soften his stony heart. With a sad little sigh, he led her away to Books & Beans. Not that it stopped her from pleading her case all the way there.

"How are you two?" Molly asked as they sat by the counter. Violet drifted next to Lola.

"It would be great, but Scott won't let me get a dog," said Violet.

"It's not that I'm not letting you; it's that I'm going to be the only person who takes care of it. She has one more year of law school. Not to mention, you'll need to study for the BAR. When will you have time?"

"Molly, tell him how responsible I am," said Violet.

"Don't let her get a dog," said Molly. Violet gasped, mouth agape, but Scott threw his head back, laughing.

"I knew it," said Scott.

"Molly, you're supposed to be on my side," said Violet.

"I am on your side, and you would have a hard time taking care of a dog," said Molly.

"Don't believe Molly," said Lola. "She hates dogs."

"How could you hate dogs?" asked Violet.

"I don't hate dogs; I just prefer cats," she said.

Violet opened her mouth to protest further, but River and Ellie's arrival distracted her enough to drop it. They spent the rest of the afternoon at Books & Beans. The coven members arrived throughout the day. After months of uncertainty and suspicion, Violet relaxed. It fell with ease.

They buried Officer Wharton's body deep in the woods. Like Derek's body before, she placed a sachet with herbs and charms with the body to keep others from finding them. A missing police officer made national news, and the coven made sure not to attract anymore attention to themselves.

Scott found a space within the coven faster than she had expected. It filled her with a warmth she couldn't name, seeing him hang out with Margaret and trying his best not to make her feel like a third wheel. He became fast friends with River. No doubt commiserating about the herbal baths, sachets, and crystals their girlfriends forced on them. The rest of the coven warmed up to him, and Violet was grateful.

Violet loved that Scott fit in with her weird little family. One day, however, Scott admitted to wanting to call his dad. It took her by surprise, almost dropping her mug on the carpet. But when he called, she sat next to him. Her hands wrapped around his. His leg bobbed up and down as the phone rang. Their conversation had been brief, with half-stuttered apologies and plans. Although it may have been premature to think so, she was hopeful. Rebuilding a relationship would take time, but Scott seemed ready to try.

Scott and Violet left Books & Beans around ten and drove home. Violet had acquiesced and moved into Scott's apartment. She turned the dreary minimalist hellscape into their home. But she didn't let him off the hook and forced him to tell her what he liked. If they were going to live together, she wanted their apartment to feel like a home for him, too. He rose to the occasion, treating his apartment as more than just the place he stayed at night. Even though some of his choices were questionable, Violet learned to compromise.

He took part in her magic. She showed him how her protection spells worked. She instructed him on where to put the black tourmaline to keep out people with bad intentions. He helped her cleanse the apartment when she thought the energy was too stagnant. He even agreed to wear a ring she had charmed for protection.

Her clothes ended up taking most of the closet, and her herbal teas took over his coffee cupboard. They had argued over how to organize their bookshelves. Scott wanted it in alphabetical order; Violet wanted it sorted by genre and mood. Scott won that battle, but his frown couldn't mask his happiness. Violet often caught him staring at her. His gaze shone with affection and love for her, along with an incredulity that never left his face. As if he couldn't believe it had worked out for him. Violet couldn't believe it had worked out for her, too.

They settled in for the night. Although they no longer needed each other to sleep, Violet still looked forward to wrapping herself up in his arms before drifting off.

She read her textbook in bed, hearing Scott brush his teeth, and waited for him to come to bed. But she didn't have to wait long, as he climbed in next to her a few moments later. He smelled of fresh soap.

His hand clutched her jaw, trying to pull her away from her book. Violet sighed, turning away and continued reading. It didn't deter him from kissing her neck. Violet's eyes closed on their own, wishing to fall into him, but she forced them open. His lips were insistent, kissing her shoulders. His hands, warmed by the shower, drifted beneath her shirt and massaged her breasts. Her eyes closed with the sensation, but she nudged him away and kept reading.

"Are you tired?" asked Scott.

"Quite."

"Why are you still reading then?" he asked.

"I have a torts test next week."

"Torts? How sexy."

"The weirdest things turn you on."

"Start talking to me about contracts and then you'll see."

Violet giggled as Scott lifted the covers, and his fingers grasped her underwear, pulling them off. She gasped as his lips pressed against her thighs. Her eyes skimmed the words, half-absorbing what she read. His tongue parted her folds, and her breath hitched in her throat as his tongue found her clit. She closed her eyes without meaning to, her body reacting to his lips. He caught her clit between his lips as he sucked on it tenderly. Passion blossomed in her chest, leaving her gasping and clutching the sheets.

The intensity of his sucking made her tighten as her orgasm came closer, but before she came, Scott stopped. He pulled back the covers, his face resting lazily on her thigh. She pushed his dark hair away from his face. His lips were puffy and pouty, and she swiped her thumb over them. He wanted to say something. She could see it in his frown. He was about to give up.

"You can get the dog," he sighed, annoyed.

"You can pick out the name."

"Thank God, because I know you would give it a ridiculous name."

"I would not," she said as he lifted himself up to kiss her.

"You'd probably name it Buster." He said in between kisses.

"What's wrong with Buster? It's a perfectly acceptable name." He said nothing, but dipped his hand beneath the covers again. He parted her and found her clit again.

"I hate the name Buster," said Scott, circling the sensitive nub.

Violet tried her best to answer, but it embarrassingly came out breathless. "Fine, not Buster."

"I'll name the dog," he said, kissing her neck.

"No."

"Fine," said Scott, stopping his slow caresses.

Violet groaned. "That's not fair."

"I never said I would play fair."

Violet narrowed her eyes, but Scott flopped on the other side of the bed.

"Are you serious?"

"Yes."

"I can be stubborn," said Violet.

"Oh, trust me, I know. But I wonder how long your stubbornness will last."

"Years."

"Please."

"Months."

He laughed.

"Days."

"Doubt it."

"Hours."

He turned, his eyebrow raised.

"Fine," she said, caving in.

Scott raised himself up and crashed into her body. His lips pressed roughly on her lips as his hips pushed against hers.

"I was seconds away from giving up," growled Scott.

Violet laughed. "I should have held out."

"Oh please, you wouldn't last a second longer and you know it."

When he finally pulled away, leaving Violet in a puddle of bliss, it was only for a moment before he dragged her back into his arms. She settled on his chest, hearing his heartbeat and breath race.

Her future, once lonely, with no one but Margaret to trust, now had more people in it than she ever had before. And a love that she never saw coming.

As his heart rate slowed and he pulled the sheets to cover them both, Violet drifted off into a dreamless sleep.

* * *

AFTERWORD

Thank you so much for reading and I hope you enjoyed it! Please consider leaving a review as it helps a lot!

If you want to know what's next for Violet and Scott, you can subscribe to my newsletter at https://www.sulaalba.com/newsletter for a free second epilogue.

ABOUT THE AUTHOR

Sula Alba is a paranormal romance author living in the deserts of the Southwest.

When not writing, she loves to photograph her cats laying in the sun, baking and reading.